SWARMED

J.D. HUFF

SEVEREDPRESS

SWARMED

Then locusts came down to the earth out of the smoke, and they were given the power to sting like scorpions.

These locusts were not given the power to kill anyone, but to cause pain to the people for five months. And the pain they felt was like the pain a scorpion gives when it stings someone. During those days people will look for a way to die, but they will not find it. They will want to die, but death will run away from them.

Revelation 9: 3; 5-6

CHAPTER 1

Why she had been drawn to this particular tree was a mystery, but as Allie Vargas stood looking up through the tangle of branches, one thing became perfectly clear—she *was* going to climb it. Any qualms about potential dangers were swept away by the casual indifference only a thirteen-year-old could apply to such a perilous endeavor.

She jumped and grasped the top of the lowest limb with small but determined hands. Swinging her legs in a pendulum motion to build momentum, she was eventually able to wrap them around the coarse bark and complete the nimble move of pulling herself onto the top. Scratches were incurred, but from here, her efforts were rewarded by progressively smaller branches that formed a makeshift spiral ladder. She began to move steadily higher.

She climbed confidently until the diameter of the limbs no longer seemed robust enough to trust her life with. It was exhilarating. A slight breeze waved the top of the tree to and fro, the feeling it created like a baby being rocked by its mother. Allie looked up and realized how close to the top she was. A bird circled overhead against the backdrop of a perfect blue sky, and she felt like she could almost reach out and touch it.

Something closer caught her attention. A long, olive-colored pod had nearly brushed her shoulder. It looked like an unripe banana, but slightly longer and more slender. She reached out and touched the smooth and leathery skin. A brisk tug pulled it loose, and after a moment of contemplation, she slid it into her pants pocket. With her appetite for adventure sated, she began to descend.

It proved to be a tedious task, a slower process than going up. She bent her head down to see where her hands and feet needed to be placed. "Nice and easy, Alejandrina," she reminded herself, utilizing her full name to add emphasis just like her Momma did whenever the situation warranted. She knew she could do it. She also knew if she wasn't paying attention, she would break every bone in her body while she bounced from limb to limb on the thrill-ride gravity would impose as penalty for her carelessness.

Caution paid off and she reached the lowest limb safely. After securing a good grip, she rotated to a position under the branch, and then swung her legs towards the ground. She landed so lightly she barely made a sound.

Allie pulled the pod out of her pocket and regarded it critically. Next, she sat on the soft, natural mulch with her back against the trunk of the gnarly tree. The pod was tougher than most fruit she was familiar with, but the tip was narrow and pointed, and she discovered that with a twist of her hand, it would break off.

The cover then split along three seams and peeled off with little trouble. Inside was a prize.

The pod was filled with tiny, pinkish-colored balls. A delicate sniff revealed a pleasant aroma, certainly a precursor to the flavor, or so her thinking went. Allie discovered that they would pop when she bit them, squirting the sweet juice inside into her mouth. They were delicious, the flavor like mixing ripe pear with pineapple. Ignoring the possible negative implications of eating an unknown food, she would be proven correct in her naïve assumption that their pleasant taste meant they were safe to eat.

Allie devoured all of the orbs and tossed the peel casually over her shoulder. She was immersed by a feeling of profound peace. She settled in, enjoying the experience.

Her eyes closed as the pleasant sounds of the forest enveloped her. Relaxed, serenaded by rustling leaves and singing birds, thoughts of the outside world evaporated. The effects of the fruit came quickly and she slipped into a dream-like state. She drifted through a happy place, willingly going wherever the effects of the fruit took her.

A vision as clear as real life manifested itself.

In it, she met a stranger. The man approached slowly, reverently. There was so much emotion on his face, so much detail in his appearance that Allie marvelled in it. The man smiled and in an unexpected moment of déjà vu, his face became fleetingly familiar. But the experience wasn't destined to last, and before it all faded away, he spoke in a voice so soft Allie could barely here it. He called her by her name.

How strange, Allie thought.

And then he was gone.

Allie woke from her dream feeling no worse for wear. In fact, she felt great. Physically, she was ready to climb every tree in the entire forest and then run a marathon. Somehow, even the scrapes she got while climbing the tree had vanished.

She had no idea that no one had ever eaten this fruit before, or that this particular tree was the only one of its kind. Discovery of the tree, a recognition of what it was and consumption of its fruit would trigger an alarm response in a dark, unknown realm. The odor molecules released when she opened the fruit pod had been sought for millennia. The door that separated the two worlds was now destined to open. But to her advantage, Allie remained completely and blissfully unaware.

She stood, dusted off the leaves and litter that clung to her pants, and started back to town, now slightly alarmed at how late it was. Mama would be waiting impatiently at the restaurant, an interrogation now mandatory. Allie's answers needed to tread a fine line between honesty and self-incrimination. Mama was not a fan of her wanderings.

Her mother was running a restaurant in Barrington, Vermont—a perfectly fine town but not exactly a mecca for Mexican food. They were struggling. With money tight and the business understaffed, it was advantageous to have a daughter who knew her way around the kitchen (or at least the area by the sink where the dirty dishes piled up). So after school, and on weekends, Allie fed the dishwasher and manually scrubbed the items that were beyond its cleaning abilities in order to fulfill "*her responsibilities*"; a somewhat subjective list that had appeared in her thirteenth year. As she arrived at Casa Comida, she braced for Mama's response.

"Allie," her mother said as she breezed past, handing her a cast iron pan adorned with melted cheese, "make sure you let this one soak. And don't use so much soap. You don't need to."

"We can't afford it," Allie said in a manner and voice designed to mimic her sole surviving parent.

"Don't be smart," her mother replied lightly, never breaking stride as she rushed back to the stove.

Allie smiled in response. She wasn't ignorant of how hard her mother worked in order to support them both. She really didn't mind all *that* much that she had to help out. Besides, there had been no questions about how she had been filling her time. She hummed a happy tune as she plunged her hands into the soapy water.

That night, nestled under an unblemished blanket of twinkling stars, Barrington experienced the strongest earthquake in its recorded history. Unsecured items toppled from vibrating shelves and bleary-eyed people awoke with no immediate idea why. Dogs barked and birds not normally prone to nocturnal activity took to the sky, squawking in alarm. But it ended as suddenly as it began and no major damage was apparent. As a matter of fact, when the sun came up the next morning, it initially seemed that nothing out of the ordinary had happened at all. The quake, in and of itself, was not destined to become a noteworthy event.

However, at the back of a farmer's field several miles out of town, the same geologic activity that caused the quake had left behind dramatic evidence. A ragged, deep tear in the earth swallowed up several acres of corn. After the ground stabilized, a smoke-like cloud of dust wafted out of the chasm, creating an ethereal haze which glowed under the full moon.

In its depths, not even audible from the surface, a soft sound emanated. It was not caused by earth or rock moving. A fluttering cadence was mixed with sporadic clicks. The sound was hardly overwhelming, but was evidence of a disturbing reality.

Something was alive down there.

CHAPTER 2

The crevasse now sat under an early morning sun, perfectly visible but undiscovered because of its remote location. From somewhere in the depths, a bug flew up. It landed on the sandy ground, wings sporadically flickering while being warmed by the sun. Had anyone been there to witness it, they would have cringed away in horror.

It was enormous for a bug, larger than many species of small birds. The olive-colored wings had a leathery appearance. The body was brighter, straw yellow accentuated by red and black stripes. The garish display was nature's emergency siren, a warning not to be taken lightly. The stinger protruding from its abdomen was ridiculously long. The implied threat was all too obvious. This bug was dangerous.

A second bug flew up and landed near the first. After a moment, they both took off; the first scouting mission undertaken by this newly revealed species.

The two would not be alone for long. Deep in the crevasse, a vast horde of bugs was about to ascend skyward. Their underground base was the launching point for their very existence in this world, and would be defended at all costs. The two bugs flew on, knowing exactly what to do—look for threats, nesting sites and food sources.

Amy Worthington had taken off by herself for the first time from the Barrington Municipal Airport and Liquor Store, a potentially disconcerting combination which could only happen in rural America, land of the free and free thinkers. The small Cessna responded nicely to her adjustments on the controls. Bob, her instructor, had not intervened at all. Now she was level at fifteen hundred feet, pondering her next step. She couldn't keep the smile off her face.

"Think I can try landing?" Amy wasn't exactly yelling, but her voice had to be raised to be heard over the noise of the aircraft.

Bob was scribbling on his ever-present clipboard. The short, frizzy hair around his bald spot looked like it hadn't had a comb run through it for the past decade. Maybe he had given up when it started falling out, Amy thought.

"You just took off unassisted for the first time. Do you think you're ready for a landing?"

Amy, a forty-seven-year-old receptionist, had been trying to find some type of tonic for a mid-life crisis. Flying seemed to work. It made her feel free and in control in an exhilarating way. Her husband sensed that she needed this and had been supportive of her taking lessons.

"I am ready, Bob."

4

Bob, a patient man (a great quality for a flight instructor), nodded. "It's the perfect day. We've got light wind blowing straight down the runway."

"Does that mean you'll let me try?" What Amy wanted was to reach a point where she could get licensed to go flying by herself. And fast. *Pedal to the medal, Amy*, she thought. Perhaps it would lead to a career change.

"We'll see. Do a 180° turn, and keep it level."

That maneuver was harder than it sounded, especially for a novice. "Okay. Here we go."

As the wing dipped on her starboard side, she couldn't resist taking a quick peek out the window. During level flight, the instrumentation blocked most of the view. Too bad, since from this elevation, you would be rewarded with an expansive presentation of everything below. Fields spread out like an enormous quilt, the seams represented by intersecting roads, fence lines and streams. Green was the predominant color now, early summer growth in full production.

But there was more to be revealed. That which had been hidden was now in plain view.

"Bob, look at that," she said.

He raised his eyes from the clipboard.

"Right there." She took one hand off the yoke and pointed for added effect.

"Hey, both hands," Bob reprimanded. She realized her mistake, quickly re-establishing her grip. Bob held to his serious expression while shifting his gaze out the window. "What is that?" It looked like an enormous dark tear in the otherwise flawless landscape.

Amy forced her concentration back to flying. "I don't know. Ever seen it before?"

"I don't think so."

"Want me to do another pass?"

She needed the practise anyway, Bob figured. "Straighten us out, first. Then go down to one thousand feet. Once we're level again, you can turn back around. Nice and easy, okay? And don't drop below a thousand."

This is exciting, Amy thought. Better than dealing with annoying customers at work or doing chores at home.

If she had been flying solo and able to make her own decisions, Amy would have flown closer and tipped the wings to get a more direct line of sight. That would present a view directly into the gaping tear. If she had done so, she would have seen motion down there.

"Watch the inclinometer," Bob chided.

Amy grimaced, refocusing. Crashing would be a very bad way to impress her instructor.

While Amy concentrated on making the most precise turn in the history of aviation, the crevasse erupted. Now behind her line of sight, an undulating cloud belched out of the opening and rose skyward. The noise and vibration of the Cessna had alerted the swarm from the depths and it reacted in a savage defensive maneuver. Tens of thousands of leathery winged insects flew with one thought in mind—destroy the intruder.

Once Amy had turned fully, her eyes eagerly sought the chasm. The view was now imperfect, even fuzzy as if seen through a smoky grey filter, and for a brief moment, she couldn't understand why. Could something be burning down there?

"Hey Bob, are you seeing what I'm seeing?"

Bob tried, but the instrumentation blocked his view. "No. Concentrate on the controls, Amy."

"It's coming up."

Amy's voice had concern in it and Bob strained to catch a glimpse. "What's coming up?" He still couldn't see anything. "Relax; there are no obstacles or other planes in this area. We'll be fine."

A large bug splattered against the windshield and Amy gave out a short scream. "What is that?"

Bob wasn't sure. They were at a thousand feet and bugs shouldn't be there. Even if they were, they wouldn't pose a threat. But whatever this insect had been, it was enormous. It seemed more like they had hit a bird. The juices from its crushed body oozed across the glass, creeping Bob out.

Another hit with the same result. Then another.

"Turn us, Amy, and climb higher!"

The erosion of Bob's calm demeanor panicked Amy even more. Suddenly they were enveloped in a dense cloud of bugs. The windshield was being hammered, dead bodies blocking the view.

"Bob, what do I do?" Amy yelled.

"Climb, Amy, climb!"

Amy pulled back on the yolk with adrenalin fueled vigor. The attempted rate of incline quickly exceeded the ability of the small engine. The stall warning buzzer sounded.

"Too much!" Bob screamed. He dropped his precious clipboard and reached for the controls. But it was too late. The plane had reached a speed too slow to maintain sufficient lift.

They dropped like a rock, both occupants knowing full well what was about to happen, screaming hysterically as the last few seconds of their lives ticked away.

The plane crashed into a yard, perhaps half a mile from the crevasse. Damage to the craft was extensive, and that was before it burst into flames.

The accident was destined to be a major news story in the Barrington area, eager but sympathetic readers and listeners soaking it up. Evidence of the bugs was incinerated and the cause would be left to speculation. Amy's lack of experience would take a lot of the blame.

The crevasse, although not hidden for much longer, would not be revealed by the crash.

CHAPTER 3

Overdue notices had become a common problem for John. Lately, they were more insistent, threats of action for lack of payment boldly highlighted. He tore the envelope open with some hesitation, unconsciously cringing as his eyes focused in on the words. In self-preservation, he would skim the letter in a perfunctory manner, and then begin the process of forgetting it existed.

The first sentence changed his plans.

"Fired!"

His full and undivided attention was locked in despite his intentions to the contrary. Indeed, this moment would remain etched in his memory for the rest of his life. It was hard to dismiss an event of this magnitude. After eighteen years, his days of working for Mylan Agricultural Products LLC were apparently at an official end. As the foundation of his financial future collapsed, all he could do was stare incredulously, mouth agape.

Paradoxically, the mascot incorporated in the company letterhead had never looked happier. The cartoon rendition of an animated cob of corn was winking and smiling as if to say, *"Don't worry about us, old pal—we had record earnings last year and with no help from you. How's your bottom line?"*

John tore his eyes away from the poison text. In reality, despite his initial shock, he had been subtly haunted by the possibility of this moment in the dark corners of his imagination for longer than he would care to admit.

So this is how it ends, he thought. No phone call, no face-to-face meeting with a chance for dialogue. He was excrement and they had decided to flush. Emotional trauma notwithstanding, John knew he couldn't stand there with a blank look on his face for the rest of the day. His back wouldn't allow it.

He turned with an effort and some assistance in the form of his despised wooden cane. John hobbled into the living room, pausing at the big bay window. It was a beautiful spring morning, at least for those who still had the capacity to enjoy it.

Why hadn't the union called to warn him? Or better yet, why hadn't they intervened proactively to stop this whole ugly process? The letter should have never been written, let alone sent.

A viable question arose from his musing. Had the company slipped up by not following proper procedure? They were required to inform the union prior to his dismissal, as dictated by the collective agreement. Any departure from protocol would render this disaster null and void. He hobbled back to the kitchen, retrieving his phone from the table.

The union president's number was programmed in his contacts. She had ridden into battle with him many times, winning countless minor skirmishes. None of them ever tipped the balance completely in his favor, but he had always maintained hope that in the end, the war would still be won, or at least a truce declared…until now.

Her phone rang a long time. John was starting to put together the message he would leave when her *I'm not available* message kicked in. But when the line finally clicked, it was a live voice that answered.

"Hello, John."

"Beverly." He had an idea how he wanted to present his case but paused to collect his thoughts.

"You got a letter."

It was a statement, not a question. "It came this morning. I got canned, Bev."

A deafening silence followed. Then, finally, "I know".

Bitter rage, suppressed so deep inside that John barely knew it existed, started to seep out. "What do you mean, "*I know*"? If you knew, then why did I get this thing in the first place?"

"John, we talked about this. Don't you remember?"

"Of course I remember talking. Many times, as a matter of fact. My take was that you were going to do something to resolve all this."

"It's company policy, John. Absenteeism has to have a limit."

"Well, it's a bullshit policy, Beverly."

"Two years away from work; that's as long as they will allow. You have to come back before the two years are up, even if just for a week so the clock can reset. It's quite generous, comparatively. It was a real coup when we got it in the contract."

He fumed silently for a moment, trying to get control of himself. "I'm sure you told me recently that you were going to do something to help me. Am I mistaken?"

"I did, John. I brought your case forward at our quarterly meeting. The membership voted on it. It was rejected. They wouldn't pay for an arbitration hearing."

"Why not?"

"Because the state rep who was attending told them we'd lose. One of the members asked him specifically. Money down the drain, John."

He felt the urge to fight fading. What would follow in its place was far worse—self-pity. He felt it washing over him, ready to usurp control of his emotions.

"There's a reason I didn't come back, Bev, remember? I can barely stand and walk. How could I survive on the shop floor?"

"They offered you modified work, way back in the beginning. You refused it."

"That was a bogus job and you know it! You were one of the ones who recommended that I decline it, were you not? It was custom designed to be so awful, they knew I'd have to quit."

"I thought you'd be better before now."

John grew quieter. "So did I."

"You know what the big problem is, don't you? Your condition wasn't caused by the job. Otherwise, they'd have to keep paying for your disability indefinitely."

"More bullshit, Bev! You know my doctor said that standing motionless for hours every day contributed to the deterioration. They wouldn't even get me a mat when I complained." He took a breath and waxed reflective. "A forty dollar mat."

"The company doctor had a different diagnosis."

"No surprise there. Why couldn't the union have me looked at by somebody else? A doctor that was, oh I don't know, impartial maybe."

"I asked for that as well."

John felt physically ill, but not in his lower back. "They turned that down too?"

"Yes. The membership seems to think you gave up too easily."

"Too easily? My back feels like there's a knife in it right now. I can't stand, I can't sleep, I can't..." There was no point in turning this into a rant. He was at a loss. "What do I do now?" He meant it as rhetorical.

A sigh was audible over the phone. "I called the national office, John. I left a detailed message."

A glimmer of hope flickered through his mind. "Is there something they can do for me?"

A painful delay elapsed. "I don't know, John. Maybe there's something I missed. It's our last chance, really."

It's not your last chance, John thought to himself, *it's mine.*

"John, I'm getting another call. I've got to go."

And there it was. His last bastion of hope was not only waving the white flag in defeat, she was in the lifeboat oaring steadily away from his sinking ship. *Nice to have known you. Good luck in your future endeavours. Sorry about the iceberg.*

"John?"

"Good bye, Beverly." He broke the connection.

An interlude of unknown duration elapsed while John sat motionless at the table. Under any other circumstances, he would have gone outside to enjoy the nice weather. But he didn't want to risk somebody seeing him and trying to engage him in casual conversation.

Hi John, how are you on this fine day?

Thanks for asking, Bill. My life, for all intents and purposes, was just destroyed. I was fired by my effing former employer. Now I'll probably starve to death. So, how're things on your side of the fence?

If he was going to break down, and he felt there was a chance he might, it would be better not to do it in front of the neighbors.

Of course, one question now stood above all others—how would Theresa react to this? He grimaced just imaging that conversation. Their relationship was already strained and this bit of news wasn't going to help at all. Her patience was wearing thin—it seemed like it only existed based solely on the premise that he would eventually reprise his role as primary breadwinner. Since his disability payments and qualification for unemployment benefits had recently expired, she would be bearing that load exclusively.

John had a flash of brilliance. Times were tough (and about to get tougher), but the fridge and cupboards were both relatively full. He would get up and make an awesome supper, ignoring the movements required in the process that would no doubt aggravate the now ubiquitous, shooting pain in his lower back. Theresa would appreciate it. The act would also give credence to the theory that he wanted to put forward; he was still able to function in a productive and positive way. He stood without groaning, considered it a victory, and hobbled towards the counter.

By mid-afternoon, a savory smell was wafting through the house. The main course was going to be lasagne. It required several different phases before all the ingredients were ready to come together, which was exactly what John needed. It was a meal that would be appealing *and* keep him busy enough to provide distraction from self-loathing and other negative thoughts. His lower back, in spite of the plan, became a negative thought that refused to be ignored. John made an executive decision to go over the dose limit for his pain medication before refocusing on the final details.

As per Murphy's Law (something John had recently become a *big* believer in), Theresa was unusually late getting home. The lasagna was well past being ready, transitioning ever so painfully into the realm of being overcooked. The oven had to be turned down so as to warm, but not further incinerate, the main course. John didn't like the color of the cheese, too dark by several shades, for his taste. He was fairly confident that it wasn't actually burnt though; it still smelled good at any rate.

"Come on. Where are you?"

John turned from the window and stole another glance at the table, observing his handiwork with satisfaction. It was set to look like Marcel's, the restaurant where he proposed to her. He even found a white candle in the hutch, now prominently displayed in the middle of it all, just waiting to be lit at the last possible moment. *Classy*, he thought.

He heard a car door slam; his impatient vigil finally rewarded. Theresa was home, all right. But for some reason, she had parked out front along the street rather than in the driveway. And instead of walking in, she was standing there, looking down the road.

"Why would you do that?" He really needed her to get inside so that supper could be served before any further damage was inflicted.

Theresa remained motionless on the road, arms crossed in what presented as a somewhat defensive posture, while a pickup truck rolled up, stopping directly behind her car. A second truck arrived; this one backing into the driveway just like it belonged there. John squinted to see through the glare on the windshield. Who were these people? Why were they here? If they were staying, he was going to come up short on food. Why hadn't she tipped him off?

Now Theresa was moving towards the house, walking with her usual self-confident gait. He decided the best course of action was to meet her at the door. He barely beat her to it, slowed because of his disability, swinging it open as she reached for the handle. He gave her his best smile. She, in contrast, looked very grim and somewhat disconcerted as to why he was filling the role of doorman.

"Hi sweetie. I've been waiting for you. I have a little surprise planned. How was your day?"

She looked ever so briefly over her shoulder before meeting his gaze. So far, nobody had exited either of the trucks.

"John…"

Her voice sounded odd, but he wasn't picking up any of the vibes she was putting out. He was too focused on implementing his plan. "Wait. Before we start talking, please come in. I want you to smell this."

She gave him a perplexed look, then glanced back at the trucks for the second time.

"John…"

"I made lasagne, okay? I hate to ruin the surprise, but you need to know why it's so important that you come inside. If you brought company, it might be a little close, but I think there's enough for everybody. It would have been better if you would have given me some warning, but…"

She looked at him with a mixture of frustration and pity. "John, I'm not coming in."

He blinked in surprise, completely clueless. "Why not?"

"I'm never coming in again, John. I'm leaving."

"What…" he tried, but couldn't formulate the rest of the question.

"I can't do it anymore. I thought I could, but it's just too much."

His lips moved, but no words came out. It was the apocalypse, unfolding in real time before his very eyes.

"These are some people from work. They're here to pick up my stuff. There isn't quite enough room to get all of it now, so they'll have to come back tomorrow for the rest."

Reality, mercifully, was gone. John was standing in a dream. The world had become subjective; the edges hazy, shimmering like a mirage.

"John, did you hear me? Do you understand what I'm saying?"

"But I made lasagne." His voice was small and quiet.

She sighed in frustration. "I need you to let them in, John. You don't have to help or anything. I wouldn't expect that. Just let them do their job."

Their job, John thought. What about his job? He hadn't even told her yet.

"I got a letter today. From the company."

She seamlessly ignored him. "I've already made arrangements. I'll let you know how to contact me once I'm settled in, but not before. And I don't want you calling me constantly or being all clingy. This is for the best, John. For both of us. I need you to know that."

"This is the best for *me*?" Some strength crept back into his words.

She regarded him and his renewed ability to speak critically. "Yes, both of us. Now, I'll be sure to leave enough stuff so that you can still survive. I won't empty the house completely. I just want what I bought, and anything that was a gift from my friends or family. You know, the dining room furniture, some of the appliances, the bedroom set, all my pictures and books, that kind of thing. Okay?"

He had no idea how to answer. He had never been so totally numb. Even his back pain was temporarily forgotten.

"Why don't you just sit at the counter while these guys work? The stools are yours anyway. I don't want you interfering. I don't want any unpleasantness. I don't want to have to call the police because you said or did something stupid. Understand?"

"You're worried that *I* might say something stupid?" Rage billowed up from the dark recesses of his soul. An erupting volcano, it pushed out his normally accepting persona and replaced it with something smoldering and dangerous. "What about saying something *insensitive*...YOU BITCH!" He didn't say it; he spat it in her face.

Her expression was indignant. "What did I just tell you? Don't go there, John."

"It's too late for that, you delusional, self-righteous cunt! And *you're* the one who dragged me here!" He stumbled back inside the house, back pain temporarily banished, and slammed the door shut with such force, he thought for a moment he'd broken it. He fumbled with the latch until he was certain it was locked.

"Fuck the hell off! You and your fucking friends! You're not coming in my house. Did you hear me? My house!"

"I'm calling the police, John. Why do you have to be such a prick about everything?"

Her voice came muffled through the door, but the message and the perceived arrogance behind it got through just fine. His anger fed on it, swallowing it down greedily in one enthusiastic gulp. Strengthened by the sustenance it provided, John ignored the implications of his actions, firing back with gusto.

"I'm a prick about *everything*? You mean like being crippled through no fault of my own? You mean like being married to a selfish, cold-hearted shrew that would push her own grandmother in front of a train if she got something out of it? You mean like getting no support or comfort from the one person I count on the most? Because if that's what you mean by *everything*, then I guess I *am* a prick. But I had a great teacher, okay? Any idea who that was?"

"Asshole."

He was already loading another volley when he heard her heels clicking towards the street, out of hearing range. The adrenalin stopped pumping and he nearly slumped to the floor. The smell of the lasagne now only heralded how oblivious he had been to the reality of the deterioration of their relationship. Preparation efforts notwithstanding, he decided he wouldn't be dining at all this fine evening. His appetite was gone.

In the end, the police came. In the end, her "friends" started to clean out the house. In the end, John decided he didn't care.

Let them take everything. Let them come back tomorrow and go through the process again. It didn't matter to him anymore.

He wouldn't be here anyway.

CHAPTER 4

Brent Rivers had been farming his entire life, (a span of fifty-seven years now), and during that time had never once given any thought to the U.S. Geological Survey. That was until a few moments earlier, when a car containing two agents showed up in his driveway.

Brent, although by nature a law-abiding man, had always harbored a mild distrust of government officials. He found accommodating these two to be a struggle. Their request to go tromping about on his private property would have been better received if they had initially formed it more as a question than a demand. As the hair went up on the back of his neck, his desire to be cooperative dwindled.

"Can you be more specific as to why you need this access? The crops are in a sensitive stage right now. I have too much invested in them to allow anything that could be damaging in any way. I'm sure you understand my reluctance."

They were both young, not long out of school he guessed, and responded to his challenge with awkward expressions. Experienced agents would have handled him with a more deft touch. Brent actually found that to be somewhat redeeming. At least they were being genuine. Something truly conspiratorial in nature would have required better preparation and a more senior employee to present it.

"Satellite imagery clearly shows a geological anomaly on your property, Mr. Rivers," replied the woman with the corn row hair. She seemed to be taking the leadership role, so he addressed her.

"Call me Brent."

She smiled, revealing a set of dimples. "Okay, Brent. Did that help?"

"No. It's pretty much what you said the first time. Can you translate into plain English?"

She turned, looking at the skinny young man beside her, yielding the floor to him.

"It appears to be a large chasm," he said. "From the air, it looks like a tear in the earth. We're here to observe it from ground level and take some preliminary measurements." He looked back at his female companion as if awaiting her approval.

"Right," she said. "Does that clear things up for you, Brent?"

"I'd say it made them foggier. There's no chasm on this property. I know every inch of it and I've never seen anything like that."

"We think it is the result of a recent event. Have you felt or heard anything unusual?"

He furrowed his brow. "We did have a tremor. It was enough to wake me up."

She smiled and her associate bobbed his head. "That could be it, Brent."

"That could be what?" Brent said.

"It could be the moment that this fissure was formed," the young man answered. "It definitely could be something very recent."

This unlikely scenario was going nowhere. Brent had better things to do.

"We can bring back some photos when we're finished," the young man said, sensing the moment of decision was upon them. "You might find them interesting." He came across like a rookie used-car salesman working hard on his first customer.

Brent waved them away. "As long as you don't do any damage, go ahead and take a look. Just use caution while walking through the rows. Check in before you go so I know you're finished and off my property."

If the girl's smile had been any wider, Brent thought her face would have split.

"We will, Brent. Thank you!"

"Let me know if I have to be worried about dropping my combine into this thing when the corn comes off this fall."

The duo was already on the move. The girl responded over her shoulder so as not to impede their momentum.

"We will!"

Brent walked away, still stymied by this revelation. Moreover, he was confident that the girl had no idea what a combine was.

The coordinates of the crevasse now forced them to walk through the field. The young man held a portable GPS device. He pointed to the right. "Over there. Not far now."

They trekked onward, weaving through the corn plants.

"Oh my God, Charles! Look!"

He stopped in his tracks. "Wow!"

A gaping tear in the surface of the ground materialised. The shoulder high corn had camouflaged it until now, exaggerating the shock they felt when it suddenly appeared right in front of them. It was bigger than they had anticipated. From beginning to end, it stretched for a good quarter of a mile. It certainly looked capable of devouring farm equipment.

"Hey," he interjected. "Watch it, Bran. We don't know how stable the sides are. That looks deep."

"Are you kidding me?" she said. "Bran" was short for Brandisha and she was fascinated with this discovery. His warning went unheeded. "This is a once in a lifetime opportunity. Do you know how many geologists ever get to discover something like this?"

He missed the point of the question being rhetorical. "No, how many?" He was following, but staying a respectful distance behind.

"None. These things just don't happen."

"Hey, that's too close."

Brandisha's view was improving. The chasm looked to be at least seventy feet wide at its most extreme. Given the sheer dimensions of the surface tear, it followed that it was a long way to the bottom.

"Come on, Bran. Step back. If you fall in, you'll kill yourself. That could get us both fired."

She was staring at the sides of the chasm, at least as much as she could see from her vantage point. A light mist of some kind rose from the depths, visible against the dark earth. It was subtle, not discernable at all once it reached the lighter colored sky. "I think it gets shallower over there." She pointed to the left of their position. "Let's check it out."

Charles was exercising extreme caution, his particular way of managing stressful situations. "Only if you get further from the edge. Our safety is of paramount importance, remember?"

"I read the training brochure. Come on."

Charles caught a whiff of something noxious. "There's something coming up."

"What do you mean, *something*?"

"I'm not sure. Smoke or some kind of fume." He tried to focus harder. "Maybe sulphur."

"It can't be volcanic," Brandisha responded.

The thought created more stress for Charles. "Are you sure?"

She gave no reply, but suddenly stopped, standing frozen in place.

"What now?" Charles asked.

She held up a restraining hand. "Shh!"

He was at a loss to understand her strange request.

She looked into the hole, then back up to the sky. All her sensory abilities were being transferred as best she could to her ears. "I hear something."

"Don't say that!"

She remained rooted in place, a picture of concentration. "It's sediment running down the wall...I think."

Charles transitioned into full blown panic mode. "It could be another seismic event, which could trigger a wall collapse. *Please* get back!"

Maybe he was right, she reasoned. If the walls had been rock, that would be one thing—but this soil wouldn't have the structural integrity to withstand a lot of vibration. And yet, the sound was so intriguing. Something was happening inside the walls of the fissure; that much seemed certain. She considered moving closer to the edge, but then thought better of it.

"Hold on," she said, while pondering her options.

"I can hear it now," Charles immediately replied.

Brandisha frowned. "No, I think it stopped."

"Let's call this in. They should send a team to investigate."

"After we drove for three hours to get here? Not a chance. Put on your big boy pants and follow me. I think access might be possible."

The corn slowed their progress, but the end of the crevasse eventually drew near.

"See what I mean?" Brandisha beamed.

As the tear narrowed, its depth decreased.

"Don't get any ideas," Charles said.

It took a moment for her to process the next part of her plan. She walked up to the very edge and peered in.

"Bran!"

"We can do this, Charles." She was moving into position to take the first downward step.

Brandisha was trying to be analytical. She was a scientist, after all. Technically, agency protocol prohibited them from entering an unknown, underground, or confined space without proper equipment. But surely the first few steps would be safe enough, even if the ground wasn't completely stable. "Charles, come over here. At least have a look before you decide."

His feet dragged as the last steps were made reluctantly. The midday sun was high enough to illuminate the interior nicely. "Wow. That is one huge fracture."

A twinge of excitement ran through Brandisha.

"Charles…" She took a tentative step forward. "I know how you're going to feel about this, but I'm going in."

He shook his head vehemently. "You'd violate every operations procedure we have. Let's get some photos first and call this in. If you make a request, they might let you be on the incursion team."

"I *am* the incursion team." Holding her arms out for extra balance, she took the first step.

Charles held his position. "You're also crazy."

Brandisha easily envisioned him nagging and whining constantly the entire time she was exploring. "Go back to the car and get some rope and the good camera. That way you can help me get out if your worst fears come true. Okay?"

"And leave you alone?"

She took another step. "I insist."

"Well…"

"Go!"

He was obviously disinclined to leave, but succumbed to her pressure. "Fine. But don't move until I get back."

There was no chance of that.

Brandisha moved steadily but cautiously into the chasm. Her footing was loose, but there were no sharp edges to avoid. It was a scree slope formed by earth and not stone. Even if she slipped, the landing would be relatively soft.

As she went deeper, it was easy to imagine how dark it would become once the sun started to drop. For now, visibility was good. The walls transitioned from light soil, to heavy clay, and eventually to rock. A slight sulphur smell was discernable and Brandisha wondered about the wisdom of not using breathing apparatus. She would hate to prove Charles and his ever-present paranoia right.

When the ground before her levelled out, she estimated it was over one hundred feet from where she stood to the surface. The atmosphere was breathable, as far as she could tell by her current physical reaction—but there was an oppressive feeling there sandwiched between the towering grey walls. Brandisha pulled out her phone and started taking photos while her resolve to explore further strengthened.

When she resumed walking, one of the things she noticed was how quiet it had become. There was no breeze down here, and the noises from the surface hadn't followed her. The walls seemed to absorb sound. Even when she scuffed her feet, the resonance vanished immediately, like it had been sucked into a vacuum. All she could hear was her breathing and the hum of her blood pumping through her ears.

After a few minutes of cautious walking, the initial thrill was wearing off and she felt like it was time to turn back. The surface became more appealing the longer she stayed down there. As she was about to turn around, something caught her eye. She squinted to sharpen her focus.

"What are you?" A dark opening appeared in the wall to her right. As she closed the gap, it became clear what she was seeing. It was an entrance to a cave.

She made the final approach with Charles-like caution, moving slowly and using the light from her phone. The opening was large enough to drive a truck through, and it was impossible to guess at the inside dimensions. Reaching the point of entry, she stopped.

The paltry light her phone cast didn't even reveal walls. It was a huge open space. Standing exposed to an unknown area while essentially blind was creeping her out. Should she enter to explore further or turn around and return to the surface? Two things then occurred to help make up her mind.

The first was the initial sound coming from the cave. It was like a stone falling and then rolling before coming to a rest. Brandisha was startled, followed closely by a wave of curiosity. The second was a different sound. It was soft, barely discernable. Hard to categorize; the best metaphor she could come up with was leaves on an Aspen tree fluttering in a light breeze. The sound got louder as she hesitated.

Brandisha stepped back. She had no clue what made the sound, but it was moving closer. In a panic, she spun around and sprinted back towards the exit.

By the time she was close enough for Charles to spot her, she had slowed to a steady jog.

"Hey!" Charles waved with no small degree of enthusiasm, glad to see his partner in one piece.

Brandisha had reached the upward slope and slowed to a walk. She returned his wave with less gusto and concentrated on her footing.

"How'd it go down there?" Charles asked. "Discover anything exciting?"

To his surprise, she nodded. "There's a cave."

Charles assumed a confused expression. "A cave in a chasm? I have no idea what you mean by that."

"It's perpendicular to the chasm. And Charles...get this—I heard something in there."

Charles blinked away his confusion. "Okay. Like what? Running water?"

Brandisha paused to think. "No. It was more like a fluttering sound."

Things came into focus for Charles. "Oh, probably bats. Did you see any?"

"Bats? Yuck! I never thought of that. No, I left when it became apparent something was moving around in there."

Charles grinned. "Finally reached the end of your reckless courage, huh? Good for you. Are you ready to call this in and then go to town and find some lunch?"

She smiled as his predictable behavior crossed the threshold from annoying to endearing. At least he had her best interests in mind. "Sure. That sounds great. We'll stop and let Farmer Brent know what's happening in his field."

They turned and walked in tandem away from the crevasse. They had barely slipped back into the corn before it erupted.

CHAPTER 5

It was an explosion of a different sort. A seemingly endless swarm of bugs burst out of the chasm and flew skyward. Ironically, it was paranoid Charles who stopped to watch the event. "What in the world…"

Brandisha joined him, standing motionless. "That's not volcanic."

The dark cloud continued to rise. It moved in a strange way, the outer edges undulating erratically.

Charles was feeling his ever-present fear starting to rise. "It's not even smoke."

Brandisha's eyes widened. "Charles, it's alive!"

Now Charles was taking backward steps. "Let's get out of here."

Before she could agree, Brandisha saw one of the individual components of the cloud flying towards her. The "cloud" wasn't a cloud at all—it was a swarm. A huge insect was quickly closing in on her unprotected face. She shrieked in fear and swatted at it wildly. She scored a glancing blow and the insect hit the ground, buzzing angrily as it struggled to regain its balance and get in the air again.

Charles, who had been watching, stepped on it and ground it under the heel of his shoe. He raised his foot and beheld the effects. The bug was now a dripping puddle of twitching parts. He stared, mesmerized.

"Charles! Come on!"

Brandisha took off running at a frantic pace.

"Wait!" Charles sprinted after her. Even though he had run some track in college, he was having trouble gaining any ground on his partner. The corn stalks weren't helping either. He gave up any attempt at minimizing the damage he was causing and simply ran through them, breaking them off as he went. He was finally caught to Brandisha as the effects of her efforts caught up with her. She was gasping loudly as he pulled alongside.

That was when the bug landed on his upper back and stung him.

"Charles?"

His eyes were as wide as dinner plates. His mouth opened but no words came out.

Brandisha hadn't seen the bug. "Charles, what is it?"

Many living creatures have the ability to formulate complex chemicals internally for a variety of purposes. Anyone who runs afoul of a skunk knows that.

Snakes generate poison, some of it deadly even to very large creatures. Spiders inject their prey with a toxin that dissolves their insides, making them easy to consume. Jellyfish emit a substance that burns skin and creates intense pain, a wonderful defense mechanism for an otherwise helpless creature. A Komodo dragon's bite kills its victim slowly while the lizard waits patiently on the sidelines for it to collapse. Some stinging insects inject a compound designed to create sharp pain. This particular insect took that ability to a whole new level.

Charles screamed. It didn't sound human. It was high pitched and desperate, like a small animal in the jaws of a predator, being mauled but not quite dead. He dropped to the ground, his body in spasms, incoherent squeals emanating from his mouth.

She knelt beside him and tried to shake him out of it. Except for the spastic twitches, he was as rigid as a stone.

"Don't worry. I'll call for help."

She felt a bug land on the back of her neck, but even then it was too late to brush it off. It stung, injected venom and immediately flew off.

Then there were two on the ground, incapacitated and suffering.

And neither had the ability to let anyone know.

Brent Rivers was seriously annoyed. The car from the USGS was still sitting in the driveway and that meant those two agents were still back in his field. He had reached the point where he felt it necessary to go and retrieve them.

Grumbling to himself, he hopped into his pickup. The drive back to the field revealed nothing. There were no signs of either of the agents. The obligatory walk through the corn came next.

"Son of a gun."

Brent hadn't believed the story about the massive chasm. But now, here it was, sprawling across the field before his very eyes.

"You've got to be kidding me." He approached slowly, wanting a better viewpoint but unsure of the danger. He stopped six feet from the edge, feeling adrenalin ramp up his senses.

Every dimension was massive. Logistical issues overshadowed his intrigue. "How am I supposed to farm around this thing?" The sides wouldn't allow for heavy machinery to get near it. And filling it in looked like it would take years.

The government already knew about it, he thought. Maybe they could do something to help. But then again, in a worst case scenario, they could declare it some sort of unique habitat and force him to stop farming around it altogether.

"Great." He rubbed his forehead as if that would make the stress melt away. He still hadn't seen any signs of the two agents. His fear now was that they somehow managed to fall in.

"Hey!" he yelled at the top of his lungs.

He waited patiently, but got no response. Brent searched his recent memory for names. He was able to come up with one.

"Charles!"

Still nothing. Something was wrong. It had to be.

"Hello!"

This time he heard a sound. It was not a voice, and indeed didn't sound human. He turned to his right towards the source. He saw nothing but corn.

"Hey! Somebody there?"

There it was again. A strange, undeterminable sound. Brent walked towards it.

"It's Brent Rivers. Where are you two?"

Again the strange sound fell on his ears. He fine-tuned the direction from which it was coming.

"Oh no!"

He saw them both. The two were lying on the ground, immobile. He ran now, reaching them quickly, and then crouched beside their prone bodies.

"What happened? Can you talk?"

Their bodies were rigid and faces strained, like they were lifting heavy weights in the gym. No words came out, just pathetic yet urgent mewing sounds. Brent didn't know much about medical issues, but these two seemed to be under extreme duress.

Whatever this was, it was beyond his abilities to fix. He stood and dialed 911.

After a long and agonizing ordeal, Brent finally found himself in the Barrington General Hospital, waiting for word on the condition of the agents.

They had been heavily sedated and were now sleeping off the effects. According to the initial report from a nurse, a muscle relaxing agent had been injected into them, as well as antihistamines to combat the allergic reaction to the insect's toxin. The attending physician, Arthur Redding M.D., walked over to Brent after being convinced the agents were stable and resting.

Brent's first question was predictable. "Are they going to be all right?"

The expression on the doctor's face was more serious than Brent would have liked. "Yes. They've been sedated and are going to sleep for a while. I'm going to keep them overnight for observation, but I would imagine they'll be fine to go home tomorrow."

He let out a sigh. "Thank God. Doctor, do you have any idea what was wrong?"

He shook his head. "Not for certain. They both had been recently stung and I suspect all their symptoms were a reaction to that. We did a full set of scans. Their heart and brain functions are fine. Blood pressure was way up when they first came in, but that was a reaction to the toxin. It's coming down nicely now. I can't see any signs of permanent damage."

"What kind of sting?"

"That's what I intended to ask you. He has one on his back and she has one on her neck. The skin is somewhat more damaged than we would see in a typical sting, and so is the underlying tissue. That seems to be ground zero for all the other problems. Were you there when all this started? Do you know what they were doing?"

Brent shook his head. "Not specifically. They went back into my field to check out a big hole. When I found them, they were conscious but unresponsive."

"A big hole?"

"They referred to it as a crevasse. Apparently it just appeared the other night when we had that earthquake."

The Doctor's curiosity was piqued by this new information. "Did you see anything that could be linked to what happened to these two?"

"No. Although, while I was waiting for the paramedics, I think Charles said the word "bug" a couple times. His voice was slurred, so it was hard to tell for sure."

Doctor Redding nodded. "I don't know what else it could be. At least that would account for the allergic component to their physical issues. The problem from my perspective is that I have never seen an injury response like this before. The tissue at the wound sites looks to be lightly burned from acid. And the seizing of their muscles was so intense that there's both muscular and tendon damage."

"I thought you said they were going to be all right."

"I did. And they will. There will be some residual pain, similar to the kind from overuse or strain. But it will fade. I took a small tissue sample from the wound. The flesh was deteriorated to the point where we had to remove it anyway. I've sent it to the lab for testing and analysis. I don't think there's any more that can be done at this time."

Brent turned to go. "In that case, I'm going home. Thanks for the update."

"Very well. Have a good night."

"Oh, wait. I was going to ask…did anyone have any luck contacting someone about these two? I imagine their employer and family members will want to know what happened."

"Yes. We bent the rules and went through their clothing to find their ID's. There was an emergency contact number on their government card. A nurse was able to eventually get through to their supervisor. I believe someone is coming tomorrow for an update on their status and to take them home, wherever that is."

That was all Brent needed to hear. "Fantastic. Thanks for everything, Doctor."

"Mr. Rivers, have you noticed any unusual insects or insect activity on your farm lately?"

It was an easy answer. He had already been thinking about it. "No, nothing."

"Hmm, okay. Just thought I'd ask. Good night."

Brent walked out of the hospital, all the while trying to convince himself there was nothing to worry about back home.

This was no doubt a one-time only, freak accident. Things would simply go back to normal and that suited Brent just fine.

CHAPTER 6

John stretched cautiously, moaning as he did so. Using his car as sleeping quarters, he concluded, was apparently in no way good for musculoskeletal well-being. More than his back now ached in the mornings. He decided to go on a short, slow walk to loosen things up. John opened the door and grimaced his way to a standing position.

Fumbling in his pocket for a moment yielded a small medicine bottle. John regarded it critically as he limped along, doing a quick inventory. No visit last night from the pharmaceutical fairy, he noted. There was enough remaining for four more days. He dry swallowed two pills, pondering what the effect of running out would have on his spinal deterioration. That, and the looming demise of his limited funds, posed serious hurdles to the continuity of what he had come to think of as the *Running from Reality Tour*.

On the bright side, this particular part of the fine state of Pennsylvania was as picturesque as anywhere John had been in this unfolding odyssey. The Poconos created a tantalizing scenic vista utilized by resorts and other tourist destinations to draw in vacationers. Standing on the edge of a drop off a short distance from his car, John could see for miles. He sighed in response to the contradiction between this beautiful moment and the exquisite agony of his life's situation.

John was now viewing everything from behind a curtain of perpetual discouragement and despair. Even the best moments he'd been able to generate since Theresa left, paled into mediocrity. He was losing this battle and he knew it. A bad ending now seemed inevitable. At that vulnerable moment, in the deep portions of his subconscious, a dark door swung open for the first time. Behind it lurked a defective notion camouflaged behind a convincing facade.

Maybe there *was* a solution to his problems. Who needed a long-term plan if they had only a short-term future? Why not reassert control over this mess and bring it to an end before it got any worse? Nobody could force him to go on. Simply say *"That's enough for me, thank you very much"* and get off this train bound for nowhere. There was a multitude of ways to punch out early and bring this suffering to an end. Nobody would even miss him. Perhaps it was worth considering.

This represented a radical change in his fundamental life view. Notably, while he didn't embrace the idea with open arms, he wasn't shocked by its appearance, nor did he immediately dismiss it. He walked back to the car, feeling the usual aches and pains, but nevertheless still fully committed (at least for now) to decline the option of rocketing off the edge of a cliff or ploughing into a bridge abutment at highway speed.

As a matter of fact, he felt motivated. The clock was ticking again—the time for lollygagging pointlessly had come to an end. He needed to regain his focus. If he was going to discover a solution to his problems, he was clearly going to have to do it soon. He drove east for several hours, entering New York State, and then turned northward for no particular reason.

Vermont eventually called to John, but in a strange language he didn't completely understand. Once he laid it out bare and had a good look at it, he really had no idea why he'd come this way. Not that it mattered much—he had to go somewhere. Why *not* here?

He was coming to the end of his adventure anyway. At last check, his bank account had fewer than three hundred bucks left in it. The gas required to do nothing more than drive around for the rest of the week would deplete that paltry amount, which left no funds for the fun things he liked to do, such as eating on a daily basis. In mild desperation, John considered the notion that he might still have access to the joint account he and Theresa had used to pool their funds (back when they actually had some). He could transfer money out of it, into his personal account, right over the phone, but that seemed like nothing more than highway robbery given the current status of their "relationship". Objection sustained, motion denied.

He pulled off the interstate onto a secondary road and decided to look for a place to spend the day.

Although lacking a cohesive purpose or schedule, the *Running from Reality Tour* continued.

Allie's mom had decided to close the restaurant for Memorial Day, a welcome reprieve for both her and her daughter. The cost of losing a day's revenue weighed on her mind, but business had been improving recently, so she decided they could afford it, if only just.

Today, she cooked but not for Casa Comida. Rather, she made breakfast at home for her only child. Allie was complimentary and ate well, but to her mother's disappointment, she was obviously anxious to be elsewhere. She could hardly sit still.

"Allie!"

Allie looked up from her nearly empty plate, a perplexed look plastered openly across her face. "What's wrong, Momma?"

"You gulp that food down like you are starving. Stop it before you choke."

Allie smiled. "I won't choke."

"So you say." Kemina shook her head. "Where do you have to be that is so much more important than spending time with your mother? Can't you enjoy this day instead of rushing through it?"

"We're spending the whole afternoon together. And then there are the fireworks tonight. I just want to go for a walk, that's all."

"Are you sure?" Kemina picked up Allie's now empty plate, depositing it in the sink. "You're not going out to meet some boy, are you?"

Allie reacted with shock. "No! Why would I? Momma, don't even say that."

Kemina appraised her critically. "Another summer is here. It will be followed by your first year of secondary school. You have become a teenager." She wagged her finger, a habit in her communications repertoire that was frequently utilized. "You are changing into a beautiful young lady. Don't tell me the boys haven't noticed."

Allie crinkled her nose. "Boys are gross."

Kemina gave her daughter an all-knowing look. "You say that now. You will change your mind."

"Why?" She stood from the table. "I can't see where they're good for anything."

Kemina hadn't been involved romantically with a man in years. She seldom had time to reflect on or regret that circumstance. "Some things." She said it mostly to herself.

"What's that?"

"Nothing, little one." She still felt a transient emptiness that was sometimes painfully acute. Thank God Allie didn't seem to suffer from the harsh realities generated by these memories.

"May I go now?"

Kemina stopped, giving her *The Look*. "Out into the country?"

"Yes ma'am." Now was the time for absolute tact.

"In that dirty ditch?"

"No ma'am. I cross at a bridge."

"Through the field?"

"Yes."

Allie was clearly trying to be succinct. *Anything you say can and will be used against you.*

"Into the forest?"

"Yes, Momma."

"What about wolves?"

Allie blinked. "Wolves?"

Kemina noted that she had finally caught her daughter off balance. "Yes, and bears."

"I don't think there are any bears or wolves in this area."

"You don't *think*? Then how do I know you are safe?" The answer to that question was of paramount importance.

"I have permission from the farmer. I have never seen anything dangerous out there. He would have forbidden me if there was risk."

"But Allie, you are just a girl. Why do you insist on wandering out in the middle of nowhere by yourself? I need to know you're safe. I feel nervous about this." Kemina wished Allie had some understanding of, or appreciation for, mother's intuition.

"Why don't you come with me then?"

Kemina smiled. "Do you know how many miles I walk every day on the hard floors in Casa Comida, little one? No, I think I'll clean up from breakfast and sit under the tree in the backyard. Maybe read a book while I drink some tea. I like the sound of that."

The final answer hadn't been clearly stated. "May I go?"

The smile was now gone. "Very well, you go. But you be very careful. Make sure you are back here for lunch. No scrapes, no bruises, no torn clothing or that will be the end of these walks. Do you understand?"

"Yes, Momma. I promise to be careful."

Kemina gave her a down-the-nose look that could have been considered haughty, but was merely a reflection of the inherent dignity that life's struggles hadn't yet been able to torture out of her.

"And no boys."

Allie kissed her mother on the cheek in response as she ran out of the house.

Humidity was building under an unfiltered sun. Her goal now in sight, Allie felt herself longing for the coolness of the trees. A stroll through the field was all that remained between her and the forest. Unexpected movement caught her eye as she made her final approach to the narrow bridge she had to cross.

Two boys climbed up the ditch bank in front of her. They had been hidden until now, their unexpected presence startling Allie into a complete stop. They reached the top, stepped out onto the road, and saw her for the first time. One of them had a crude spear fashioned from a sharpened stick in his hand. A frog, legs limp and dangling, was impaled on the point. Her uncertainty about her current situation was apparent in her static, gawking position. The boys stared back. Allie realized that it was way too late, and she was way too close, for any evasive action to appear casual. Whatever she did now, whether turning back, walking past, or just standing there, would look and feel forced and artificial. She had a wisp of concern waft through her emotional state.

One of the boys, Brad Merritt was his name, grinned. "Hey, look who it is."

Allie forced a smile. "Hi." Her voice projected no self-confidence. She had seen them at school, but they were not her classmates. She pegged them as seniors, from the other grade eight grouping.

"It's that Mexicano girl."

The second boy, Lonnie Attwater, held the spear but said nothing. He had also assumed an uninviting smile.

"You're the burrito family, right?" Brad said. "Tacos for breakfast every day. Aren't you illegal immigrants or something?"

Allie felt obliged to say something in response. "No."

"Yeah, that's you. Don't lie." Brad's hair was jet black and thick. His front teeth protruded slightly, giving his open mouthed visage a kind of wolf-like appearance. He wasn't bulky, but he looked…solid, strong. He took a step in her direction, almost as if to gauge her response.

"I'm just walking." Not *much* of a response, but it was all she had.

His expression was bold and defiant. He took another step, this time spreading out from his leering partner, covering a wider area. "Just walkin', huh? Well, this is *our* road. You shouldn't be here."

She noticed that her breathing was accelerated. *So this is what fear feels like*, she thought abstractly. A moment ago, she'd been happy and relaxed.

"What're you gonna do to pay for using it?"

She didn't understand the implication, but it suggested something bad.

"I'll leave. Sorry." It was a feeble response. Why did she have to apologize anyway? It was a public road. Desperation was creeping into her thoughts. This was bad, but it wasn't yet awful. Her mother's warning of danger flashed through her mind (boys, bears and wolves), followed by a pang of regret.

"No, you're not going anywhere." His slow but purposeful approach, now being matched by Lonnie, had brought him close enough to run her down if she decided to bolt. That was a predatory response she didn't want to invoke. She was now quite sure that there was blood showing on the exposed tip of the spear. As subtly as she knew how, she slid her foot backwards.

"My mom will be expecting me." Another weak response, she knew. *Perhaps* it would be better than nothing. *Perhaps* it would buy her some time until this worked itself out. *Perhaps* they were just bluffing—teasing her. *Perhaps*. But it didn't feel that way.

"Hey, look. She's got little Mexican boobs." Brad grinned, pointing. Both sets of their eyes locked on shamelessly.

Allie felt a cold chill. She had been in denial about the physical changes that were starting to manifest themselves, another unwelcome side effect of the dangers of being thirteen. She was wearing a light tee-shirt and shorts. She suddenly felt underdressed.

"Hey, is it cold or somethin'? I guess this ain't like the Mexican weather, huh? Look at those little nipples standing up."

She slid back another step, the duo matching her movement. She resisted the urge to cover her chest with her hands. She was no longer bothered by the heat of the day. As a matter of fact, she wasn't bothered by or even aware of anything but the need to get out of this place.

"Come on. Show us those little titties. Lift up your shirt and we'll let you go." Brad's eyes glistened in cruel anticipation. The spear carrier guffawed at the humor in this amusing scenario.

Allie was consumed by the horror and helplessness of her situation. She had no intention of showing anything to anybody.

"Do it!" The boy's voice was now loud and demanding. The look of expectancy was replaced by anger. "Take your shirt off or we'll take it off for you. Then you can walk home without it." A smile returned to his face but there was nothing pleasant in it.

"No." There was little defiance in her tone. It was a reflection of how she wanted this to be resolved. She hated the feeling that her own free will was being taken away from her.

"Last chance. Do it or maybe we'll pull your pants off, too. Then you can just walk back into town naked."

Lonnie, the boy with the spear, responded to the last statement. He whipped the crude weapon in a whistling arc, the impaled frog flying off when it reached its apex. The body gyrated through the air, landing on the road with a pitiful splat. Allie wanted to ignore her own peril and weep for the poor thing and this violent, pointless end to its life. Why he felt the need to have his crude lance unencumbered was a mystery to Allie. Perhaps he had grown weary of looking at the dead amphibian. Then he spoke.

"Let's do it." There was no hint of jest in his tone. It was the voice of a boy, carrying an adult implication.

"You want to?" Brad asked. His tone wasn't threatening, but reflective and thoughtful. Either he was a good actor or Allie had entered into the worst scenario that she could have imagined. This couldn't be what it seemed. These were boys from town, after all. They went to the same school she did. They weren't officially out of elementary school yet—they couldn't be ready to turn into violent criminals. This was all designed just to scare her, she rationalized. It was working well. Then she looked at the sprawling body of the frog and concluded she might have to make a run for it after all.

That was the moment Brad decided to stop all pretext that this might be a charade. He walked with boldness right up to Allie, standing in front of her, smiling with no semblance of humor at all. Allie couldn't make her own body respond to her commands. She stood rooted in place, incapable of anything but dread.

His arms shot out and he pushed her—hard. It was an unexpected move and Allie lost her balance, falling to the gravel. She scraped her elbow. From the level of pain it generated, she figured it must be bleeding. Her Momma was going to be mad if any got on her clothes, she thought as tears welled up in her eyes. Brad grabbed her arm, pulling her to her feet, making her grimace with pain.

"You had your chance," he hissed. He twisted her wrist until her arm was wrenched in an unnatural position. He did it hard, and she cried out as she felt more pain.

"Shut up or you're just going to make this worse." He loosened the pressure on her arm, but just a little. "You might as well do what we want. It'll be over faster that way."

The other boy stood in front of her, leering.

"I wanna pull her pants down."

Maybe this wasn't even real. Allie tried to use her mind to teleport away. It didn't work.

"Okay. But I'm first. You get sloppy seconds."

The euphemism held only a hazy meaning to Allie, but that was more than enough. She knew one thing; this was going to end very, very badly.

CHAPTER 7

John was lost. The surface of the narrow road he was on turned into gravel without warning or fanfare. Although he had no exact destination in mind, he still preferred to know where he was. But he didn't, and like any man, he hated the idea.

The corn looked healthy, John supposed, though he had no real interest in it. It made him think of his former employer, and that was downright unpleasant. At least it was too early in the growing season for there to be any grinning cobs of corn dangling off the side of the plants.

What kind of folk live out here? John pondered after the notion of asking for directions flickered through his mind. And wouldn't that be a great conversation? *Hi, I don't know where I'm going, but I sure as hell don't want to be here. Can you help me get away as fast as possible?*

His phone rang, startling him and interrupting his morose line of thought. It was his first call in quite some time. His phone display showed an unknown number. He slowed the car to a crawl, but didn't stop. There had been no one else on this road for some time. He figured he was safe enough.

"Hello?"

"John."

It was Theresa. He found himself incapable of response.

"John?" It was no longer a statement, but had an inquiring tone.

"Yeah. It's me."

An awkward silence ensued. John felt loathing. He pondered hanging up.

"Where are you?"

John frowned. "I'm in the magical land of *none of your damn business*." It sounded harsh and he regretted it, but only a little.

More silence followed.

"I was worried about you, John. You just disappeared. Nobody has heard from you."

The idea that she was worried about him seemed unlikely. The car crunched its way along the fine stone path.

"Well, I'm fine," he lied.

"John, we still have things to work out. Things to take care of."

The peaceful setting and the slow pace couldn't keep his blood pressure from rising. "Oh, don't worry about that. I think you pretty much took care of everything." Perhaps a better solution would be to throw the phone out of the window, into the ditch. He considered it, but then thought better of it.

"Look, I know you're angry with me. But what about the house? It can't just sit there empty. Aren't you coming back?"

"I don't think so," John said.

"We'll have to sell it then. I can't do that on my own."

"Then I guess you're pretty much screwed." That put a smile on John's face, even though the premise was nonsensical. The delay would also hurt him financially.

"Don't be an ass. If we sell in this market, there should be a little money for us to split when it's all settled. And you've got stuff in the house. Even in a garage sale you could make a few hundred dollars. Maybe even a few thousand. You can't just leave it there."

A little money, John thought. That would be good right about now. But returning seemed only slightly more appealing than driving headlong into a big tree. "Okay, I see your point. The problem is that I'm a long way from home right now, and I have no plans to return."

"Ever?"

Was there a hint of concern in her tone? "Not now. I don't have any concept of my future beyond the next few days."

"John, I can move some of this along if I know what you want and have verbal consent to do so. But legal issues arise with selling the house. The bank and realtor will need your signature to do anything."

John couldn't face the thought of returning. "What about an electronic signature?"

"I don't know. I'd have to ask. Are you that determined not to come back?"

John could now see people along the side of the road ahead. He closed the gap towards them at a snail's pace. At least he could find out where he was, and how to get out of here.

"Look, can you find out?" he said. "If you'll sell my stuff, I'll split the money with you or something."

A slight hesitation, then, "How would I get it to you?"

"Just deposit in our account and I can withdraw it from there."

During the following interlude, John imaged he could hear her mental gears spinning. Maybe his ability to do that had slipped her mind. As his car approached, he could now discern that the people he saw were in fact just kids. They should still be able to give him directions though.

"I guess that would work. How much do you want for this stuff? There are some big items still here."

Something about the dynamics of the group had captured John's attention. When he responded, his voice sounded distracted. "Whatever you can get. I could use a little cash. Sooner would be better than later."

"It's going to take some time to get answers and organize this without any help from you."

The accusatory tone was lost on John. He had bigger fish to fry now. "Just do the best you can, Theresa. Thanks." He hung up without any further ado, cutting off a string of expletives that followed in reaction to the sudden dismissal. He squinted to pin-point his focus as he approached the trio on the road.

Allie felt her shorts give up the brief struggle to save her from what the boys had in mind. They slid down with disappointing ease after clearing the slight bulge of her young hips. She was crying now, not even realizing it. Her Momma had been right all along. *Boys, bears and wolves.* They posed a danger and she had been oblivious.

A car horn blared. It was right on top of them and was loud enough to cause all three of them to jump. The boys whirled around. Even Allie, despite facing the direction from which it had approached, didn't see it coming. She had been a little distracted.

It pulled alongside and stopped. The window was down, and a man with an angry face started yelling. John had seen more than enough to get good and riled up.

"What the hell is going on here?" he demanded. "What are you boys doing?"

Neither boy had anything to say. They turned and started walking away. It was way too casual a walk for what they had been caught doing. John decided to risk it, opening his door. He didn't want them to see how immobile he was. But he was fuelled by righteous anger and couldn't help himself.

"Hold it right there. You two can wait until the police get here."

John hadn't called 911 yet, but the bluff worked fine. Both boys bolted, running with Olympic fervor down the middle of the road.

"Hey!" He yelled it out with gusto, but it was all he had. He watched just long enough to be sure that they were not giving any thoughts to coming back.

"Bastards." He turned his attention to the girl.

She was pulling up her shorts, snuffling and crying. John approached her cautiously.

"Hi sweetheart. Are you okay?" The question was undiluted idiocy, but it was all he could come up with on short notice.

She attempted a smile, which failed to be convincing. "Yes. I'm fine." She then burst into real tears.

John was afraid to approach her, to touch her. But he followed his protective instincts regardless of the risk. He put his arm around her shoulder. She threw her arms around him and cried. It didn't last long, however. She had some steel in her backbone, John thought.

"I'm sorry. I'm all right now. Honest."

John observed her. "You don't seem all right. I think you should go see a doctor."

She looked horrified, and not for the first time since this whole escapade started. "No! They didn't do anything." They were going to though; she was certain of that. "I just need to go home."

John considered it. "Let me at least give you a ride. Okay?"

She seemed reluctant. John didn't blame her in the slightest. "I can walk. They're gone now."

John was still able to see them. "There is no way I'm leaving you now. If you walk, I'm going to follow you in my car until I know you're safe in your house."

She seemed to lose the will to argue. "All right. If you could drop me off, that would be fine."

John smiled. "Okay, now you're talking. You can give me directions on how to get back to the main road while we're driving. I seem to have gotten myself a little bit lost."

"All right." Allie walked over to the far side of the car, opening the passenger door.

John put the car in gear and his magical journey resumed.

"Home so soon?" Kemina had a relieved smile across her face. It didn't last long.

Allie walked in, determined to present herself as if nothing had happened. But the moment she saw her mother's face, her emotions let loose. She ran to her, grabbing on in a tight embrace, sobbing.

"What is it, little one? What happened?"

Kemina noticed a man standing awkwardly in the doorway.

"Who are you?" she asked sharply.

He seemed to have trouble finding a suitable response. "I'm John. I just wanted to drop her off. I also wanted to make sure somebody was home."

The eyes blazed, burning into him. "Why was she in your car?"

"He was helping me," Allie cried, forcing herself to intervene. Her mother pushed her gently out to arm's length away, regarding her with a critical eye.

"Helping you with what? I don't understand."

"I…" It was all she could manage before losing control of her emotions again.

Kemina held her while staring daggers at John. He walked closer, hands outstretched with open palms, trying to look harmless in the process.

"I was driving down the road out there," he said, pointing out the door for clarification. "I was just out of town, where it turns into gravel. I saw this young lady along the edge of the road. There were two boys there with her."

"Boys?"

"Yes. They were…"

"Why were you with boys?"

Allie struggled to regain control. "I didn't know they were going to be there."

The eyes, still blazing but now tinged with confusion, swung back to John.

"They were…" John was astonished at how difficult it was to talk to this woman about what had happened to her child.

The eyes continued to drill into him.

"When I got there, she, umm…"

"What happened to my daughter?" The voice was strained.

"Momma, I'm okay," Allie managed.

"Then tell me what happened."

She sobbed but that was all she could manage.

John cleared his throat, which seemed to be closing up. "She was, umm…they had…well…"

"Tell me!"

"Her pants were pulled down." It was easier to just blurt it out.

"What!" She had an expression of abject horror on her face.

Allie clung to her mother, sobbing.

John decided to push this along. "I don't think anything happened. They ran off when I drove up. She told me that she was all right, but I insisted I give her a ride home. I wanted to be sure there was somebody here for her before I left."

The room was silent except for the soft sounds of emotional release, now emanating from both of them. John was acutely uncomfortable.

"Maybe it wouldn't be a bad idea to see a doctor," he said. "But it's up to you."

Kemina's eyes had softened when they met his gaze again. "Thank you for bringing her home."

"You're welcome." He weighed his options. "I didn't call 911. Do you want me to? I can do it from my cell."

She shook her head. "I will take care of her. You have been very kind, but I don't think there is anything else you can do."

He nodded in agreement. "Very well. Sorry to have met you under such difficult circumstances. I'll just see myself out."

That he did with great relief.

CHAPTER 8

Geraldine Stafford wasn't that old (in her thirty-seventh year and in good shape to boot, thank you very much), but she was definitely old school. The laundry had been hung on the line despite the nice electric dryer she had recently purchased for days where the weather didn't cooperate. As per the forecast, the sun had been shining and sufficient time had passed to ensure no moisture was left in the clothes. Geraldine lugged the laundry hamper out, deposited it under the line and started removing shirts and pants.

Anything worth doing was worth doing with enthusiasm. She grabbed the clothes and tossed them into the hamper with vigor. Geraldine wanted to get done and they still had to be folded and put away once they were brought in. What she didn't know was that there was something undesirable in the fresh smelling laundry, hidden in the rumpled pile, temporarily caught in a rolled up sweater.

Getting through the doorway with the bulky hamper was a chore, but she had done it before and knew the trick. Soon it was on the living room floor, and she was folding clothes and sorting them into piles on the coffee table. That was, until the phone in the hamper rang.

That certainly was what it sounded like. It wasn't a ring, but a persistent buzzing sound coming from somewhere in the remaining pile. As Geraldine rummaged through the clothes in order to find the source, it occurred to her that her phone was sitting on the kitchen counter. How odd.

The bug had been in the sweater when she pulled it from the line, and by now it was good and angry. She felt something hit her hand that was too hard to be any kind of cloth. An instant later, she was stung.

At first it felt like her hand had been shut in a car door. She recoiled, yanking it out of the basket. Eyes wide from pain and fear, she stood and took a couple of wobbling steps away from the hamper. Then the pain ramped up exponentially and she collapsed onto the floor, moaning.

Her kids returned home some time later and found her still there. Unable to get any kind of coherent response despite her eyes being wide open, they called emergency services.

"Mad" Myles Jankowski didn't give a crap about the fields and whatever was growing in them, but he liked the flat, open roads with little traffic and a virtually nonexistent police presence. President of *The Savages*, a regional biker gang, he seldom got the opportunity to ride alone. But this day was so perfect, he made a spur of the moment decision to hit the road with no escort. As President, he had enemies from rival gangs that would do him harm if the opportunity presented itself. Here, on the open road in the middle of nowhere, that seemed unlikely. Besides, at slightly over six feet tall and a smidge north of three hundred pounds, he could take care of himself.

He had been riding for over two hours and had to find somewhere to refuel. It was time to pay attention to the road signs. He had that thought a split second before the bird flew into his forehead and nearly knocked him off of his Harley. Some kind of body fluid and pieces of flesh got in his eyes and blurred his vision, burning as they did so. He pulled over quickly while he still had control.

He peeled off his half-shell helmet and tossed it without regard as to where it would land. He grabbed for the sloppy remains spread across the upper part of his face with both hands. It was a gooey, disgusting mess. And it wasn't a bird at all.

His forehead had a sharp, sudden pain slice through it. He grabbed in reflex and pulled away more residue. There, twitching in his hand, in a puddle of crushed parts, was the ass end of a large bug. Protruding from it was a long stinger with a single yellowish drop of liquid oozing out of it.

The pain in his head exploded. He screamed and grabbed it, losing his balance. Both he and the bike toppled over. His leg was pinned, but that was of no immediate concern. The pain in his head consumed his every thought.

It felt like a long, jagged shard of broken glass was being slowly and tortuously pushed through his skin, his skull and into his brain. On top of that, a feeling of pressure like an SUV had driven over his head and stopped with the tire sitting on it, gave him reason to think his skull would split and his head would burst. It was the sum total of every pain he had ever felt in his lifetime, condensed into one hellish presentation. He screamed, not a bellow from a powerful man, but high pitched like a small animal caught in a trap. He would have given anything, paid any price, not to endure even one more second of the absolute torture that was consuming him. Relief was all he could think of, but that blessed event was a long time away. To him, it would seem like an eternity.

Two miles down the road, a red sports car with its convertible top down was zipping along the quiet road. Randy Sanderson couldn't keep the grin off his face. It felt like summer was finally here and he was loving it.

A gigantic bug flew out of nowhere and settled on a course that lined it up with Randy's face. He couldn't help but flinch when the disgusting thing hit the windshield and splattered into a gooey mess before his very eyes.

"Oh, gross!" Randy turned on the wipers and spray wash simultaneously, but the immediate result was an even bigger smear. Persistence paid off, and soon the guts and juices started to relinquish their hold on the previously pristine glass. Randy had no idea what he had hit, but before he could speculate too much, a disturbing sight came into view. A biker was lying on the shoulder, his cycle seemingly dumped awkwardly on top of him.

"Oh no!"

It had been less than three minutes since Myles had been stung when Randy stopped and did a Good Samaritan investigation. Unable to get any coherent information from the man, and incapable of lifting the heavy bike off of his leg, Randy called 911. It took forty minutes for an ambulance to arrive.

By then, Myles had begged for death numerous times in an incoherent, smeared voice. It did not come. But the pain stayed, chewing on his nerve ends like a Rottweiler on a bone. Myles, now incapable of sustained cognitive thought, managed only to fleetingly wonder numerous times why he couldn't pass out from the pain. No answer was forthcoming.

Dr. Redding seldom visited the hospital lab. Today was the day to make an exception.

"Hello Alice," he said to the slender woman in the lab coat.

"Arthur! How are you? Haven't seen you for a while."

"I don't suppose you'd believe me if I said I've been busy."

She smiled. "I might. There's lots of that going around lately."

"Have you had a chance to look at that tissue sample yet?"

"Are you referring to the sting victims' samples?"

"Alice, why did you pose that in the plural form? I only sent one."

She responded with a shallow smile that was not meant to reflect happiness. "We've had a total of four victims so far, including your two."

"Four? All stung by the same insect?"

"It sure looks that way. All have major entry wounds. All were incapacitated yet conscious. On a brighter note, all are responding well to standard treatment for an allergic reaction."

Dr. Redding filed and collated this new information. "What else can you tell me about these two new victims?"

"No similarities, at least nothing obvious. First one was a housewife, source of sting unknown. The second was a big biker guy who hit one of the bugs while driving. It got him in the forehead. Ouch."

The doctor cringed. "It seems your research into this might be more important than I originally thought."

Her smile sweetened. "All my research is important, Arthur."

"You know what I mean. What have you discovered?"

"First of all, we both know my research falls only within the parameters of chemical analysis, so there's still a lot to learn outside of that. Now, let me give you a summary. That sting consists of a very complicated venom. I found things I still don't understand. Do you know what kind of insect did this?"

He shook his head. "No. That's one of the reasons I wanted to get this analysed. I talked to the two original victims and they described an insect the likes of which I've never heard of before."

She turned back to her desk and retrieved a sheet with the chemical breakdown on it. "Well, we have a blend of the usual bee and wasp components. Melittin is the main chemical in bee stings and there was some of that. It can kill and break up cells, and that explains the deterioration of the tissue. A bee sting, however, wouldn't do damage on a scale that large. The rest of the bee compounds I found are relatively benign. Now, here is where it starts to get strange.

"I found piperidine alkaloids. They are known to cause severe pain. But this chemical is generally found only in fire ants. How it got mixed up with whatever this bug is remains a mystery to me. And it doesn't stop there. Amongst other things, I found acetylcholine. This compound stimulates pain nerves, but it too is commonly found only in stinging ants. It accentuates the pain of a sting."

"You said amongst other things. Is there more?"

"Yes. There were other toxins utilized by hornets and wasps. Some I simply couldn't categorize. The funny things is, to me it seems like the sting is designed to both inflict severe pain and incapacitate the victim, but also to keep them alert and fully aware. Cruel little bastards. If you think this is really important, we'll have to send more samples on to a better equipped lab."

Dr. Redding took a moment to ponder his response. "Not yet. Can I ask you another question?"

"Sure."

"The victim's bodies experienced severe muscle seizures. They were basically locked in position when they got here. I think that's where a lot of the pain originated from. Can anything you found explain that?"

She took off her wire rim glasses and rubbed her eyes. "No, nothing that I've been able to identify would explain that. I understand the pain aspect, however. I used to wake up with a charley-horse in my calf when I was going to the gym on a regular basis. It felt like my leg was being crushed in a steel vise."

"Here's hoping an insect can't inflict that sort of suffering. Thanks for the help, Alice."

"Should I be stocking up on repellent?"

He didn't smile. "I feel like I have no idea what is happening. I need to find some kind of expert, whoever that might be."

She repositioned herself in front of her microscope. "Whoever that might be."

He turned to leave. "I'll figure it out."

CHAPTER 9

John discovered that he was in Barrington, Vermont. Although he had never heard of it before, he decided it looked like a suitable place to spend the night. He cruised around, seeking a safe place for his car.

He found a small parking lot across from the town library, located two blocks from the main street. It was quiet, visible from very few homes. Since the library happened to be closed, there was but a single car taking up residence there. Now he just had to figure out where to eat.

The portion of the main street where most businesses were located didn't seem to be that lengthy, and he felt like he needed the exercise, so John walked. He found an interesting diner, but it was closed after lunch. He ignored the Mexican restaurant, concerned about how the spicy food might affect his digestive tract even before spying the *closed* sign in the window. A small cafe looked a little too hoity-toity for his tastes. That left the sub shop as his last resort.

John got an assorted on white with everything (why not?), and then found a bench beside the war monument. He sat alone, eating and pondering. He'd be broke in another two or three days. Maybe it was time to officially abandon the *Running from Reality Tour*, and head back home. John laughed as soon as the thought manifested itself. He had a house, but it could no longer be considered a home. He had no job, no wife and no good thing waiting for him. He pictured himself six months from now, living under a bridge, eating out of dumpsters. The thought was swept away before it could ruin his demeanor. No point getting teary eyed out in public amongst strangers.

He finished his repast, forcing himself back onto his feet. He meandered through several of the small shops that were open before he started to feel conspicuous. It was easy for the locals to pick him out as a newcomer. He was garnering too many stares. Besides, he never liked the feeling of walking out of a store without making a purchase. An ever-present paranoia made him imagine that somebody was going to peg him as a thief and make him empty out his pockets. He picked up a copy of the town paper (twelve whole pages), and a crossword puzzle book before heading back to his car. An evening of news and word games lay before him, followed by a night of tossing and turning through agonizing pain.

He could hardly wait.

John woke with a start. The sky lit up in a brilliant flash of red followed by a booming crash. In a baseball field, one block down from where he was parked, someone was lighting off fireworks.

John sat upright, grimacing as he did so. He was momentarily confused, but then it came to him. "Oh, Memorial Day. How did I forget that?" He liked fireworks and he wouldn't be able to sleep now anyway. He exited his car and walked in their direction.

It was dark enough that he felt like he could blend in with the crowd. After hobbling up to the edge of the field, he stood there like he belonged and watched the sky. He contributed to the 'oohs' and 'aahs' generated in appreciation for the bigger bursts. For a small community, it was a pretty good show. John allowed himself the pleasant illusion of being a part of things. Several people exchanged short snippets of casual conversation with him in the gloom before the show wrapped up.

John walked back slowly (no problem there) in order to let the crowd disperse, wanting to avoid anyone watching him settle in for the night. He didn't think sleeping in his car was illegal, but that didn't alleviate the uncomfortable feeling it generated. He wasn't homeless (yet), and he didn't want to present himself as if he was. He also preferred not to get mugged by some ne'er-do-well or rousted by the local constabulary.

John circled around the block once before all the stragglers appeared to be gone and he felt safe getting back in his car. As he slumped into the seat, the small space that had been his home for the past several weeks suddenly seemed restrictive. He shut the door, but lowered the window. It felt like he could hardly breathe. Once again, issues were arising. The feasibility of the *Running from Reality Tour* was waning.

The sound of a foot scuffing the ground nearby startled him. He turned to see someone standing very close, their features somewhat obscured by the streetlight shining over their left shoulder. For the moment, he could only speculate on who they might be, or what they might want. He assumed the worst.

"Can I help you?" His tone was defiant.

"I thought it was you."

John, having figured out her identity, allowed himself to relax somewhat. "You're that girl's mother."

She nodded. "Kemina."

She was giving him a good visual going over. John didn't care for it. It felt like an invasion of his privacy. In the period of silence that followed, he overcame his innate urge to fill in the gaps with conversation. She had approached him, after all.

"Are you sleeping in your car?"

The question startled him with its bluntness. He could sense no trace of antagonism or ridicule in her tone. "I suppose the blanket and pillow gave it away."

She didn't reply. Her lack of response threw him off.

His tone slipped back into defiance. "It's not against the law." For all he knew, it might be.

"Drive back to my apartment. You know where it is. You can sleep on the couch tonight."

Her offer made him uncomfortable. It also offended him. "I couldn't do that. I don't even know you. Besides, I'll be fine. It's not like this is my first night."

She shook her head. "I can't let you sleep here. You can leave in the morning, or do whatever you want, but tonight I insist you stay with us."

"Sorry, no. It's not safe for you to invite a complete stranger into your home."

"You helped Allie. You are a good man. Give me a few minutes. I'll leave the door unlocked. The couch will be made up when you get there."

John couldn't come up with any other arguments. He supposed he could just ignore her request, driving off to park somewhere else as soon as she was out of sight. The whole idea of going with her was disconcerting as hell, but he found himself leaning towards responding in the affirmative despite his misgivings.

"Are you parked nearby?" he said.

"No. I don't own a car."

"Then at least get in and let me drive you back. I can't accept your generosity if you won't accept mine."

"Very well." She started to walk around the car. John took the opportunity to clear the passenger seat of clutter. She opened the door, climbing in casually as if she had done it a million times before.

John started the engine. "You might have to give me a few directions. This is my first time in Barrington. Everything is more confusing in the dark."

She nodded. "Turn left out of the parking lot; then left again at Main Street."

Apart from directions, there was no other conversation between them. John didn't know what to say. They drove for a short time, until the apartment building appeared.

"You can park along the side of the street. Just pull over here."

John did as he was told. He turned off the engine and the car grew silent, but his passenger didn't exit.

"Do you have clean clothes?"

It seemed like a strange question. He hoped he didn't smell that bad. "Yeah. I have a bag in the back."

Another awkward silence ensued.

"What is your name?"

"John."

"How long have you been living in the car?"

He struggled not to be annoyed. "Not that long. Why do you ask?"

"Bring in all your clothes. I will put on a load of laundry now so they will be clean in the morning. You can shower before you go to bed. You will feel better."

And smell better, too, he supposed. John sighed.

"What is wrong?"

"I don't know." It was partially true. "I mean, on one hand what you're offering sounds awesome. On the other hand, me accepting it seems weird. We are complete strangers. Why would you compromise your safety to do this? You don't know me at all."

"I lived out of a car once." She opened the door, stepping out. "Come on. Bring your clothes in with you." She walked off as if it was a done deal.

"Okay." John stepped out into the cool night air, wondering what he had just done.

CHAPTER 10

"Hey Zak. Look at this." Jed pointed to a large growth hanging from an old oak tree. His eyes narrowed as his facial expression assumed a look of complete concentration.

The Brogan brothers had gone out looking for adventure. In their case, that usually meant shooting or burning something while consuming alcohol. Each of them was carrying their gun of choice.

"What is that?" Zak asked.

They walked slowly forward in the kind of unison that comes naturally to siblings and people who spent plenty of time together.

"That is so weird." Jed squinted to the point where his face was distorted. "I ain't never seen nothing like that before."

It looked like a green leathery sack. The surface was smooth and Jed (barely) suppressed an urge to walk up and touch it with his hand. He had by no means completely given up on the idea, but two things made him hesitate. First was the sheer size of the thing. Second was the sounds coming from inside. He heard scratching, clicking and buzzing. Something was definitely alive in there.

A flitting sound and movement drew their eyes simultaneously. A large insect landed on the sack. After a moment of searching, it found a small slit and crawled inside. The opening had been invisible to the brothers until now.

"Dang, son. That is one dog-ugly bug." Jed took a step back.

"I think it's a bee." Zak also moved away from the sack.

"A stinging bee," Jed added. "And a big one."

"Hey." Zak broke out in a smile. "I got me an idea."

Jed was not clairvoyant, but knew where this was going. "Talk to me."

Zak pointed. "See that old maple over there that fell in the wind storm last year? Let's use it for cover and blast this ugly thing all to pieces."

Jed nodded. "You really are the brains of this here outfit. Let's go!"

They walked away, cautiously at first, then running pell-mell while laughing like school boys. They crouched behind the fallen trunk, utilizing the cover to totally conceal themselves.

"If this don't work, we'll come back after dark with some gasoline." Zak drew a bead on his target.

Jed lined up his shot as well. "It'll work. Watch this."

Zak, feeling a hint of competitive spirit, managed to fire first. "Ha! You're just too slow, old man."

Jed fired too. Silence fell after the echo from the shots faded. "Did we do anything? I thought it might blow up or something."

"Yeah, I wanted to see some pieces fall off." Zak readjusted his aim. "Guess we'll just have to keep shooting."

Jed froze. "Hey, you see that?"

Zak might have been deficient in some ways, but his eyesight was razor sharp. "Shoot yeah."

The bugs began to pour out of the sack, taking to the air.

"Get down!" Zak hissed as he squatted low enough to be completely hidden by the tree.

Jed followed suit. "Dang, dang, dang. What do we do now?" He had a sudden and powerful desire to be somewhere far away.

"Just relax." Zak gave him a stern look. "Don't move or make no noise. It ain't like we was hitting it with a stick. They don't know what happened and they don't know we're here. Just cool it for a few minutes and then we'll go. Okay?"

Jed couldn't stay still. "I just wanna see what they're doin', that's all."

Zak gave him a strained look that conveyed everything he wanted to say, but it didn't matter. Jed slowly stood up and peered over the trunk. "I think they're gone," he said in an exaggerated whisper. That was the moment one landed on the back of his extended hand and stung him deeply.

Jed sensed that something had happened. "Zak?"

Zak felt like he had grabbed an electric cable. The jolt of the toxins kicking in literally knocked him on his rear. His nervous system gave him the feeling like he was being torn apart by wild animals. And that was just the first level of the pain.

Jed knelt beside him. "Zak? Zak, can you hear me?"

Zak couldn't respond. All of his thoughts and capabilities had been hijacked by incomprehensible pain. His whole body was full of kidney stones and they were all moving. He could only gasp short breaths and whine like an injured kitten.

"Buddy, hang in there. I'm going to go and get help." It was a perfectly good plan, at least until Jed was stung on the back of his shoulder. He felt a sharp pain that immediately got his attention. Then his back muscles spasmed and threw him to the ground. His nerves told him he was being cut in half by a dull blade. Then the toxin circulated into his head and his brain exploded in a kaleidoscope of suffering. Thoughts were impossible to organize during the torture, but it did seem strange that he couldn't pass out. Death became the sweetest dream and the goal above all others. Jed would have mortgaged his entire future to be anywhere else, not experiencing this agony.

The opportunity didn't present itself.

A chiming sound woke John from a fitful sleep. For a brief moment, he had no idea where he was. He reached from his prone position on the couch, picking the phone up off the floor.

It was a text from Theresa announcing that she had sold his grandmother's hutch. She assumed this was okay based on their phone conversation from the previous day. She got a good price for it and had already deposited the money into their joint account, adding her blessings for him to withdraw the entire amount. It should be enough cash that he could afford to renew his prescription. He might even be able to continue to eat until he could get back home again. Regardless, he felt a pang of regret that an heirloom was forever gone.

"You're awake."

His savior from the previous evening stood appraising him. He hadn't heard her approach.

"Get dressed. You can give me a ride to the restaurant."

His back felt kinked, but it had been worse. Much worse. Sleeping on this unfamiliar piece of furniture hadn't helped. He suppressed a groan, swinging his feet onto the floor. "What restaurant?"

"My restaurant. Hurry or I'll be late."

"You have a restaurant?"

"I want to leave before Allie sees you. Get up and get moving."

John conceded. In the bathroom, his reflection revealed bloodshot, tired eyes, and skin that seemed to be sagging where it never had before. Already overloaded with negative thoughts, John's coping mechanisms allowed for imagining himself as a young Brad Pitt. He refocused his vision away from the mirror as quickly as possible.

She wasted no time encouraging him when he emerged. "Come on. Your clothes are in the bag by the door. Don't forget them."

John snagged it with one hand on the way out.

"Shut the door."

He complied. "Not to sound too presumptuous, but it's the Mexican one, right?"

She smiled a little. "You are very perceptive."

John performed a U-turn on the street. There was no other traffic about. "Thank you for letting me stay. It was very kind of you."

"De nada."

John had the route figured out, and was pleased in a small way not to need directions. "Is there a bank in town?" he asked.

"There are two. Both on the main street."

"Great. Thanks." He had a withdrawal to make. They reached their destination quickly.

"Go behind the restaurant," she said. "There is parking there."

"Wouldn't it make more sense to drop you off out front?"

"Not if you're coming in for breakfast."

John winced, but not from his back. "I stick to just two meals a day. I'm trying to maintain a nice, slim appearance."

"Nonsense. I will cook something for you before you go." She didn't word her response as if there was to be any debate.

"You're very generous. Thank you." In silence, he pondered what breakfast would look like in a Mexican restaurant. Stress and medication already had his digestive system under duress.

"Turn here."

They parked in the back. John followed her in through the rear entrance.

"Go out front and turn on the lights." She wasted no time busying herself in the kitchen.

After a short search, he located the switches. Once the room was illuminated, he took a moment to assess the interior. It was simple and elegant, adorned by a number of hanging plants. She hadn't overdone the decorating in any way to drive home the Mexican theme. He liked it.

That was when he looked out the front window.

"Who would do this?" Her frustration was obvious.

"I don't know." It was the only answer John could think to give. Maybe in celebration of the holiday, someone had partaken in a drink or two, discretion blurred in the process. It looked like a full dozen eggs had been thrown against the glass, the gooey mess now congealed into an ugly smear.

"Have you got a bucket and water?" John said. "Maybe some soap and a step ladder?" Perhaps it wasn't completely dry. It would be as soon as the clouds broke and the sun had a chance to work on it.

Kemina raised an eyebrow. John had some obvious mobility issues. She waved his suggestion away. "I will clean it."

John, after years of living with Theresa, knew he was dealing with another strong-willed woman that would have to be manipulated into doing anything that went against her first impulse.

"Not a chance. You can't make me wait now that you've put the idea of food in my head. Forget my initial reluctance—truth is, I'm starving. Besides, I used to work part-time for a cleaning company back in my college days. I know how to handle this."

She conceded, but didn't look thrilled. "Very well. Come back to the kitchen with me. I'll find you what you need."

It was the first time in weeks that John was going to do something useful. He was struck by how good it felt. Now to see if his back would be in agreement.

The mess actually came off easier than John had anticipated. He didn't stop until the frame and sills were spotless, and the glass shone streak free. He admired his handiwork, noticing that his back didn't feel too bad. Perhaps this would be one good deed that would go unpunished.

"I'm done," John announced as he walked into the kitchen, burdened by his cleaning apparatus.

"Just drop those things," she said. "I'll put them away after. Your breakfast is ready."

He followed her back into the dining room, taking a seat at the table she indicated. Breakfast was an omelette filled with green onion, red pepper, cheese and some as of yet unknown herbs. There was also toast on the side. She poured a cup of coffee for him as he observed her handiwork.

"This smells great. Thank you so much."

She walked around to the other side of the table and took a seat. John didn't care much for an audience while he was eating, but he was not in a position to dictate her actions. He picked up his fork, spearing a bite.

"So, what are you doing next?" she asked, staring at him steadily while waiting for a reply.

It was a tough question. The answer was speculative. "I guess I'm still working that out." He didn't owe her any more of a response than that, and they both knew it.

"You did well cleaning the window."

By now he was chewing. He nodded silently until he could swallow. "Thanks."

"I could use some help. I have some jobs to be done."

John, surprised by the direction of the conversation, put down his fork and held up both hands defensively. "Whoa. Look, you've been super nice to me, and I truly do appreciate it. But I won't be staying here in...Barrington."

"But you said you don't know what you're doing next. Why *not* stay in Barrington?"

John had resumed eating and shovelled in another piece of omelette. He pondered while he chewed. "Okay, fine. The truth is..." He hesitated, imagining Tom Cruise yelling *you can't handle the truth!* "I'm in the process of running away."

"Running from what?"

He frowned. "Everything. My life. Or lack thereof to be more precise."

"How far?"

"Pardon me?"

"How far will you run?"

He sighed. "I don't know."

"Barrington is not far enough?"

"It's not that, exactly. Look, I'm only passing through. There's nothing for me here."

"I just offered you something."

He smiled. "A few odd jobs aren't going to fix my situation."

She stared relentlessly. "What is your *situation*?"

He fired off a frustrated look in retaliation. "You want to know my situation? Will that be enough for you to let me finish my breakfast in peace?"

She leaned back, shrugging in an uncommitted response.

"Fine. My wife just left me. My back is screwed up. My former employer just fired me. That pretty much sums it up. Can I eat now?"

Her expression softened. She didn't appear to have anything more to say. She stood up, walking back into the kitchen. John finished his meal feeling like a bit of a jerk for being so short with the woman who was currently filling the role of being his personal benefactor.

"More coffee?"

He jumped a little. He hadn't heard her return. "Sure. One more cup would be great."

She poured with the steady confidence of someone who had done it many times before. "Why not stay one week? You could help me. Then you can run away some more."

John, out of respect, pondered the logistics of her proposal before rejecting it. "Look, many of the reasons why I left in the first place would preclude me from staying here."

"What reasons?"

John raised an eyebrow. "Has anyone ever told you that you're kind of pushy?"

"No. What reasons?"

He shook his head. He considered standing up and walking away.

"Tell me," she said. "What can it hurt?"

"All right. You deserve to hear about my good news after all this pestering. I'm sure it will cheer you up for the rest of the day."

"Speak."

"Fine. It's my back. That's what brought me to this. That's why I lost my good job. That's why I lost my mediocre wife. That's why I'm living out of my car, having no hope for the future. That's why I might not even be able to do your odd jobs."

"Is it that bad?"

"Yeah, it's that bad. On a good day, it's just numb. On a poor day, it's a little tight and achy, like right now. But then there are times when the pain is so severe, I can't do anything. It's debilitating. It's almost like being stabbed with a knife that's coated with the flu virus. I sweat and get nauseated from the pain. I can't get comfortable whether I stand, sit or lie down. It's unpredictable. It can happen anytime. Sometimes I aggravate it by doing certain things. Other times it comes on for no reason at all. It's already destroyed most of my life, and you know what the icing on the cake is?"

She shook her head.

"It's going to get worse. Maybe much worse." He sighed. "It's a progressive deterioration, and there's nothing anybody can do about it. How's that for good news?"

"Nothing can be done?"

He stared out of the now sparkling clean window. "There's a surgical option, but there's no guarantee of success. And it comes with a load of negative side effects."

"I see."

John took a sip of coffee. He needed to get moving. The bank would be open soon. "Is there a pharmacy in town?"

"Yes. PharmaDeal. It is also on the main street. You can't miss it."

"Great." He chugged the rest of his drink. "I have to go." He pushed his chair away from the table, standing up. So far, no bad side effects from the window cleaning.

"Give me three days."

"What?"

"Three days to do odd jobs. I will pay you a little, feed you, and you can stay at my apartment. Then you can go on your way."

"I really can't."

"You would be a great assistance to me. I am falling behind on maintenance."

"Just hire it done."

"Maybe I can't afford to."

There it was. There was nothing like a snippet of the truth to cut through the murkiness of a drawn out conversation.

"I see." He suppressed another sigh, making a snap decision. "I'll tell you what. In response to both your persistence and generosity towards a complete stranger, I'll give you two days. Today and tomorrow, then I'm gone. Okay?"

"Yes." She smiled a little, softening her expression to the point where her entire appearance changed.

"Right. I need to go to the bank and the pharmacy. After that, I'll come back and you can give me my marching orders."

"Good. I will have a list for you."

"Well, don't forget my back. If you put anything like "carry my safe up to the attic" on there, I'll have to politely decline."

"Finish your meal. I will not interrupt you anymore. Do what you have to do, then come back and see me." She walked off as if that was that.

John, after noting that he didn't have a real agenda anyway, decided that he could live with a delay before restarting his journey. Refilling his pain medication, however, was an entirely different matter.

CHAPTER 11

Brandisha and Charles had been released from care, both feeling exponentially better. Leaving the hospital was great—leaving Barrington would be even better. Their supervisor turned and looked at them before putting his car in gear.

"Are you sure you feel like driving yourselves back?"

They both nodded.

"Yes," Brandisha replied.

They still had pain where the stinger had penetrated their skin, but compared to the previous agony, the dull ache was like a day on the beach in Maui.

"Off to the farm it is." He drove away, talking as he did. "Can you tell me again about what happened?"

Charles gave his partner a look that bequeathed the speaking duties to her.

"It will all be in our report. But in summary, somehow there was an enormous swarm of bees living underground in the chasm. I guess we disturbed them. They came out by the thousands and before it was over, we each got stung." It was an understatement on a massive scale.

"And that's what put you in the hospital? So, are you guys allergic to bee stings?"

"Not that I know of," Brandisha said.

"Me either," Charles added.

"Okay. I'll read about it in your report. So tell me about the crevasse."

This was a somewhat more palatable topic.

"It's incredible," Brandisha said. "It's deep and long. And there's a tunnel opening near the base of the wall. I think that's where the bees came from."

"So you're saying it warrants further exploration?"

"Definitely." This response was voiced simultaneously by both of them.

"Keeping the potential danger in mind," Brandisha expanded.

"You two get back to the office straight away. I'll use your report as the basis to justify some future research."

Allie enjoyed learning, or at least she did until this wonderful, most recent phase of her life began. A fundamental change had occurred, and she was now finding school unpleasant for the first time. With her heightened awareness, she was keenly mindful of the presence of the two boys who had threatened her. They seemed to be everywhere. She spied them multiple times on her first day back after the "incident". This caused her great anxiety.

Once, on the way to the library, she had to walk past both of them in the hall—a most traumatic event. She forced herself to stride along (*why weren't they in class?*), faking disinterest as best she could. She didn't think they had noticed her, until she turned the corner and heard one of them yell something about Mexicans smelling bad. It was stupid and childish, but it was meant for her, and it was meant to hurt. Knowing that full well didn't make it any easier. The words accomplished their goal. Then they fired an incoherent question about whether or not she enjoyed the eggs. Unaware of the window at Casa Comida, she had no idea what that meant.

After school, Allie walked part-way home with a group of girls from her class—an unusual deviation from her preference towards being alone. Living on the edge of town, she eventually had to split from the security of the group. She covered the rest of the distance alone, looking around like a rabbit in wolf-infested woods. Allie made it, relieved to shut the door behind her. But there was still another problem to resolve in this new reality; how to get back to the Dream Tree.

Hopefully, the boys being out there in the country was a one-time deviation from their normal schedule. She had to risk it, but also wondered if there wasn't a better way to get the fruit on a regular basis. After some deep thinking, an idea presented itself. She wasn't sure if it would work, but feasibility could only be determined by a test. Her agenda was set—she would chance a visit.

Allie went to the Dream Tree, racing like never before. To her great relief, she didn't see any boys. She came prepared to do a serious harvest.

She climbed up, loading her backpack with pods. Then she jogged home, opened them and deposited the orbs in an empty, well-rinsed margarine tub. It was impossible to see what was inside of it once closed, and Allie alone used the stuff; her mom preferred butter. Allie hoped that would be sufficient to keep them undetected. If they kept while refrigerated, she would not need to make another trip to the tree for some time.

Allie got to the restaurant on time, scuttling through the doorway just as the clock struck the five o'clock hour. There was an average crowd seated at the tables. Several of the regulars waved at her as she walked past.

"There you are." Her mother was busy at the stove when she entered the kitchen.

"Hello, Momma."

"Can you stir this? Make sure no lumps form."

"Yes, Momma."

"Turn off the heat once it is thickened."

"I will." Anything was better than washing dishes.

"You're a good girl."

Yes, a good girl who snuck out when she wasn't supposed to, and made a covert plan to add a secret ingredient to the food, Allie thought.

"Oh, the spray nozzle on the sink works now. You can use it for rinsing."

That was exciting news. She kept her focus on the task at hand. After several minutes, she noticed the back door to the restaurant was ajar. A man was tinkering with the handle. Somehow he looked familiar. She squinted to better focus. He turned and made eye contact.

"Hi. Remember me?"

She did now. It was the man who had given her a ride back home after her life-changing encounter out in the country. "Yes. Hello." Why would this man be working on the back door?

"Nice to see you again." He returned his focus back to his work.

Allie felt uncomfortable in the restaurant for the first time. She walked towards the dining hall door and looked out at her mother, serving a table. Allie waited for her to return.

"Why aren't you at the stove, little one?"

"That man." Allie gestured furtively. "Why is he here?" The question was whispered for the sake of discretion.

Her mother looked about as if she wasn't sure which man Allie meant. "Oh yes. He is doing some odd jobs for me. He will be staying with us for a couple days."

Allie's eyes widened. "Staying with us? Why?"

"Because I need some help, and he needs a place to stay."

This was a shock. Guests were unprecedented for them. And a man, of all things.

"Don't trouble yourself, Allie. Just do your job, like a good girl."

"Yes Momma." Her tone was dubious, but she turned back towards the stove as her mother had instructed.

Allie had decanted a few of the orbs to a smaller jar, bringing it to the restaurant in her jacket pocket. She wondered if heat from cooking would have a detrimental effect on the qualities of the fruit. A trial was the only way to know for sure. She picked what she perceived as the right moment, and after looking around to be sure no one was watching, she emptied the jar into the steaming pot she was stirring.

"Yes!" she whispered as she tucked the jar away in her pocket. Several swirls from the big spoon and the fruit disappeared, becoming one with the sauce. Now she had to wait. This was the first time she had added the fruit to anything. Allie couldn't wait to find out what the positive effects would be on all those who ate it. A negative reaction was something that hadn't crossed her mind. She hoped the flavor of the original dish wouldn't be adversely affected.

"Whatcha doin', kiddo?"

She jumped and whirled around, eyes bulging. The man who had been fixing the door stood behind her. How had she missed him? *Calm down, Alejandrina*, she said to herself. "I help out in the kitchen. It is my job."

He nodded. "Good for you. The younger generation seems more interested in indulging themselves than contributing, in my opinion. You give me hope for the future."

There was some humor in his eyes. Allie deduced he was joking. "Thank you."

"I've got to talk to your mom. See ya, kiddo."

"Goodbye." She was relieved to see him walk away. He was very stealthy. In the future, she would have to be more careful. That had been way too close.

The man was already there when Allie arrived at the apartment early that evening. He was sitting on the couch, watching television. He turned towards her when she entered.

"Hey."

"Hello." She didn't know what else to say. He made her feel uncomfortable.

"My name is John, by the way."

"Okay."

"I just made myself at home," he said. "Do you need me to move, or change the channel, or…whatever?"

"No, I have homework to do. I'll work out here on the table."

"Is this too loud?"

"No. Thank you for asking."

The apartment grew quiet except for the soft drone of inane television chatter. Allie set out her books on the table.

"Not to be too intrusive or anything, but what were you really doing in the restaurant tonight?" He turned, looking at her over his shoulder.

Allie felt a small chill. "I help out. I clean mostly, but sometimes I help with cooking as well."

"That's not what I meant," he said. "Didn't I see you add something to that food you were cooking?"

Allie froze. She had been raised not to lie, so that left her backed into a corner. "I've added ingredients to the food before." It was a careful choice of words.

"Okay. Maybe I shouldn't be so nosy, what with me being a newcomer and all, but you seemed like you were being a little sneaky about it."

Perhaps a change of direction would derail this particular line of conversation before it got any worse. "I have a lot of homework. I should get started."

"Well, don't let me interrupt."

Mercifully, he stopped talking. She took the opportunity to refocus on the task at hand. Writing a twenty-five-hundred word essay on the role of unions in the American workplace was staring her in the face. She retrieved the old laptop from her bedroom. After looking at the screen with a sigh, she started working.

John struggled through the evening news broadcast. He wondered how many legitimate reports were ignored in order to come up with the disturbing, manipulative tripe they had just offered up. His own story would fit nicely. *Man abandoned by employer and wife to suffer through crippling spinal degeneration.*

"Yeah, that's got a nice ring to it," John said.

"Were you talking to me?" Allie asked.

"No, sorry." John stood up slowly, stretching cautiously as he did. "Just talking to myself. One has to grab intelligent conversation wherever one can find it." After a moment's contemplation, he walked into the kitchen. "Don't mind me," he said. "Just getting a glass of water."

She mumbled softly in reply.

"Am I bothering you?"

She looked up, surprised. "Oh, no. It's this assignment." She sighed again.

John ambled over casually. "Oh? What are you working on?"

"An essay."

John grimaced. "Yikes. I never liked those. What's it about, if you don't mind me asking?"

"Unions."

John snorted. "I've had some experiences with unions lately."

"I have to be either for or against, and defend my stand," Allie said.

"Really? For or against? What position did you take?"

"I've actually changed my mind three times so far," she said. "It's hard to come up with enough information to fill in twenty-five-hundred words either way."

John nodded. "Sure. Pro-union or anti-union—either way, the real problem is that the best position lies somewhere in between the two extremes. No doubt your research is giving you conflicting information."

She turned to meet his gaze. "Do you know anything about unions?"

"You could say that."

She considered her options. "How do you know about them?"

"I worked for a unionized company for nearly twenty years."

This revelation indicated a potential new source of information. "Are you for or against unions?"

John pulled out a chair, sitting down beside her. Allie decided that this didn't bother her.

"That's a tough question for me right now. Emotionally, I want to say against. But logically, even I have to admit that the unions serve a purpose. Therefore, I would say I'm somewhere in the middle."

She frowned. "I don't think that helps me."

"I have an idea," John said.

Anything was worth considering at this point. "What is it?"

"Why not do your essay from the perspective of middle ground?"

"Middle ground?"

"Yes. Neither for nor against. Just lay out the facts as they exist. Then do a summary at the end where you could lean one way or the other, should you feel so inclined."

"I'm not sure. That's not what she asked for."

John smiled. "Do you think your teacher would punish you for some independent thinking?" he said. "They should be teaching you kids how to reason for yourselves. Making logical decisions is more valuable than memorizing information or having someone else's political or philosophical opinions driven into your head. It's more likely to stay with you that way."

"I don't understand," she said.

"It's up to you, but if you want to comprehend life as you grow up, you must realize that extreme views are always wrong in some fundamental way. They exist because they have some sort of personal political agenda supporting them. Find the middle ground, Allie. That's where truth lives."

"So..."

"So write about both points of view followed by a great summary at the end. Did your teacher seem to be leaning in one direction or the other?"

"No, I don't think so."

He shrugged. "There you go." He started to stand.

"Can you tell me what you know about unions?"

He settled back in. "You must have done some research by now, right?"

She nodded.

"I doubt I could tell you anything that you haven't already found. But I always enjoy presenting a long, boring monologue of my opinions, if that's what you want."

"Yes, please."

It was the first time in forever since anyone had expressed a desire to listen to what he had to say. John was flattered. "Fine. I'll start with the positive side. Feel free to interrupt if you have any questions." He cleared his throat and started talking.

CHAPTER 12

Kemina walked through the door, surprised to see her daughter sitting at the table with the new, temporary handyman. They were so engrossed in what they were doing, they didn't seem to register her presence.

"You're still up, little one. What are you doing?"

Allie turned towards her. "John has been helping me with my essay. He knows a lot about unions."

"Oh?" She put her hand on her daughter's shoulder, looking at the sheets strewn about the table. "You have been writing many notes, I see."

John, now distracted from the assignment, was stretching while he sat. "Twenty-five-hundred word essay and according to the computer, she is a little over twenty-seven right now."

Kemina nodded. "Very good, Allie."

"She's a very smart girl," John said.

Her mother smiled. "I know."

Allie looked uncomfortable. "Momma, let me finish please. Just a few minutes and it will be done."

"Don't be long. You need your sleep."

Allie, knowing that her mother had turned towards the counter, rolled her eyes in response. John caught her attention and winked.

"I brought supper for you." Kemina indicated a container on the counter.

"Thank you," John responded.

Allie had one last item on her agenda. "How was business tonight, Momma?"

"It was an interesting night, Allie. People kept eating, asking for more. I started thinking that I would have nothing left to bring home."

Allie was exuberant on the inside, but kept a straight face. The fruit had worked its magic, or so she thought. "I'm glad."

"Maybe things are turning around. We are getting a little busier. I might have to start cooking more."

"And hire more help?" Allie asked.

This was an old topic of conversation. "I have good help," she said. "The best."

The microwave beeped and John pulled out a steaming plate. "This smells great."

Allie scooped up her work. "Just a thought."

"I will think about it, Allie."

Allie grinned. "I'm glad. Good night, Momma."

"Good night, little one."

John started to eat. The rice based dish was indeed very good.

Allie looked back as she walked out of the room. "Thank you for your help, John."

"My pleasure. I hope you don't get an "F"."

She laughed as she walked away.

Neufeld Community College had lucked out. Graduation Day dawned clear and warm, with no rain in the forecast and blue skies predicted for the entire day.

Chairs had been set up on the lawn, one area for graduates and another for visitors. The stage was decorated and the sound system tested and ready. By early afternoon, people started arriving. Both parking and seating were achieved with the assistance of a small army of volunteers. Things went smoothly, and the chairs were soon filled. The graduates filed in and sat on their preassigned place.

Wonderful, Dean Wilkinson thought before taking the stage and addressing the crowd. *Couldn't have turned out any better*.

Things could have been better for Tim McCarther. His older sister was graduating, and for reasons he didn't understand, his mother had insisted that he attend the ceremony. Tim couldn't have cared less and was already bored and fidgeting. His original plan was to bring his phone to use as a distraction, but that had been nixed by his mother. So he sat on the uncomfortable chair, sun beating down on him, surrounded by people he didn't know with absolutely nothing to do. As the voice of the man on the stage droned on, Tim looked up at the sky and wished for something interesting to happen.

That was when he saw the dark cloud.

It wasn't all that big, nor was it even a cloud in a traditional meteorological sense. But it was almost directly above them and seemed more interesting than the speech. As Tim watched, it undulated randomly, expanding and retracting with no apparent rhyme or reason. It was dropping, getting closer by the moment. Whatever the cloud was made of suddenly pulled apart and dispersed, all but disappearing from Tim's sight. He thought about telling his mother, but knew this was not a good time.

Professor Samuel Webster took his cue and stepped up to the microphone. He had the pleasure of presenting the first academic award of the day. The recipient was the perfect choice. This young man had worked hard all year to reach this level of achievement and deserved the recognition as much as anyone.

Professor Webster did what he did best—orating a splendid description of the student and all his efforts to overcome the plethora of challenges that all students faced. When he finished and called the young man up to the stage, many eyes in the audience were no longer dry.

The young man made it up the steps and approached with a smile on his face, knowing this was a moment he would remember for the rest of his life. He didn't know the reason would be radically different from what he was anticipating. A bug landed on the side of his gown and stung him on the hip through the thin material. The boy first showed surprise and annoyance, then shrieked and dropped to the stage. He ignored the extended hand Webster was offering to help him get back up.

What was that? Webster thought before kneeling to assess the boy's predicament. Other staff, many of whom had first aid training, were also approaching to lend aid. The crowd was murmuring, looking both concerned and restless.

"Ladies and gentlemen," Dean Wilkinson said through the PA system. "Please remain calm. Everything will be all right."

But he was wrong. A horde of the bugs had noticed the crowd. Enraged by the presence of all those people, they began to attack. Screams now filled the air.

Tim forgot about being bored.

His mother grabbed his shoulder and pulled him to his feet. "Let's get to the car. Hurry!"

He followed, unable to completely ignore the people who had fallen all around him who were screaming in agony. "What is it? What's happening?"

His mother swatted away an enormous bug with her program, which thankfully continued on towards another target. "Run!"

She had worn heels, but Tim had trouble keeping up. They reached the car, climbed in quickly and slammed the doors shut with gusto. While they sat wide-eyed and gasping, one of the bugs landed on the windshield.

"What is that?" Tim screamed.

She had never seen anything like it before. The ridiculously long stinger was tapping against the glass, making soft ticking sounds and leaving tiny droplets of yellowish venom.

"I'm calling 911," she announced as she dug for her phone in her patent leather purse.

"It's really hot in here," Tim whined.

"Don't put the window down!"

He recoiled from the volume of her scream.

"I'll turn the air on." This she did while dialing emergency services.

The responders had a super stressful experience. Dozens of people were immobile, suffering from obvious, extreme pain. The source, according to those who hadn't been stung, was some kind of insect. This quickly proved to be true when two of the paramedics got stung themselves, while several others had close calls.

Triage was finally rejected in favor of evacuating everyone from the area as quickly as possible. Treatment and prioritization could happen once a safe environment was reached. Ambulances, fire trucks and even police cars were used to shuttle the victims away. Once at the hospital, the emergency room was swamped and extra staff members were called in.

As he allowed himself a brief moment to take an overview of the chaos, Dr. Redding quickly came to a conclusion.

Although not on this scale, he had seen this before.

John finished the last item on his to-do list around the middle of the afternoon, just before the supper crowd started to trickle in. His back started the day tight, but had now progressed to undeniably sore. He was worried about the effect all this exertion was having. He wondered if he'd be able to move by the next morning.

"Kemina?"

She was busy in the kitchen, a multitude of dishes in the early prep stage. "Oh, there you are."

"The list is done," he said.

"Very good. So the oven door does not screech when it is opened now?"

"Nope."

"The floor by the window is no longer a tripping hazard?"

"Perfectly level."

She nodded. "Should I try to find more?"

"No."

His tone wasn't what she was expecting. "Is something wrong, John?"

"It's my back."

"Sore?"

"Getting worse. I might have mobility issues by morning if this keeps up."

"Did I make you do too much?"

He shrugged. "It's hard to say. Sometimes this flares up for no reason at all."

She nodded. "Go back to the apartment and get comfortable. There is a jar of camphor ointment in the bathroom cabinet. Try to put some on. Just relax. I'll bring you something to eat when I come home."

John had been kicking around the notion that he should get in his car and leave. His two day commitment was over anyway. Time to go back and clean up the mess he had left behind.

"Well, have you nothing to say?"

John forced a smile. "I have plenty to say. But this is America. I also have the right to remain silent."

She turned away as if the matter had just been settled. "I will see you later on. Thank you for your help."

He decided that sleeping in the car might not be the best idea right now, anyway. One more night at the apartment couldn't hurt. That was assuming he could get out of the car by the time he drove there.

Allie was arriving home from school when John pulled up. She waited for him, holding the door open in a polite gesture while he approached. As he tried to walk up the cement walkway, Allie noticed that he couldn't quite maintain an upright posture without grimacing with every step.

"Good afternoon, young lady," he said from a slightly stooped position. "How was your day?"

"It was okay."

"What? Just okay?" John walked in past her. He couldn't stop himself from wincing as he stepped over the threshold.

"It was fine." *Fine as could be with those boys haunting my every waking moment,* she thought glumly. She watched him amble over to the couch, and then obtain a seating position by letting gravity drop him in place.

John looked up and saw her staring. "What?"

"Are you all right?"

"Yes, I'm fine," he said.

"John, what is it?" Allie had reached the point where she was comfortable calling him by his first name.

"It's not your problem, Allie. Just go about your usual evening's business. Trust me, I'll be fine." John didn't seem to take sympathy very well. "Go write an essay or something."

As women in his life had been prone to do, she ignored his suggestion.

"Did you get hurt at the restaurant? Did you fall off a ladder?" She had heard about his window cleaning job.

Despite everything, John managed a subdued laugh. "No." He shook his head while studying her expression. "Allie, it's my back, okay? Sometimes it gives me trouble. This is nothing new. It will pass. I will deal with it. Now would you *please* go find something else to do?"

She looked dubious, but turned away

"After you hand me the television remote."

She delivered it with a smile, but made no further comment.

"Thanks." John grunted as he repositioned himself.

Allie had an hour before she was to be at the restaurant. She cast a sidelong glance at the man on the couch, then walked away wondering.

When Kemina arrived home, John was established in a lengthwise, semi-prone position. He had been up once to use the bathroom; so far his lone foray off the couch.

"How do you feel?" she asked.

"Okay." There was no enthusiasm behind his response.

She shook her head. "No, you're not. Have you taken any medication?"

"Yeah. I have my prescription."

His face was haggard and he was moaning softly, even when he talked. Kemina wondered if he knew he was doing it. A light sheen of sweat glistened on his forehead. "You didn't use the camphor ointment." It was a statement, not a question.

'No. I didn't think I could reach back there to apply it. I'm a little motion restricted at the moment."

"I will put some on for you. Can you stand up?"

John assumed a pinched expression. "I *could* stand up. But I don't think I will unless the apartment is on fire. And please don't light it just to motivate me."

She leaned in towards him. "I will help you. Come on."

"Why?" John's voice was strained and he made no effort to move.

"You can stand up and I will put on some ointment for you," she said. "It will help."

60

"I doubt it. I've tried everything before."

"You tried camphor ointment?"

John was cornered. "No, but I've used about a million different cream and oils. When I get like this, nothing helps. I just have to survive until it works itself out. That's all."

"Get up. Come on." She reached for his arms, starting to pull him up.

"Fine," John hissed through clenched teeth.

Kemina hoped her confidence in the ointment would be confirmed by a lessening of his obvious pain. Seeing him up close, she had a small twinge of doubt.

CHAPTER 13

John woke to the sound of a moan coming out of his own mouth. His current body position was causing an unacceptable amount of pain. He knew that moving to change it would cause even more in the short term, but with no other options, he forced himself to roll over.

"Ow!" Even as the exclamation was still coming out of his own mouth, he tried unsuccessfully to suppress it. Using some newfound leverage, he was able to achieve a sitting position. He sat gasping air, feeling hot and sick. The pain was severe. John lowered his head, focusing on controlling his breathing.

After a minute or so, he raised his head, opening his eyes. He became aware of light and movement in the kitchen, and turned his head cautiously towards it.

"Allie?" He was surprised to see her. It must have been the middle of the night.

She smiled, giving him a quick wave.

"What are you doing up?" No doubt she had heard him.

She walked towards him, something in her hand. "I made you a snack," she said.

John, although he had not eaten earlier, had no appetite. "Did I wake you up?"

"No. Sometimes I can't sleep."

"I know the feeling."

She extended a small dish towards him. "I made you pudding."

It was such a genuine gesture, John couldn't say no. "Thank you. You're a good girl." He accepted the bowl and spoon, not wanting to reach too far and re-aggravate the stabbing knives. "You should go back to bed."

"I will. I have to put a few things away first, but that won't take long."

John figured that he would be spending the rest of the night sitting just like he was now, staring into space. Sleep was impossible when he was terrified of moving. The pain was now severe. Sadly, that was a significant improvement from several minutes earlier when it was acute, something he had no intention of sabotaging.

"Do you promise to eat that?" she said.

He caught a whiff of the pudding, a blend of butterscotch and some other sweet ingredient. She had loaded it with fruit from the old tree, but John didn't know that. "I promise."

"If you eat it right now, I can wash the dish before I go back to bed."

John positioned the spoon in his free hand. "You know, if your mom found out you were up because of me, I'd be in trouble."

She watched him scoop a small amount and put it in his mouth. "Do you like it?"

In truth, the fruit (whatever it was) and the butterscotch didn't blend as well as they could have. But, it wasn't unpleasant. John felt a slight flicker of appetite. He would not say anything to hurt her feelings, regardless.

"It's delicious, Allie. Thanks."

She stood staring until he had eaten it all.

"Here you go." John extended the bowl back to her waiting hands. "Thank you again, Allie. That was very nice of you."

She took his offering, but didn't move away. "How are you feeling now?"

John did a quick assessment. "Better. I guess I was a little hungry."

She beamed in response. "Great! Have a good night then." She walked into the kitchen with the lithe movement only the young were capable of, while John looked on with envy. As she finished cleaning up, John pondered what the remainder of his night would look like. If he could reacquire a horizontal position without making himself scream, maybe he could get a few minutes of fitful sleep.

In the end, he did better than that.

That night, John had the most vivid dream of his life. The details were so lifelike; it was as if he was still conscious. *This isn't real,* he reminded himself while in the midst of it.

He was standing in a vast, park-like area with no idea how he got there. The trimmed grass was lush, deep green, and bordered by numerous flower beds. They sported bright colored blooms which added spectacular splashes of color. Both sides were flanked by a thick, manicured hedge, with larger trees growing beyond it. It was beautiful.

The ground sloped upward to his right. At the top of the ridge was a mansion. Though its actual size was hard to ascertain from this distance, the home was clearly enormous. Light reflected off of the manor with dazzling brightness. There were huge pillars at the front. Before them a gigantic fountain spewed crystal clear water high into the sky. John felt a tugging on his heart strings. He wanted to walk to the house and see it up close, but his feet seemed rooted.

Refocusing his attention away from the mansion, John noticed a wrought iron bench a short distance away. Sitting on it was a strangely dressed man. The figure drew John's attention as if he had his own gravitational field. He smiled, waved, then made an unmistakable *come on over* gesture.

As John approached, the man became more visible. He was young, maybe thirtyish, with a slight build. His hair was a bit too long to fit in with current fashion trends, and he had a short beard of light brown hair. He wore what appeared to be jogging pants and a tee-shirt, with sandals on his feet, but that wasn't exactly right. It was only how John's mind catalogued it in order to process what he was seeing.

"Hello, John."

His voice was the Vienna Boys Choir accompanied by the Boston Symphony Orchestra. The effect was astonishing. It brought tears to John's eyes.

"It's good to see you." The man extended his hand. John shook it in reflex. As their eyes met, John was destroyed, every molecule and subtle nuance of his being disintegrated, followed somehow by a spontaneous reconstruction as a new being. It took but an instant to happen, and it took his breath away.

"Here, get comfortable."

The only response John could come up with was a weak nod.

They sat side by side. To John's surprise, he *was* comfortable. There was no discernable back pain at all. He turned, looking into the most amazing eyes he had ever seen. It was as if all the stars from a clear night's sky were twinkling in them.

"John, I'm glad you're here. I need to talk to you."

John found his voice. "All right."

The man smiled and the effect was like the sun breaking over the horizon as it heralded the arrival of the best day in John's life. "Good."

John waited.

"It's the tree, John."

John felt panic for a brief moment. *What tree?*

"A great danger will come."

John nodded. *What tree?*

"Protect the girl."

John was in exquisite agony. He couldn't find his voice to ask. *What tree?*

"At the appointed time, this will happen."

What tree? What tree?

The man put his hand on John's shoulder. "You'll know. The girl will show you. And John?"

"Yes?" Thank God, his voice finally worked.

"It's never a coincidence, John. It's all meant to be."

It was ending. John could sense it.

"Can I see your house?" His mouth, now functional, seemed to spit out the words of its own accord. The man smiled in response.

"It's not *my* house, John."

What did that mean? John had felt so sure of it. "Then whose?"

"It's yours."

With that, it all faded away as reality flooded back in. John had never felt such acute disappointment.

He wanted to stay.

CHAPTER 14

"What is that?"

Janine Walker was taking her morning break, a welcome reprieve from talking to unhappy taxpayers on the phone, fielding complaints ranging from the high cost of dog tags to unfair parking tickets. Working at the Civic Center was a great job and she knew it. But there were days when she suspected there had been a full moon on the previous night and this was shaping up to be one of those.

"What are you talking about?" Rob Kruger sat with her, enjoying the morning sun and a Marlborough with his coffee. He was a draftsman in the engineering department and was knocking on the door of retirement. Due to some unhealthy lifestyle choices, he looked to be around a hundred years old. His raspy voice reflected decades of tobacco use. "I don't see anything."

Janine knew how to sit strategically, taking the breeze into account in order to avoid Rob's industrial strength, second hand spewage. She stood and stretched before taking a few cautious steps. She pointed at a tall, immaculately trimmed shrub. "In there. There's something inside the branches."

Rob was no entomologist; neither was he a choirboy. Anything pertaining to bugs was not worth his interest. However, Janine's rear view was another matter. *Not a bad backside for a middle-aged broad*, he thought as he stared shamelessly.

"Do you see it?"

I sure do, he thought to himself as he refocused his eyes. "I don't see anything."

She pointed with more enthusiasm. "Right there, in the tall one. Inside the branches."

Rob saw it now. It was hard to discern any details from where he sat, but he would not be standing up to investigate until his smoke and coffee were both gone. "Yeah, I see it. So what? What is it?"

She took two more slow steps towards it, and then stopped, reacting to an internal alarm going off in her mind. She had no idea why, but it was screaming *danger*. "I don't know."

Two insects, frighteningly large, flew up to the shrub and landed, disappearing quickly inside the dense greenery.

"On my God! It's a bee's nest." Now she was stepping carefully backwards, eyes still focused on the nest.

Rob refocused. The tight fitting jeans were a positive side-effect that he doubted Levi Strauss had ever envisioned. Nonetheless, thank God for Casual Fridays. "Well, stay away from it. You know what they say; leave them alone and they'll leave you alone."

"Who says that?" she asked as she reached the table. She neglected to sit.

"You know—them. I've heard it somewhere."

"Rob, I saw a couple of the bugs. They were huge. I'm not taking any chances. I'm going back inside."

"Okay, suit yourself. I've got time for one more smoke." Rob was well known for milking it. With his seniority and crusty demeanor, nobody bothered to make an issue of it.

"Be careful then." With that she was off, her heels clicking on the cement and hips swinging in a way Rob still couldn't ignore.

As Janine reached for the door, it swung open from the inside and Mayor Drew Dickens walked out. They exchanged some sort of pleasantry and then he walked towards Rob's table. This was something Rob could have lived without.

The mayor reached the table but remained standing, looking like some sort of conqueror surveying his realm. "Beautiful day, Rob. Summer's not far behind now."

Rob lit his second smoke, instant justification for his break overage. "I guess so."

"Don't forget those foreign investors. I'm going to have them meet you when we're doing the tour. Just say hello, no need for prolonged conversation. As far as that goes, we won't have time for it anyway."

This was music to Rob's ears. "I can do that."

Now the mayor was staring towards the shrub. *What is it with you people and bees?* Rob wondered.

"Have you seen this?"

Rob took another drag, savored it and then exhaled slowly before answering. "Seen what?"

"Damn. There's a bug nest in there. I was going to bring the investors out here and let them enjoy the sun while I nailed down this deal."

"I've been out here and they haven't bothered me," Rob said.

A man of action, the mayor was pondering a quick solution. "Do you suppose if I poked that thing with a stick, they'd all fly away and rebuild their nest elsewhere?"

Now Rob was mildly interested. "I don't see why not."

"I suppose it will take hours to get an exterminator here."

Rob liked where this was going. "You should take matters into your own hands, Mayor. Show that decisive quality the voters like so much."

The mayor looked around. Revealed to his inquiring eyes, leaning on the brick wall of the Civic Center, was a rake that the grounds crew had been using earlier. "That's perfect."

Now, Rob was all in. This could prove to be entertaining.

The mayor returned, rake in hand. He held it out like a weapon designed for a medieval joust. "If you want it done right, then do it yourself."

Rob figured this would be the moment for hesitation and the mayor could use further encouragement. "Give it a good poke," he suggested. "Let them know you mean business."

The mayor approached, extending the rake handle like a warrior's lance. "It's bigger than I thought."

He's going to back down, Rob thought. "One good jab should do it. Maybe pull it loose and let it fall. That should be the end of it."

Bolstered by his innate belief in the virtue of action, the mayor closed the gap, tightened his grip and speared the nest with a sudden burst of reckless energy.

Rob actually clapped his hands in response, waiting for the bugs to do something. "Good job. That'll teach 'em a lesson."

The rake handle was stuck. The mayor pulled and the nest fell so suddenly, he almost tumbled over backwards. He could hear angry buzzing now. "I think we should go back inside."

Rob enjoyed this show of cowardice. "I'm almost done here." He still had two swallows of coffee and half a cigarette to finish.

The mayor hustled past, stealing an over the shoulder glance at the shrub. He moved with a fearful gait that made Rob's grin grow ever wider. He chucked the rake into the flower bed with no thought to exactly where and how it landed and disappeared into the Civic Center.

Rob took the last drag from his smoke. "That was fun. Thanks, Mayor."

One of the bugs flew past Rob's head, the sound of heavy wings easily discernable. Rob cringed in reflex and reconsidered his stance on the humor of the situation. Janine had been right—the bug was huge.

He reached for his coffee. "Time to go."

Another bug landed on his forearm and immediately plunged in its huge stinger.

Rob felt like someone had smashed it with a sledgehammer. His entire body jolted in agony, like he had fallen off the edge of a cliff and was rolling uncontrolled down a steep, rocky incline. Pain was everywhere. It consumed his thoughts. If life meant this kind of suffering, he would give it up without argument. He tried to stand up from the table, but his legs buckled and he collapsed onto the cement. He was the only target in close proximity to the nest and several other bugs stung him in quick succession. He was now incapable of movement or rational thought. Breathing took effort, possible only in short, unsatisfying gasps. His tour of hell was unimaginably horrible, and had just begun.

Janine, looking out of the glass door, saw him collapse. The bugs swarming around him were visible even from that distance. She called 911.

Out front, a hired car was dropping off the foreign investors. They exited the Escalade and stood on the sidewalk, stretching out the kinks from the two hour ride. They expected the VIP treatment.

The bugs which were now descending upon them had other ideas.

The first thing John noticed was light coming in through the window. Somehow he had slept and made it through the night. The second thing he noticed was that his back felt good. Tight, maybe, but no shooting pain. He sat up incrementally, testing and analyzing the results as he did.

"Good morning," his early-rising host said.

John swung his feet onto the floor. "Hi."

Kemina observed him from the kitchen. "So, are you leaving?" She was nothing if not straightforward.

"Yeah. I guess so," John said.

"I have a proposal."

"You keep making those."

"How is your back?"

John risked a stretch. "Not bad, really. It was a rough night, but it feels good now."

"Good enough to do more work for me?"

John stopped, reflecting. Something had changed, but he couldn't get a grip on what it was.

"Three more days," she continued, sensing he was not committed to leaving. "I have enough work to keep you busy for that long. You can leave once it is all done."

John tried twisting slightly from side to side, expecting pain, but getting none. "I'll tell you what," he said. "I'll stay for three more days and then I'm leaving, even if your list isn't finished. And, if my back starts acting up again, I'm done. Okay?"

"Yes, okay. Get ready and come with me."

"You need a ride?"

"Of course. Hurry along now."

"I need a shower."

"No time."

"But..."

"There is a shower at the restaurant, just off the pantry in the back."

John noticed it earlier. It was an old plastic stall with a drain and a shower head.

"Does it even work?"

"It will. It is on your list. You can use it as soon as it is repaired."

"Okay." She was rushing him now to the point where he wasn't thinking right.

"Come on, you slothful man. Let's go."

John looked around, perplexed, sensing that he was missing something but still not awake enough to bring it into focus. Kemina stepped behind him, pushing on his shoulders. "Come on, move! I will need time to make us breakfast and you have a busy day ahead. Grab your keys and let's go."

"Take it easy," John said. "You're going to develop hypertension if you don't learn to relax."

"Just march."

John began to suspect, as she swept him out of the house, that she didn't want to give him time to rethink his decision. If that was her strategy, it was working.

When his phone rang a few minutes later and an unknown number came up, John could only think of one person it could be. He was thankful Theresa had waited at least until he had arrived at the restaurant before calling. He didn't want to have a discussion that could turn antagonistic with Kemina sitting right beside him in the car.

"Hello?"

"Hi John. It's me."

Well, that was informative, John thought, surprised at how his immediate reaction was one of disdain. "What's up?"

"How are you feeling?"

Was this a gesture of concern? "I had a bad night last night, but I feel better now."

"That's good. Where are you? I can hear an echo or something."

John didn't feel obliged to give her too much information. "I'm at a restaurant right now. Just waiting for breakfast."

"I see. John, there are two things. I have a yard sale organized for two days from now. I've been promoting it. I think I can sell most of your stuff from the house. Also, I have a broker lined up to put the house on the market. She thinks we'll come out ahead if we can find a buyer." She paused, then, "Is there any way you can come back to help?"

"Not that quickly. I'll never make it."

A moment of dead air time. "I'll need you to sign the sales agreement for the house, John."

"All right. I'll be back early next week. I'll do it then."

"All right, John. I appreciate it."

"Anything else?"

More dead air. "Yes. John, do you remember Terry from accounting? He was at the last office party we attended."

A vague image came to mind. "Yeah, I think so. Sort of."

"I moved in with him," she said.

John, although knowing this contingency was likely, still managed to feel shocked. In his mind, behind all the antagonism, there had been a possibility that they might yet reconcile and get back together. Now that dream lay in spasms on the ground, caught in the latter stages of death throes.

"John, don't get all pissy. At least I had the decency to tell you myself. I didn't want you to find out through a Facebook posting or something like that."

"I'll see you next week." John hung up. *Screw it*, he thought to himself. He had spent enough time caught up in a Theresa generated funk. More than enough. He walked to the kitchen to see how Kemina was making out with breakfast.

CHAPTER 15

Mayor Dickens had chaired his share of meetings, ranging from large public gatherings with media present, down to one or two other people under a shroud of secrecy. This one was small and discreet—but in a move that seemed counter-intuitive, a local reporter had been invited. It had been the mayor's idea even though he didn't feel comfortable about it. Despite the intimacy of the small group, he would be careful what he said. Words had a way of finding their way into print.

"Folks," the mayor said from his office doorway, "please come in."

The reporter entered first. They shook hands briefly.

"Hello Brian. How are things with you? The Gazette still hanging in there during this digital age?"

Brian smiled. "Funny you should ask. I think that topic might work its way into our conversation."

"Please, have a seat. Just drag the chair to any spot you think is appropriate."

The mayor knew the name of the next person waiting in the doorway, but had never met him before. "And you must be Doctor Redding."

"Arthur Redding, MD. Pleasure to meet you, Mayor. Thank you for seeing me on short notice."

"Please be seated, Doctor."

The final two participants, a trim grey-haired man and a tall, younger blond woman, were new faces.

"And you must be from the FBI. I appreciate you getting here on such short notice. As a matter of fact, when I called, I didn't think the Bureau would be interested to this extent. I was looking for help which I thought would come in the form of a referral to another department."

The man shook the extended hand. "The number of victims and the severity of the attacks put most terrorist activities to shame. Also, I've had experience with unusual cases before. I'm Robert Specht, pronounced 'speck' despite the spelling, and this is my partner, Jan Collins."

"Nice to meet you both," the mayor said. "Grab a hot drink if you wish. There are enough chairs for all of you, so pick a spot and get comfortable."

There was coffee on a small side-table which drew Specht like a moth to a flame. He went about the business of preparing a cup.

"I don't see the need for any degree of formality with just the five of us here," the mayor said. "Doctor, why don't you get us started? You have some information which should set the stage for our subsequent conversation."

"Actually," Dr. Redding said, "I was talking with Brian in the lobby. I think he might be the better choice to kick things off. If he doesn't mind, that is."

Brian smiled. "I'll talk all day about any topic you want."

The mayor returned to his desk, mug safely balanced in his hand. "That's fine. Brian, tell us what we need to hear. And despite your previous pronouncement, I'm going to assume you understand the value of being succinct."

"Not in the slightest." He adjusted himself in the chair. "I'm going to refer to a story I wrote and was printed in today's paper. In reference to your question about the status of the Gazette, I'll have you know today's edition sold out, more copies were requested by several retailers and on top of that—the story was picked up by several state-wide media outlets."

Dickens knew what was expected. This was where he scratched the dog behind the ears as a reward for a job well done. "Excellent work, Brian. Your talent is wasted here in Barrington with such a small audience."

Brian soaked up the praise. "May I assume you have read it, Mayor?"

He shook his head. "Normally the answer would be yes. But today was one of those days where everything was somewhat rushed, chaotic and out of sync. Please enlighten me as well as our other guests."

"Neufeld Community College held its graduation ceremony yesterday. Or perhaps I should say, they attempted to hold it."

"I was invited but couldn't attend," the mayor said. "What do you mean, they *attempted* to hold it?"

"It was interrupted," Brian relied. "Honestly, I don't understand how you didn't hear about this."

"I've been busy tending to the needs of my constituents. I was to be sequestered in an all-day meeting today regarding a possible investment here in Barrington by a large, overseas distribution company. It represented potential for lots of jobs and future tax revenue. Unfortunately, we had the freakish bad luck of having a serious insect attack that involved the investors. I fear we are now off their list of potential locations. Please, continue to enlighten us."

"Straight to the point it is, then. The ceremony had just nicely started when a swarm of bugs appeared unexpectedly. They proceeded to sting a large number of people, incapacitating them. The ceremony was cancelled and local emergency services responded, although stretched to the limit by the scope of the attack."

The mayor frowned. "What a strange and inexplicable thing. Is everyone all right?"

"As much as I feel like I need to keep talking, I'm going to defer to Doctor Redding regarding the medical side of the conversation."

Redding looked grim. "We anticipate that everyone from the graduation ceremony will recover. That's not to say that the immediate symptoms of the stings weren't painful to the point of being debilitating. But based on experience from earlier sting victims, we know the effects can be managed and will fade relatively quickly. By tomorrow afternoon, most if not all should be released. I'm afraid the news isn't as good for the staff here at the Civic Center." Doctor Redding looked at the mayor. "Do you mind if I elaborate or do you wish to speak to this?"

The mayor sighed. It had been a long day and he was feeling the effects. "I'll make a brief statement at this time and then you may continue."

The doctor nodded in agreement.

"A long-time employee, Robert Kruger, was stung earlier today. He collapsed as a result. Emergency Services responded and he was transported to Barrington Regional Hospital where he subsequently passed away. His family has been notified and frankly, we're all in shock here. Worst of all for me is that I initiated the attack by poking the nest which was located in a shrub just to the rear of the building."

Collins was flipping through the notes she had brought. "He died from the sting? Isn't this the first known fatality caused by these bugs?"

Doctor Redding fielded the question. "Mr. Kruger had underlying health issues that I believe contributed to his death. He was a long-time smoker, a borderline diabetic and didn't exercise or eat a healthy diet. The stress of the toxins appears to have put him in cardiac arrest."

Now it was Specht's turn. "Did you say there was a nest right here?"

The mayor nodded. "Just off the back patio area."

"Is it still there?"

"No. A local exterminator came and bagged it up. I assume it's been incinerated by now."

Specht frowned. "How was he able to safely remove it?"

"He was wearing a protective suit. He also said it appeared the hive had been abandoned, but as to why, I have no idea. I only poked it once and the little buggers seem to be quite willing to defend themselves."

For a moment, Specht was lost in thought. "You've had a lot of stings here. Is this a new phenomenon?"

"We've never had anything like this before," Doctor Redding answered. "That is, until the past week. Since then, we've seen numerous victims, all of whom had identical symptoms—extreme pain, muscular contractions to the point of paralysis, and the inability to react or even speak coherently despite being fully conscious."

"It gets more interesting," Brian said. "I interviewed numerous people who were at the graduation when it happened, and even some of the first responders. They described an insect that I've never heard of and can't find anywhere online. It's huge and aggressive. I took some photos of the remains of several bugs that were killed during the attack. I'm trying to find somebody who can identify them, but so far, no luck."

"Our lab technician analysed the venom," Redding added. "It's unlike any that we know exists. It's all very puzzling."

"An invasive species? Is that what you're saying?" The mayor looked like he had reached a new level of concern.

"That possibility still exists," Dr. Redding said. "But the internet has worldwide reach and there's no obvious info about it there. This could be something new."

Collins looked dubious. "I could accept a new species as the answer if this was the middle of the Amazon rainforest, but here in the American heartland? I don't see how that could be possible."

"Then where did these things come from?" the mayor asked. "And maybe more to the point, where are they now?"

"I may have a possibility as far as origins are concerned," Redding said. "The first two victims were stung near a deep hole at a local farmer's property. They were from the USGS and knew about the hole. They were there to investigate it."

"Deep hole?" Collins didn't seem satisfied with the vague description.

"That's all I know," the doctor said. "I have the farmer's name if you want to contact him."

"We'll get that info before we go," Specht said.

"Thank you for taking this seriously," Dr. Redding replied.

"I only hope we can be of some service," Specht said. "This sort of thing is a little off the beaten path for us."

"What I need," the mayor interjected, "is some realistic idea of how much danger the people of Barrington are really in. That, and a way to eradicate these things."

"I know some people who are good at that sort of thing." Specht quickly drained his cup. "Give us a couple days and we'll sort this out."

"Keep me posted," the mayor said.

Collins looked up from her notes. "Any good motels around here?"

"Let's keep our priorities straight, partner," Specht said as he looked around the room. "Where can I buy a good cup of coffee in this town?"

CHAPTER 16

Specht was drinking coffee while he drove. Collins gave him a dirty look. He noticed (it was meant to be anything but subtle), but he wasn't sure if it was the distracted driving or the audible slurping that had her upset.

"Something to say?" he asked in his smooth, baritone voice.

Collins rolled her eyes. "It's not like an FBI Agent should be familiar with the law or anything like that."

He smiled and took another slurp. "If you drank coffee, you'd mellow out. It's something to consider."

She held back her initial response, but barely. He was her superior, after all. "Caffeine makes you hyper. Honestly, Robert, I don't know how you come up with these hackneyed supporting arguments to reinforce your flawed world views. Didn't you graduate summa cum laude?"

"Education and opinions go hand in hand."

"Not *wrong* opinions." She squirmed in her seat. "How much further?"

He took a sidelong glance. "You're the navigator. You tell me."

"Never mind. Besides, I have a more pertinent question. Why is the Bureau investigating a bug infestation in the first place? Shouldn't it be some expert in insects rather than criminologists who don't know the first thing about bees?"

"I feel like this isn't the first time you asked me that."

She put on an artificially huge smile. "I feel like you haven't given me a credible answer yet."

Specht drove in silence for a few moments before replying. "I believe we are currently in an 'observe and consult' capacity. As far as why it fell on you and I specifically—you know my reputation."

Indeed she did. It was the reason she had requested him as a partner.

Specht had, through no initial effort or desire on his part, been involved in several extremely odd cases. He picked up a reputation (which he despised) for solving mysteries with some sort of macabre or weird otherworldly component to them. As they piled up, he was surprised to find that some agents found this appealing. Some even looked at him with a measure of awe.

But that wasn't what he was referring to in this case. His superior seemed to be counting the days until he could get Specht out of his hair. Nearing retirement and feeling insulated from reprisals, Specht could be recklessly disrespectful to his boss should circumstances merit. If there was a case that nobody else would find appealing, especially if it got Specht out of the office, his boss was going to assign it to him.

Jan pondered the connection to her original question. "First of all, how could I not want to partner up with someone who killed a werewolf? Secondly, are you saying these bugs are some kind of monsters?"

"I didn't kill the werewolf; he nearly killed me. I just happened to be there when it happened. And besides, it turned out to be some nut job wearing an animal skin."

The artificial smile returned. "It looks good on paper, though. Best report I've ever read."

Specht grimaced. "Stephen King used to call on a regular basis looking for writing tips. Now, regarding the bug situation—I have no idea what they are. And when I mentioned my reputation, I meant from my boss's point of view. He seems to like getting me as far away from the office as possible. That's probably why he was so willing to deploy us on such an unusual mission. I think he's hoping I'll get stung."

Collins was enjoying how uncomfortable Specht seemed to be with this whole line of conversation. "Robert, that's a terrible thing to say about the Midwest Director of Operations."

"Not really. Terrible would be me recommending you for a transfer to another department. Let's refocus on the task at hand. A number of people were attacked and stung at a graduation ceremony yesterday. And two USGS agents were stung prior to that at what we have come to believe is ground zero for this unfolding fiasco. A number of other attacks have also occurred, all within the past week, all in this immediate area."

Collins was multitasking—listening to Specht talk and monitoring her GPS. "We're close. Another few minutes and we get off onto a secondary road. It won't be far after that."

"In keeping with my reputation, here's where it gets weird. According to the USGS report that I received during the meeting as an e-mail attachment, these insects were seen emerging from a recently formed fissure."

"Wait—so, like from underground? I guess that must be the hole that was mentioned."

Specht nodded. "This is preliminary information, keep in mind."

"I know there are burrowing wasps," Collins said. "I used to see them on my grandfather's farm. They live underground. They dig holes about the diameter of a standard pencil. They are big and scary."

"This hole is a bit larger and deeper than that. And the insects are unprecedented in size and stinging ability as well."

Collins turned to look at her partner. "Could it really be a new species?"

"The possibility exists."

"Robert, this is a highly modernized and developed area. How would that even be possible?"

"That is partially what we are supposed to find out."

"Exactly how dangerous are they?"

He shrugged. "Don't know. That's another thing we're supposed to find out. There are bee suits in the trunk for our protection."

"I definitely see the weird component now. Turn at the next left."

"Don't look so stressed, Collins. With a sufficient supply of coffee, even this could turn out to be fun." He turned and smiled. He knew about her phobia.

Collins wasn't a fan of spiders and bees. "I'd rather it was a werewolf."

Special Agent Specht was pleased with how the conversation with the farmer had gone. Brent Rivers, the owner of the property, was a goldmine of information. The time had now arrived when Specht transitioned to being more worried about his company car getting dirty than getting stung. "You're confident we can drive back to the place where the first attack occurred on this path?"

"Oh yes," the farmer said. "It's a dirt surface, but it's quite smooth and dry as well. There's enough space at the end to turn around. You shouldn't have any problems."

"And you haven't seen any more of these things since the incident?" Collins asked.

Brent shook his head. "No. But to be fair, I haven't been back to the crevasse again."

Specht had a thought. "Do you have any livestock outdoors?"

Brent nodded. "Yes, about twenty head of cattle out behind the barn."

"Have any of them shown signs of being stung?"

"No. Not that I've been able to tell."

Specht nodded. "I'll take that as a good sign."

Collins didn't seem entirely comfortable whenever the conversation turned to being stung. "You say it's a very painful experience?"

The look on Rivers' face was pained by the memory. "The two agents I found were completely incapacitated. They were conscious, but couldn't even talk, let alone do anything else. Worst of all, they had an expression of acute agony on their faces."

She made a face. "Sounds unpleasant."

"More like debilitating, from what I saw."

Collins turned to her partner. "Maybe we should suit up now."

"I'm sure we'll be fine until we get back there," Specht replied.

If Brent hadn't known better, he would have thought Specht was enjoying his partner's uncomfortable reaction to the situation they were in.

"Do be careful," Brent suggested. "And if you don't mind, I'd like to hear about whatever you find before you go."

Specht seemed agreeable. "That's fine. Thanks again for giving us access. Come on, Collins. I'm sure you're anxious to get started."

Collins insisted on suiting up the moment they got out of the car. Specht put up a mild argument simply for the sake of watching her stress level climb. In truth, he wanted the protection as much as she did.

Walking through the corn while in the bulky outfits was awkward at best. But once the crevasse came into view, all else was forgotten.

"Are you seeing this?" Collins asked.

"If you're insinuating that my eyesight is in some way deficient…"

"I wasn't expecting it to be this huge."

Specht took a moment to do a detailed scan. "Wouldn't want to fall into it."

"With that thought in mind, what now?"

Specht pointed to his left. "We walk this way. According to the preliminary report, access is possible from that end."

"Access? Are you insinuating that we're going in there?"

"Not at all. Insinuating is a very uncertain term. I'm telling you plainly, we're definitely going in. And by the way, this is the first time I've seen you so nervous."

"I'm not nervous," Collins said. "I'm just frigging terrified of stinging bugs."

Specht chuckled. His partner was the bravest agent he'd ever worked with. But everyone had their own kryptonite. Now he knew hers. That kind of information could come in handy. "If only we had a flyswatter and some insect repellent. Oh wait; we're wearing a bee suit."

"It's more than the bugs," she replied. "What do we know about the integrity of the walls? Is the atmosphere safe to breathe? What about footing?"

Specht didn't answer immediately, but pondered her concerns. He had already thought of the same issues. He had no intention of being careless. "As far as entering the crevasse, the USGS agent suffered no ill effects. Let's walk around and at least have a good look from above. After that, we can make a decision about what comes next."

"You mean no ill effects until he got stung."

"She. And it happened up here, not down there."

"Even worse on both accounts."

Specht was formulating a response when a bug landed on the screen mesh surrounding his face. It came out of nowhere and the sheer size of it shocked him to a stop. "Collins?"

She noticed he was no longer walking forward. "What is it? Change your mind already?"

"You could say that."

She turned and saw the bug. "Oh…"

Specht couldn't think of anything to say. The bug was arching its mid-section for added leverage as its ridiculously long stinger punched through the screen. Only inches from his face, it could have been a knife blade as far as the level of menace it generated. The bug was way bigger than Specht had imagined it could be, and it clearly meant to sting him. His list of options was short and so he took the first one that had occurred to him. While the stinger was still protruding through the screen, Specht swung both hands upward. They met in the middle, crushing the bug between them. Its wings continued to flutter as it dangled by the stinger. Specht swiped at it a second time, pulling it loose. It tumbled awkwardly to the ground. Specht looked down at it, trying to control his breathing.

"Robert?" Collins was also peering down at the twitching bug. "Is that its stinger I'm looking at?"

"Yeah. Nasty thing, isn't it?"

"Robert, I have two questions."

"Okay." His voice shook ever so slightly.

"Did it actually sting you?"

"No. The screen was able to keep it away."

"Good. Secondly…what material are these suits made from?"

He knew immediately where she was going with this. "Cotton."

"I think we get back in the car."

She was right. The screen had been rigid enough to keep the stinger at bay, but the soft material would not offer that protection.

"Let's go."

Neither had anything smart to say during the brisk walk back.

CHAPTER 17

John was picking away at his plate with limited enthusiasm. Maybe what he really needed more than breakfast was to get to work. It was time to tackle the shower.

"Is it your back?" Kemina was giving him a serious look from across the table.

"No." John forced a smile. "It feels good. No problem. As a matter of fact, I think I'm going to get back to work."

"You're not eating. Why?"

He emitted a long sigh. Would it be good, therapeutic even, to get this out? He had an image of Kemina putting him in a headlock, refusing to let him leave until he confessed all. He shook his head.

"What is it? Tell me."

"My wife just called. You know, to say hello, to update me on how things are going back home, to tell me she's moved in with another guy...that sort of thing."

"Oh, John." Her volume dropped off significantly. "I'm so sorry."

He waved off her sympathy as he stood. "No, don't worry about it. This is hardly a surprise. If it was, shame on me. Now, if you'll excuse me, I have a shower to fix."

"Are you all right? Would you like to go somewhere to be alone? Allie will be off to school—so you can have the apartment if you want."

"No," John answered in a decisive tone. "The best thing I can do right now is to keep busy. I'll be in the back if you need me."

"Very well. Just so you know, I am going to leave for a few minutes. I have some things to pick up. Don't worry, the door will be locked and I will be back soon."

"Fine. I'll let you know when I'm finished back here."

John worked the entire shift, keeping busy in the kitchen after the shower was fixed. His day ended when he left with Kemina after the restaurant closed. *How does she do this six days a week?* he wondered. He was tired and a little sore all over. His back was tight, although nowhere near the pain of the previous night. It was just enough to get him concerned. What was he thinking anyway...doing so much after having such a bad night?

Allie went off to bed before the two adults retired. John sat on the couch, waiting for Kemina to call it a day before he settled in. He hoped he would get a good night's rest.

"John?"

She had emerged from the bathroom in her robe, stopping on the way past.

"Yes?"

"Thank you for your help today. It made a big difference."

He managed a smile. "You're welcome." He decided not to give away how achy he was.

"Goodnight, John."

A short time later, he was tossing and turning on the couch.

He was sleeping fitfully when Allie came out to get a drink. During these times when he was physically distressed, he could be easily awakened from his shallow slumber.

"Hmm?" At first, consciousness only rewarded him with confusion.

"Shh. It's me, John."

"Oh. Hi Allie."

"I'm just getting a drink," she said. "Sorry to wake you."

"Don't worry about it."

The drink was a process that only took a moment. She paused on her way back to her room. "John?"

"What?"

"How is your back? Is it better?"

How unique that a young girl would allocate resources in her active imagination to care about his sore back. "It's okay," he said. "Way better than yesterday. Thank you for your concern."

"John? Can I ask you a question?"

John was thinking that every moment spent awake now would stretch exponentially while trying to get back to sleep. "I'm pretty sure you already did. What else do you want?"

There was a brief hesitation. Then she said something that almost made him fall off the couch.

"Did you have a funny dream last night?" Allie asked.

How could she have known about that? "Was I kicking and screaming in my sleep?"

"No. I just wondered. Goodnight, John."

"Allie, wait." He struggled to a more upright position. "You just made the most authentic psychic statement I've ever heard in my life. You can't walk away like it was nothing." He reached out, gently grasping her hand. "I had the most vivid, realistic dream of my life last night. How can you know about it?"

"I...was just guessing."

"Allie." His voice was soft, but his tone was indicative of his doubt.

Her voice fell to a level where he could barely hear it, even in the quiet of the house. "I can't say."

"Why?"

"You'll be mad."

That answer surprised him. "Allie, why would I be mad? You knowing that I had that dream is an extraordinary thing. Please tell me."

"I..." She hesitated yet again. "It was the pudding."

John furrowed his brow. "The pudding?"

"Yes. That I made for you last night."

"I know what pudding you mean, Allie. Why would it make me have a vivid dream?" What he was beginning to suspect was almost too horrible to connect to this sweet girl.

She stood mute.

"Allie, answer me. Did you put something in the pudding? Something that made me hallucinate?"

"No." She was fidgeting to the point where she couldn't stand still. She amended her original response. "Yes."

John couldn't believe it. A million questions and disturbing scenarios were swirling in his head. "Allie, this is very important. You have to tell me what you put in the pudding, okay? I need to know. It could have made me very sick. What was it?"

"It wouldn't make you sick. I think it made you better."

"Allie, that sounds sweet, but I think you might be delusional. Tell me right now. What was it? Where did you get it? Was it something the kids at school gave you?"

"No!" Now her voice was steady and strong. She reminded herself to lower it or she would wake her mother. This was not a conversation that Momma should be part of. "It wasn't drugs or anything like that, John. I wouldn't do that."

"All right. That's good. I believe you. But you still have to tell me what it was." John had visions of strange mushrooms, or the slime off the back of some South American toad swirling through his mind.

"It was…the fruit."

"Fruit?" His tone was dubious.

"Yes. I was pretty sure how you'd react to it."

That made no sense, but John was committed to getting the truth. "What kind of fruit?"

Allie seemed almost paralyzed. John patted the cushion beside him. "Allie, sit down for a minute. You need to tell me about this fruit."

She sat obediently but said nothing.

"Is it from Mexico? Is it something your mom uses in the restaurant?" *Do they grow hallucinogenic fruit in Mexico?*

"Momma doesn't know about it," she said.

"Is it something that is fermented? Is it like wine?"

"No. Just fruit."

John sighed. "Allie, there is no magical fruit that makes people have strange dreams that I'm aware of. Tell me more."

Why had she put herself in this predicament? Allie wondered. Maybe she *wanted* to tell an adult about it. This man seemed trustworthy enough. She knew he had some depth of moral character.

"It comes from the Dream Tree."

That raised more questions than it answered. "Allie, my dream last night— the one you somehow knew I had—was partially about a tree."

Her eyes grew wide. "Really?"

"Yes." What exactly was going on here? "Allie," he said, "you have to tell me. After eating this stuff, I have a right to know. What exactly are you talking about?"

She turned to meet his eyes. Then she told him the story of the Dream Tree.

They stood by the open refrigerator door, bathed in its soft light. Allie held the container with the fruit in it while John looked it over.

"This is it?"

She nodded while being careful to maintain a safe grip. "Yes."

"I've never heard of anything like it before. You say it came from a tree just outside of town?"

"Yes."

"Pull the lid off, okay? I'd like to have a smell."

She twisted it off, extending the tub towards him. John bent down with caution, taking in a sniff of the aromatic fruit.

"Hmm. That's not bad."

"No. It is delicious."

"This is what you put in the pudding?"

"Yes." She nodded.

Curiosity was beginning to assert itself. "Allie, what would happen if I ate some right now? Just a spoonful?"

She smiled. "It would make you feel good."

He shook his head. "That is so weird. How many times have you eaten it?"

She shrugged. "I don't know. Four or five times, maybe."

John marvelled at her apparent ignorance of the potential negative consequences from eating an unknown substance. "It never made you sick?"

"No," she said. She took a moment to formulate her next words. "It healed me."

Without context, her statement made no sense to John. "What do you mean, Allie?"

"The first time I climbed the tree, I scraped my arm bad enough to make it bleed. I knew Momma would see it and be mad at me. I ate some fruit, then sat and had a rest. When I got up to walk home, the scrape was gone."

John, though dubious, wondered what she had stumbled upon. "This tree is just growing in the middle of a forest, you say. It's not surrounded by an electric fence or anything like that?"

"No. Why would it be?"

"It's not in an orchard or field?"

"No."

John opened the silverware drawer, selecting a tablespoon. "You're sure it's safe for me to eat?"

Allie nodded.

"I hope you're right." He was definitely old enough to know better. "My curiosity is overwhelming my common sense."

He dipped the spoon in, scooping up a small amount of the pink orbs. He sniffed them again.

"It's okay," Allie said. "I promise."

He still had doubts, but figured if a little girl could manage it, he could too. He popped the spoon into his mouth, slowly chewing the contents.

"Well?" Allie looked at him with hope in her eyes.

He swallowed and shrugged. "It tastes pretty good."

"How do you feel?"

Something was happening, but it was subtle. John couldn't really describe it. "I feel okay."

"Just okay? Maybe you should try some more."

The effects were increasing. His expression gave it away.

"What is it?" Allie asked in a subdued voice.

"You were right. I feel...good. It's not like my senses are distorted or anything; it's more like they're sharper now. I feel strong. My back pain is fading."

"Have more."

"No." John thought that this experiment had gone far enough. There were still too many unknown variables. "Let's put it back for now. I'll see how well I get through the rest of the night. We can talk about this tomorrow, okay?"

She nodded. "Just not in front of Momma. Thanks for listening to me, John."

"Yeah. Thanks for trusting me enough to share your secret." *And thanks for the magic carpet ride,* he thought.

She closed the fridge and walked away. John pondered his current physical and emotional state. Compared to the previous night of agony, this was quite pleasant.

CHAPTER 18

The plan for this day was that John, despite his newly assigned duties as sous chef for Casa Comida, could sleep in. Before Kemina herself had left the house, however, a loud, intrusive knocking startled him out of the semi-dozing, relaxed state he had been in. "What?" He looked around, trying to get oriented.

"Someone is at the door," Kemina said, walking towards it. The rapping repeated.

She swung it open while John looked on. A police officer was standing there. A surprised expression washed across her face. "Good morning, Officer."

He was business-like from the onset. "I'm Constable Moody with the Barrington Police. I'm looking for Alejandrina Vargas." He consulted his note pad.

"Allie? What could you want with her?" The first words out of Kemina sounded challenging, a circumstance she hadn't intended.

"Is she here?"

He was too serious; almost confrontational. His demeanor was putting her off.

"She is just getting up, but yes, she is here. What is wrong?"

"She attends Barrington Elementary?"

"Yes."

By now John had heard enough to motivate him to get off the couch.

"Can you get her up? I need to talk to her."

Kemina seemed flustered and hesitated.

"Ma'am? I really must insist."

"But can't you tell me anything first? I am her mother."

John intervened at this point. "I'll wake her up, if that's okay."

The officer stepped partially into the apartment. He craned his neck to get a better view. "Are you the girl's father?"

Kemina was first to respond. "No. He is a friend."

"Not the girl's father?"

"No. He died."

"I don't recognize this individual. How long has he been in Barrington?"

"Just a few days."

John woke Allie up as gently as possible. He'd heard enough of the conversation to be concerned with both the direction and the tone. He walked back out while Allie got dressed.

The officer stiffened his posture, apparently not thrilled for the extra company. "What is your name, sir?"

John, a born and bred American, was feeling that this officer was being a little too intrusive and evasive for his tastes. Rights, unlike rules, were not made to be broken. "I'm John. What seems to be the problem, Officer?"

"The problem right now is a lack of answers and cooperation. What is your last name?"

"My last name is Wakefield. I don't see any lack of cooperation here."

"It's what I'm seeing that matters. Is the girl coming out?"

John was afraid he might say the wrong thing. Why was this officer so deep into the tough guy routine just to talk to a little girl? "Look, I don't want to come across as confrontational, but we have every right to ask you why you're here."

"The girl's parent does. I still don't know how you fit into all of this."

Kemina held up her hand to John. "It's all right."

Allie walked out, still blinking the sleep out of her eyes.

"Is this the girl?" The officer stepped in further.

"Yes," Kemina said. "This is Allie."

"Allie, we need to talk." She blinked in surprise but could muster no other reaction.

He looked around the apartment. "There's no need to do this from the doorway. Can we take a seat at the table? We can avoid any curious neighbors that way."

You could also avoid any other potential witnesses, John thought. Kemina nodded.

"Not you," Constable Moody said to John as he approached. "If you're not the girl's father and nobody can explain to me what your relationship is, or even why you're here, then you have no business sitting in on this."

John was steaming. "I'll sit on the couch," he offered before any suggestion could be made that he should leave the apartment altogether. The way this was playing out, John wanted to hear what this guy had to say.

The cop frowned, but didn't say anything contrary. He gestured for the other two to sit at the table. He followed them, and took a seat himself. "Allie, you attend Barrington Elementary?"

"Yes." It was an easy question, but her voice was strained.

"You and your mom moved here recently?"

"About a year ago."

John wondered what that could have to do with anything, but held his peace for the moment.

"Allie, I was recently approached by someone at your school. They told me some rumors about you that were very disturbing. I need you to tell me the truth about them."

Allie looked stunned, but didn't say a word.

"What rumors?" Kemina asked, sharing the same stunned expression.

"I'm getting to that."

Same belligerent tone, John noted. What could this sweet little girl have done that was so serious?

"Apparently you've been talking to your classmates about two of our local boys. Do you know who I'm talking about?"

Our local boys, John thought.

Allie's face was white. "Boys?" She could barely spit it out.

"You've been telling people that they did something bad to you. Is that right?"

"I…" Her hesitation came across like an admission of guilt.

"Making baseless accusations of a sexual nature is extremely serious. They can ruin someone's life. And it is against the law. We call it slander, and you can get into a lot of trouble for it."

John was really hot. This was the most one-sided, closed-minded position he had ever heard anyone take. This from a police officer!

"But, those boys…" Kemina tried to defend her speechless daughter.

"Those boys what? You can't make open-ended accusations."

John had heard enough. "Wait a minute. I saw them with her. They had her cornered out in the middle of nowhere. They were pulling her pants down against her wishes. That's hardly innocent activity."

John earned himself a scathing look. "I didn't ask you. I don't even understand why you're here or why you have any interest in this. Besides, if that's true, then why hasn't there been a complaint filed? Surely, if this was legitimate (he returned his attention to Kemina), you, as her mother, would have contacted the authorities. Your daughter should have had a medical examination. That never happened. Subsequently, this assault never happened as far as the police, the law and common sense are concerned. These boys are minors. They have a lot of rights. These accusations have to stop, and I mean now."

It was all becoming clear to John now. An immigrant, who felt like an outsider in the community; two local boys known by everyone; Kemina didn't report it because she was afraid of this very thing.

"Tell me that you understand what I'm saying to you," Constable Moody said with a tone and demeanor which were overbearing.

Allie's eyes teared up. "Yes."

The fury rose within John. He used everything he had to keep himself from leaping up and screaming at this guy. That would only make things worse.

"Good. I hope you mean it." He swung around, looking at John. "What's your role in all of this?"

John was about to explode. Somehow, he kept his voice under control. "I'm afraid I don't have a "role". Sorry."

"No role? How about an explanation then? Who are you, and why are you here?"

John wasn't an immigrant and wouldn't be that easily intimidated. "I'm just a person who is staying for a little visit, which is perfectly legal. And, I'm an American whose best friend is a criminal defense lawyer; something to think about before you say anything threatening." It wasn't true, but John couldn't resist throwing it out in his anger.

The cop stood, his chair making an ugly scraping sound against the floor.

"Don't mouth off at me." He pointed his finger like it was a gun. "This is a nice, quiet town. We don't need troublemakers here. Keep this up and you're all going to need a good lawyer."

He spun on his heels, walking towards the door. "I'd better not have to come back here again."

He walked out, letting the door slam behind him.

The trio left behind sat dumfounded. The whole episode seemed surreal and artificially confrontational.

What the hell was that? John wondered.

Moody decided to stop at the local diner for bacon and eggs after his confrontation with the immigrant family. He was feeling good and that gave him an appetite. He had been on the force for fourteen years, and grew more confident every day that he would rise to the position of chief when it became vacant. Being proactive and nipping problems in the bud, like he had just done, only served to confirm his readiness for the position.

He saw himself in the role of the respected lawman everyone could count on. It was his duty to clean up this little town and keep it that way. It never occurred to him that Barrington was devoid of major crimes and always had been. Moody's view of what constituted a threat to the community was warped by his lifelong exposure to small town living and the homogenous mindset that came with it. But ignorance was bliss. The constable hummed a happy tune as he drove along, waving at all the law-abiding citizens along the way.

Unsubstantiated threats wouldn't fly. Brad Merritt wasn't a troublemaker. He was a local boy, born and bred. Maybe a little rambunctious at times, but all boys were. His mother had made some mistakes too, but that wasn't the boy's fault. In the end, he would turn out to be a fine man.

Of this, Moody had no doubts. After all, he should know. Brad Merritt was also his nephew.

CHAPTER 19

"Okay, we're in business." Specht sat his phone face down on the table.

"We found a bug expert?" Collins was finishing the best Mexican food she had ever had. The risky decision to eat at Casa Comida had paid off.

"We've been rescued by the Department of Plant and Soil Sciences at the University of Southern Vermont. Dr. Sanders and his team have dropped whatever else they were doing and will be leaving shortly for Barrington. It's not all that far. They should arrive mid-afternoon."

"Fantastic." Collins pushed her now empty plate away. "Did you notice the dessert menu? I think I'm actually going to try something."

"And risk your girlish figure?"

"I'll burn it off running away from the bugs later on."

Specht looked around, saw the waitress and gestured for her to come over.

Collins frowned. "You didn't have to do that. I'm not in any hurry. I haven't even figured out what I'm having yet."

"Relax," Specht said. "Give me some credit for independent thinking. I have a plan for how we can spend the afternoon while waiting for the university team. Let me ask you something—how enamored are you with our motel accommodations?"

Collins wrinkled her nose.

"That's what I thought."

The waitress arrived. "Yes, how can I help you?"

Specht had read her age, her accent, her likely nationality and the dignified manner in which she conducted herself. Deductive reasoning was how he did his job. "Excuse me for asking, but are you the owner of this restaurant?"

She smiled. "Yes. Is there a problem?"

Specht reciprocated the smile. "Not at all. The food was great. I think we're even going to try some dessert."

"Very good. Do you know what you want? I can make a recommendation if the menu doesn't give you enough details."

"I think I'll take you up on that. But I have another question first."

The waitress waited patiently. "Yes?"

"My partner and I are from out of town. We have a meeting in a couple of hours or so, but nowhere to go until then. Would you mind if we set up our laptops here and worked at the table? We would be quiet."

"You are welcome to stay until three. After that, I need to get ready for the supper crowd."

"That's perfect! My name is Specht and my partner is Collins."

"I am Kemina," she responded.

"Very good. Now Kemina, please tell us about your dessert options."

Specht and Collins eventually packed up so they could get to the variety store parking lot by three, despite the pleasant atmosphere and excellent coffee at Casa Comida.

"Let's go back for breakfast tomorrow," Specht said. "I want to try the Mexican omelet."

"If we have to stay another night, I'm in for the omelet." Collins pointed as they entered the parking lot. "And there they are." A white van, unadorned except for a small logo sporting the university's name, was already parked there.

"Let's go meet the team." Specht had a take-out coffee in hand when he stepped out of the car.

A portly man climbed out of the van. Mere moments out of the climate-controlled vehicle, the skin on his forehead was beading up with sweat. "I'm Sanders." He extended a hand which Specht shook.

"I'm Specht, and this is my partner, Collins."

He shook her hand as well. "I can't tell you how excited I am to be here." He gestured towards the van and two young people exited. "This is Jules and Millie, both graduate students of mine."

"Good afternoon, ladies," Specht said. Collins simply nodded and smiled.

"So," Sanders said, "have you actually seen this insect?"

"We've had the pleasure," Collins replied.

"One landed on the mesh of my bee suit yesterday and tried to harpoon me in the face," Specht added.

Sanders grinned, his eyes twinkling. "Excellent. How big was it?"

"The bug or the harpoon?" Specht asked.

"If the stinger was ridiculously long, it probably wasn't a stinger at all," Sanders said. "It was likely an ovipositor, used to place eggs. Unless it is the modified type, it can't even be used to sting."

"It was long," Specht confirmed. "And the bug itself must have been around five inches or so."

Sanders' jaw dropped. "It can't be a hornet or wasp if it's that large. The biggest one in North America would be less than half that size. Girls, are you hearing this? Any ideas?"

Jules was the taller of the two, with multiple tattoos showing and dark hair that had been shaved off in a marine style cut. "Giant salmon fly, maybe. They can grow up to three inches in length."

Millie, whose long sandy hair was in a ponytail, had put on makeup for this excursion. "The only other thing that would come close in size would be a dragonfly."

Specht shook his head. "I know what a dragonfly looks like. This thing was a cross between a wasp and a locust in my opinion."

All three university people paused to think.

"Can you describe the coloration?" Sanders asked.

"Greenish leathery looking wings. The body was brighter. Yellowish with red and black stripes along the sides."

Sanders came to a fascinating conclusion. "I have no idea what that is, but I can't wait to see it. Can you show us where it was when you saw it?"

Specht nodded. "Of course. May I ask what you have for protection first?"

"We have full suits," Sanders said. "Every body part will be covered."

"So did we," Collins replied. "But we have doubts as to how well it actually works against something this large. Cotton isn't exactly one step down from Kevlar."

Sanders seemed dismissive of their concerns. "You probably had a cheap, entry level suit. Ours use heavier material, with all seams and access points triple protected. We'll be safe, don't worry. We've done this many times."

Collins and Specht exchanged a glance.

"Then let's go for a nice, short drive," Specht invited. "Follow me."

Allie had been too upset for school. Neither John nor her mother could get her to shrug off the residual emotion from the police visit. Kemina eventually left for the restaurant. The two of them remained behind to cope as best they could.

John had nothing to do to distract himself. Allie was sitting at the kitchen table, sniffling.

"John?"

"Yes, Allie?"

"Did I do a bad thing?"

Which thing are you talking about? "It's hard to make perfect decisions when you're a kid."

She pulled another tissue out. "It was a mistake."

John stood nearby, not wanting to get into her personal space. "What was?"

"The tree!" She burst into tears.

John waited for her to regain some composure.

"Look what happened because of me!" she said. Whatever shred of dignity she might have been clinging to disappeared as she blew her nose.

"Allie, that cop was out of line."

"If I hadn't been going to the tree, those boys never would have…" Her emotions got the better of her again at this point.

"So that's what you were doing out there," John mused. It had never come up in conversation before.

"Now," she spewed out with an effort, "those boys can just laugh at me and do whatever they want!"

John strolled over and stared out the kitchen window while Allie rode her emotional rollercoaster.

"I'm sorry." Allie got up and walked back into her room, closing the door.

John sighed. He wanted to do or say something to fix the problem, but couldn't think of anything useful. His mind eventually went back to the tub of fruit in the refrigerator. It seemed to be calling to him. He found it hidden near the back of the bottom shelf.

"So, you're the source of all this trouble." John held the container at eye level, meditating on the small pink balls inside. On impulse, he pulled the lid off. He lowered his nose gingerly, performing experimental sniffs as the tub drew closer. It smelled good. Was his mouth starting to water? He was struck by an impulse to grab a spoon and eat some. Fruit for breakfast was a sensible, healthy choice. Why not?

It tasted better than he remembered. He sat back down at the table, container in one hand, and spoon in the other. He began to ladle the fruit into his mouth, slowly building momentum.

After several minutes, the tub was empty, and John was rinsing it in the sink. He had no idea how hard it would be to get more, but after the trouble it had caused this morning, maybe he had just done everybody a favor. But the news wasn't all good. Disconcertingly, he was beginning to feel strange.

When Allie came out of her room, John was sitting on the couch and didn't acknowledge her presence. She walked to the kitchen for a glass of water. As she filled it from the tap, Allie saw the margarine tub in the sink. Perplexed, she reached for it. It was empty. Had he dumped it down the sink? That thought made her angry. She turned to look at John again. This time she had her answer.

He was staring without moving a muscle. She walked into his line of sight, waving her hand to get his attention. There was no response. "John?"

Nothing.

"John, are you okay?"

He continued to stare. His expression didn't change. Her concern for his health and well-being began to rise.

"John, can you hear me?" She put her hand on his shoulder. His face was blank.

"John!" She shook him until he snapped out of it.

"What?" He looked around, disoriented. His eyes met hers. "Allie?"

She nodded. "Are you all right, John?"

He had to think about it. "Yes. I'm fine."

"Did you eat the fruit?"

His eyes grew wide. "Yes. All of it. Sorry." His profession of guilt was perfunctory; he seemed distracted.

"That's okay. How do you feel?"

"I feel... great." He stood up. His expression changed as surprise and concern mingled together.

"John, what is it?"

"My back."

"Is it okay?"

He walked away from her. Then, without moving his feet, he pivoted at the hip until he could see her again, looking over his shoulder. "Wow!"

"What is it?" Allie was becoming panic stricken. Her obsession with the Dream Tree had already caused enough trouble.

"I haven't been able to turn like that for, I don't know, five years."

"Really?"

"Yeah, really." He continued to experiment with subtle movements.

"I'm glad you feel better, John."

The look of concern returned. "Allie, there *is* something strange about that fruit."

She sat down on the nearest chair. "Tell me about it."

"I just had a…dream, or vision, or…something."

"I've had them too," she said.

"This one was very vivid; do you know what I mean?"

She nodded. "Like it was real?"

"Yes. It was very real."

"Do you remember it?"

"Oh, yes. Allie, what were your dreams like?"

She wasn't sure what he meant by that. "Like yours, I guess. Like something that was really happening."

"So they seemed real to you too?"

"Yes."

"Allie, the one I just had was *exactly* like real life. I could smell things, I could feel things. Did you ever have one like that before?"

She wrinkled her nose. "Not like that."

"Allie, that container full of fruit I just ate…"

"Yes?"

"Have you ever eaten that much before?"

"I don't think so. Why?"

"I think the amount consumed might affect the impact it has."

Now she was curious. "Why do you say that?"

"My vision." He started to relive it in his mind. "And my back feels better than ever. Like new." A nagging doubt remained. "Allie, what if this stuff has some negative side-effects that we're not aware of? What if we're harming ourselves by eating it?"

She had no answer. She hadn't bothered to reason that out. "Can you tell me about your dream?"

"Why?"

"I wonder if it's like the ones I had, that's all."

"Oh," John said.

Allie could sense his reluctance. "That's okay. You don't have to."

"Allie, no offense. It's just that part of my vision was very personal, and I might need some time to work it out before I'm comfortable sharing it."

She nodded. "Okay."

"Allie?"

"What?"

"Can you show me the tree?"

"Really?"

He nodded. "Yes. Right now."

That put a smile on her face. "Yes! I'd love to. You'll have to walk into the woods with me."

"No problem. The way I feel, I might climb the tree myself."

Allie laughed as she imagined it. "That wouldn't be a good idea."

The chasm was now in view. They all stood in a line, staring. Neither Specht nor Collins had any desire to get closer, especially unprotected.

"The access is to our left." Specht couldn't stop looking around, trying to see if there were any bugs in the area.

"That is way bigger than I expected," Sanders said. "As far as you know at this point, this is ground zero for these insects?"

Specht, who was usually calm even under duress, felt the hair go up on his arms. "Yes. And I would like to humbly suggest that you folks suit up. I would also like to return to my car before anybody gets stung."

In his line of work, Sanders had seen what he considered to be irrational fear of insects many times. "Of course. Is there anything else you can tell us that might be of value before you go? Any small detail at all?"

Specht and Collins were turning to leave.

"Just be careful," Specht said. "I don't want to hear about you on the evening news tonight."

As they walked off, Millie leaned in towards Jules. "What did he mean by that?"

"Ladies," Sanders was all smiles as he anticipated the thrill of discovery. "Time to suit up."

CHAPTER 20

John stood at the base of the tree, looking skyward through the maze of branches. He failed to see anything that could justify the intrigue. "Where's the fruit?" he asked. "I don't see any at all."

"It's at the very top," Allie responded. "You have to climb part way to see it."

John tried to work out the logistics. "You climb this thing?"

"Just watch me!" she said, her face beaming with pride.

"Are you sure it's safe? That is a long way up."

"I'll be careful." She jumped up, grabbing the lowest branch.

"I don't mean to pressure you, but if you fall, I'm quite certain your mom will kill me."

"Don't worry," she said, as she swung her leg over the branch. "I've done it before."

"What are you going to do when you get up there?"

"Pick a whole bunch."

"So, you're going to the very top?"

"Almost." She was upright on the branch now, moving towards the centre of the tree.

"Please be careful. You're way more important than the fruit."

"Stop talking. You're distracting me."

He wasn't sure he even wanted to watch at this point, but found that he couldn't tear his eyes away from her progress. The higher she went, the more concerned he became for her safety. Soon she was only partially visible, the spreading branches obscuring his view.

"Watch out below!" Her voice seemed filtered out by the maze of leaves. A long pod hit the ground by his feet.

"Hey, watch it." He bent over, noting his functioning back, and picked up the pod. The outer covering wasn't anything special. "How do you open this thing?"

"Just wait!" More pods started to rain down.

John took a few steps back. "If you insist." He started swivelling at the hips, first one way, and then the other. He didn't know how long his back was going to feel this good, but he was determined to enjoy it while it lasted. "Don't leave the poor tree barren!"

"They grow back." More pods landed on the forest floor.

John started arranging the pods in a nice, neat pile. By the time he finished, Allie was swinging down from the bottom branch, landing gracefully.

"That's a good amount," she observed.

"It is," John agreed, although her rationale seemed entirely subjective.

She sensed something in his tone. "What?"

"It does bring some questions to mind."

Allie pulled a crumpled garbage bag out of her pocket. "Like what?"

"How long do these things keep? You've got quite a pile there. It would be a shame to have them spoil."

She was scooping them into the bag. "I don't know. The ones in the fridge were there for a few days and they were fine."

"You've got a lot more than that now. What are you going to do with this many?"

She continued working, undeterred. "You're right," she said. "We need a plan."

"Allie, just to be clear—the only people who know about this are you and me…correct?"

"I'm pretty sure if I told anybody they wouldn't believe me." She lifted the bag. "That's all. Let's go."

"Good idea. I'd better get you home and get myself ready for work."

They trudged along, side by side, feet crunching on leaves and small twigs.

"John?"

"What, Allie?" he said.

"Are you going to stay?"

It occurred to John that she had no knowledge of the arrangement between him and her mother.

"I promised to help your mom for a few more days. Then I've got to get back home."

"Where is home?" The question was a funny blend of innocence and intrusiveness.

John concluded there was no harm in sharing some peripheral information. "I live in a place you've never heard of. It's more or less a part of Pittsburgh. Standard suburbia; not a bad place in most regards."

"I've heard of Pittsburgh. Sidney Crosby plays there."

"So you're a hockey fan?"

"I'm a Sidney Crosby fan," she corrected. "He's cute."

"Not a perspective I've ever operated from. But I suppose."

They crunched more leaves.

"Why did you come here, John?"

"Well, that's the million dollar question. I'm not sure we have enough time for me to answer. Let's just say that I needed to get away."

"To Barrington?"

"I didn't have a specific itinerary. Barrington just sort of happened. Me being a little lost might have played a role."

"You can't be a little lost, John," she said. "You either are or you're not."

"Wrong. Men *can* be a little lost. There may be other degrees as well, now that I think about it. Trust me on this one."

She laughed, and it was a sweet sound. John thought back to the boys that were with her when they first met and decided that it might be fun to hang them from their toes. What the hell were they thinking? She didn't need that kind of post-traumatic crap bouncing around in her young mind.

She swung around and locked eyes with him. They were sparkling with energy. "I have an idea. Could you help me?"

"Help you how?"

"I won't know until we get back home. It depends." After the police visit earlier, John reminded himself not to do anything that would contribute to the delinquency of a minor. Barring that, he would be happy to assist.

"All right, kiddo. Let's get back before we're missed."

Later, John went off to the restaurant feeling better about Allie's emotional state. He felt up to spending a busy afternoon in the kitchen, and wondered if his new and improved physical condition would have allowed him to continue working at the job he had lost.

Life is funny, he concluded. After further reflection: *yeah, hilarious*. He started cooking and thought about what Allie had organized back at home. When he left, she was making Dream Tree jam.

Allie had unwelcome visitors that afternoon. She had just cleaned up from making jam, putting the last of the jars away, when a loud rap on the door announced their arrival. With her mind elsewhere, she opened the door without hesitation or concern. It took but an instant to realize her mistake.

Brad grinned at her with mean humor. "Hey, what's for supper—tacos?"

Lonnie, his usual accomplice, stood nearby, laughing.

Her blood turned to ice. How could they have the nerve to show up at her door?

"What do you want?" She managed to be a little bit challenging.

"Oh, don't be like that. Aren't you glad to see us?" It was neither funny nor clever; the driving force behind it was blatant cruelty. There was an ample amount of that to fuel its effectiveness. "Besides, Mama Maria and her boyfriend Poppa Luigi are cooking burritos, right? They left you all alone here. We thought you might be lonely."

"He's not her boyfriend."

"Are you serious? I bet they're doin' it on the counter right now. You're so stupid."

Allie felt her muscles turning to stone. She wanted to shut the door in his face but couldn't move for some frustrating reason.

"Aren't you going to invite us in?" He took a step forward.

Her paralysis broke. "No, I can't. Go away." She shut the door with enough force that it slammed. Would he have the nerve to force his way in? She grabbed the deadbolt, securing the lock.

"Hey, we just wanted to have some fun," he yelled, loud enough to be heard by her and the neighbors.

"Go away," she whispered, taking a step back from the door.

"We'll be back."

Moronic laughter filtered its way in. Allie felt darkness closing around her.

"If you do something for us, we'll leave you alone."

The voice was only slightly more subdued.

"It'll only take a minute. We can help if you want. Let us know when you're ready."

How could it be that these two dolts could come up with a simple plan to terrorize her but she couldn't come up with any way to deter them? Why couldn't the police show up now and see them harassing her? Any residual happiness from visiting the tree melted away. She retreated further away from the door, feeling alone, afraid and sorry for herself.

When she summoned enough courage to approach the window and look outside, there were no signs of them. But that wasn't enough to wash away the residual fear and disgust she now carried. Allie sat, contemplating a future full of wretched self-loathing. Another unpleasant thought occurred to her.

Could it be that this was all her fault?

Sanders and his team had made their way to the bottom of the crevasse. They were moving further in, walking slowly and cautiously. After all, their speciality was insects, not geology.

"Why do the walls look like that?"

Sanders looked to the side and saw that Jules had stopped walking.

"Like what?" They were walking down the centre of the chasm and the walls were now some distance away.

She started to edge closer to the side. "I don't know—green and shiny. Is that some kind of metal?"

Emeralds would be a nice discovery, Sanders thought without any actual hope of it being true. "No idea. Let's not forget what we came for."

Jules was getting closer. Details came into focus. There was subtle movement on the walls. She wasn't looking at metal at all.

"Shit!"

Sanders grew immediately concerned. "What is it?"

Jules' voice had a hint of awe intertwined with the concern. "There are millions of them. The walls are covered."

Sanders still couldn't discern what she had seen. It was dark and dreary enough to obscure his view. "Covered with what?"

She turned to make eye contact and Sanders could see the haunted look on her face even through the mesh. "Bugs!"

The walls exploded. The air was instantly filled with buzzing, leathery wings. Jules was right, Sanders thought. There were millions of them. He felt his suit getting heavier as they landed all over him. His mesh visor was crawling with them, literally, and he could no longer see to walk. He heard the girls scream.

"Don't move! Just stay still." Movement would only agitate them more.

He saw the stingers being pushed through the protective screen, aiming for his face. He had second thoughts about the ability of their suits to withstand this kind of onslaught.

We're in trouble, he thought as the girls continued to scream.

Kemina noticed something was different as soon as they entered the apartment. With uncanny accuracy, she walked into the kitchen. There, spread out on the counter, was a proliferation of jars, all full of pink jelly. Allie, prepared to be defensive or elated depending on how her mom reacted, came out of her room.

"Allie, what is this?" Her tone was neutral, but implied concern.

"I made jam."

There was a moment of silence. "Jam?"

"Yes." Allie was still optimistic, but hope was fading as the seconds passed.

"You are a silly girl. Come over here."

She approached, receiving an enthusiastic hug. Allie was elated.

"But how did you do this? Where did you get everything you needed?"

"John helped."

Kemina gave him a quick look that was suspicious in nature. "Oh, he did, did he? It is funny he didn't tell me about it."

He held his palms up in a surrendering gesture. "I was sworn to secrecy."

Allie released her embrace, and Kemina picked up a jar. "Allie, what did you make this from? I don't recognize it."

Allie had given the answer to that question a lot of thought. An incomplete but skillfully crafted response was loaded and ready to go. "The farmer I know had some of these growing on his property. I got them from there. He told me I could." He told her she could *walk* there; magical fruit had never been discussed.

"But what kind of berries are they?" She held the jar up to the light, admiring its pinkish hue. It made a nice presentation.

"I don't know what they're called. Gooseberries maybe?" There was such a thing; Allie had done the research.

"Gooseberries?" Kemina repeated the name with distaste and distrust.

"Open a jar, Momma," she said. "Try it."

"Now? You just made it. It won't be set."

"It will be fine. Even if it is still a little runny, it will taste good. You will like it." Allie *really* wanted her mom to try it. She still wasn't certain that prolonged heating didn't take away from their healing, dream-inducing qualities. She wanted an answer to that question as well.

"All right. Maybe just a bite." She sensed her daughter's eagerness.

"Wait. Let me put down a piece of toast to spread it on."

"That's not necessary. I'll just use a spoon."

Allie already had the bread in the toaster. She popped it down, sealing the deal.

Kemina opened the silverware drawer, pulling out a tablespoon. "John might like a piece of toast." She twisted off the lid, sniffing. The spoon went in and came out filled with pinkish jelly.

"Go on," Allie encouraged. "Try it, Momma."

She did. Her eyebrows shot up in apparent surprise. "This is good."

Allie was delighted. "I'm so glad you like it!"

Kemina mused. "It's like…pineapple marmalade. Sweet, but not unpleasantly so." She doubled dipped for another scoop.

"John, would you like some on toast?" Allie asked.

He smiled at how this scenario had played out. "Sure, that sounds good, Allie. Thank you."

Kemina dropped the spoon in the sink, unaware of how close she had come to experiencing the more dramatic effects of the fruit. The list of restaurant needs and responsibilities swirling in her head kept her from pondering the finer details of anything as mundane as fresh-made jam.

"Make sure you get to bed at your usual time," she said to Allie. "Tomorrow is another day."

CHAPTER 21

Specht and Collins received the official word that they would be staying another night. They secured their rooms and headed out for supper. There had been no word from Sanders and his team.

"I can't wait any longer," Specht said as they left the restaurant. "Let's go for a drive and see what's happening at the crevasse."

"You're going to get the car dirty," Collins said, knowing full well how much that annoyed him.

"If only I had someone I could get to wash it for me."

Collins shook her head. "Let's wrap this up and go back to crime fighting."

The drive wasn't long. Once they arrived, Specht maneuvered slowly along the path beside the field, avoiding the dreaded dust as much as possible. The car soon arrived at the access point.

"The van's here. I guess they must still be gathering data," Collins said.

"Let's go." Specht opened his door.

"Why didn't we pick up some repellant at the hardware store?" Collins said, making light of her phobia as she stepped out.

The van was still sitting in the exact same place it had been when they left earlier.

"I already tried the phone. Time for something less hi-tech." Specht cupped his hands around his mouth like a mini megaphone. "Sanders! Can you hear me?"

They both stood motionless, listening. Moments ticked away silently. Neither wanted to move any further from the safety offered by the car.

"Damn," Specht said. "I think we've got to go in."

Collins wasn't thrilled. "Into the crevasse? I have several concerns about the wisdom of that."

"The team could be under duress. If they can't move or talk, which seems possible based on what little we know, they may be in desperate need of a rescue. If that's not our job, then what is?"

"Couldn't you stick with sarcasm?" Collins said. "Shaming me really hurts."

Specht, despite his words, was hesitating. "I wasn't expecting this. We have no protection."

"Don't we still have the suits we used before?"

"You mean the ones that didn't work? Yes, they're in the trunk."

"Better than nothing."

"I suppose." He cupped his hands and yelled again. There was no sound in response. He turned back towards the car. "Yelling at the top of my lungs isn't working. Let's suit up."

"Robert!"

Collins' voice was so urgent, Specht crouched in reflex as he spun around. A bug flew inches over his head, the wings making an audible sound.

"Back in the car!" he yelled.

They jumped in frantically and slammed the doors with gusto.

"I really hate those things," Collins gasped.

Specht hated being forced into inaction. "We need to think. There's got to be something we can do."

"We're still not certain of their status. Otherwise, calling in support would be justified."

"What kind of support do you call for something like this?" Specht watched another bug fly closely past the windshield. "There are still a lot of them and they're very active. Either Sanders can't hear us because of the suits they're wearing, or they've been overcome by the bugs."

"Two radically different scenarios. Only one of them requires an active response."

"Hold on." Specht looked towards the west. "The sun is setting. Bees are generally not functional nocturnally. I got rid of a hive on the corner of my garage once simply by waiting until dark and then knocking it down. Let's wait a few more minutes and then we'll try again."

"Robert," Collins replied, "I'm not sure how much I trust the finer details of your knowledge of bugs—no offense intended."

"We'll try again in fifteen minutes. At the first sign of an active bug, we retreat back to the car."

"And to think," Collins said, "until this assignment, getting shot seemed like the worst case scenario for this line of work."

Time slowed to a crawl, and fifteen minutes became an eternity. The sun painted a colorful splash across the horizon as daylight faded.

"Let's go." Specht swung his door open cautiously. "Keep your eyes peeled."

Collins followed suit. "Don't worry about that." Her eyes darted about in all directions.

"Let's head to the place where we entered. Hopefully we can see into this thing well enough to spot the team."

"If we make it in one piece," Collins said under her breath.

No less than three times they saw a bug fly past, easily visible now against the paling blue sky. But this time, none of them flew towards them, seemingly interested only in getting back to the chasm. Fighting no small amount of trepidation, the agents kept walking. They reached the end of the chasm soon enough. All was quiet.

"I can't see the bottom," Specht lamented. "It's dark as night in there."

"Me neither," Collins agreed. "Should we risk yelling?"

Specht hesitated. Neither of them was outfitted for a descent into a major geologic anomaly. "No. Let's risk it and enter. If we don't go now, it will be too dark to see. A fall might be every bit as bad as a bug attack. Follow me before I change my mind."

Specht took the first step where the ground sloped downward into the actual crevasse. Soon they were descending slowly but steadily. Darkness was overtaking them as they went. It was no surprise to Specht that Collins saw the team first. Her eyesight was amazing. She placed her hand gently on his shoulder, and then pointed ever so slightly to the right side of the chasm. He could now see three figures lying prone on the ground. There was no sound or sign of movement.

He turned to look at his partner. "Remember the bugs are likely not nocturnal."

She had to respond despite the seriousness of the situation. "You should take a moment to record that thought. It'll look great on your tombstone."

"I'm not speculating—I've done some research. Bees and wasps are immobile after dark. They aren't equipped for night flying. Besides, these folks need help and they need it now." *Assuming they're still alive*, Specht thought to himself.

"Let's do it."

They approached cautiously.

"Use your phone for light," Collins suggested. "It's better than nothing." She bent over one of the girls, while Specht checked on Sanders.

"Shit!" Specht hissed.

Collins turned her attention to her partner. "What is it?"

Sanders' face was hard to see even with the light from the phone. What little he could make out would haunt Specht for some time. The expression on Sanders' face was one of pain and horror, and worse—he was fully conscious. His eyes were wide open and moving as if trying to see something that was moving quickly. His lips were also moving but no discernable words came out.

"He's alive," Specht said.

Collins turned her attention back to the two girls. In a moment, she had the answer. "The girls are alive too." Collins stood and faced her partner, frustration apparent on her face. "What do we do now? How are we going to get them out of here?"

He looked up at the top rim, all the while thinking. It was a long way up. "I don't know. We're going to need help."

He looked at his partner and watched as the expression on her face changed. She was staring towards him, but not directly at his face. She had assumed a look of pure terror. Specht slowly looked over his left shoulder, the direction Collins was facing.

He saw what she saw. The walls were moving. Under the soft glow of her phone squirmed untold thousands of huge insects, wings starting to twitch.

"Turn that light off!" Specht hissed.

Collins pawed frantically at the tiny keyboard. The light began to dim and soon they were in darkness.

"Are they still moving?" Specht asked.

"I can't tell. We need to get out of here stat."

Eyesight became of paramount importance. Hers was superior. "I'll follow you," Specht said.

Collins couldn't wait to get out, but hesitated regardless. "What about them?"

Specht, based on what they had just seen, was willing to bet that without light, the insects would remain docile. Or so he hoped. "We'll have to call emergency services for an extraction team. We need the help, bugs or not."

Collins started moving as fast as she could, given the uneven footing. Relief was tempered by concern. She hated leaving the victims behind.

The medical team took what seemed to be several lifetimes to arrive. Once there, Specht gave specific direction to the paramedics. Minimal, sporadic lighting, be wary of the uneven footing, and then get the victims up and out of the crevasse quickly before doing any diagnosis or treatment.

After enduring too many stressful minutes waiting at the top, patience was rewarded as the team finally made it out safely. Specht breathed a sigh of relief. If he and Collins had arrived during daylight to look for Sanders and his team and wandered unknowingly into the hole, the insects would have swarmed them too. He suppressed a shudder.

"Special Agent Specht?" One of the paramedics had approached.

"How are they?"

"Hard to say. Alive, but definitely under some as of yet unknown physical duress. I think it's safe to assume they've been stung. We've already administered a shot that should start to mitigate the effects of the venom. We need to transport them now. We can work on them more while on the way to the hospital, but doing it here is going to waste valuable travel time."

"Absolutely. We'll follow you." He was both curious and concerned about the victims. "Take good care of these three."

Collins stood nearby, looking unusually pensive. Specht gestured her over.

"They're being transported now. I want to follow. Are you okay with that?"

"Definitely."

Specht had a thought. Distraction might be a blessing for her. "Do you want to drive?"

"Oh, I see your plan. That way you can blame me for getting it dirty. No thanks. I'll just sit and stare out the window, if that's okay. I have some fresh images that I want to scrub out of my brain before PTSD can set in."

Specht was no stranger to that. "Whiskey might help, but I'm fresh out. Let's go."

CHAPTER 22

John had just fallen asleep, an accomplishment that was destined to fail. Something woke him and he decided to find out what it was before dropping off again. He opened his tired eyes and saw a blurry representation of Allie. "Hey," was the best he could muster while waiting for his mind to come back to full power.

"Hi John," she whispered.

"What's up?"

"I couldn't sleep."

"So…misery loves company?"

She hesitated. "Pardon?"

He shook his head. "Nothing. Can I help you or something?"

"Yes. I'm sorry I woke you up, but I was afraid you might not be here much longer. Are you leaving soon?"

Like mother, like daughter. "Yeah. Two more days and then I'm on my way. You didn't wake me up just to ask me that, did you?"

She gave a slight nod of her head. "I'll miss you, John," she said, sniffling.

"Oh." He sat upright, patting the now available cushion. "Here, have a seat."

She sat beside him, posture perfect. Weren't kids supposed to slouch?

"I'll miss you too, Allie. You're a nice kid."

"Do you have to go?"

"Yes," he said. "I have things to do, which I've put off long enough."

"What about when those things are done? Can you come back then?"

John couldn't remember being so popular. "Your mom asked me the same question earlier."

"What did you tell her?"

"I said yes. I will come back one more time."

"Good. And stay?"

Right to the point, no subtlety. "I don't know. I haven't decided where my future is."

"Oh." She sniffled some more.

John put his arm around her shoulder. "Hey, you've only known me for a short time. You haven't seen the jerky side of me yet."

"John," she whispered between sniffles, "I need a good thought in my head."

"I see. Well, I've never heard it said that way before."

"Can you tell me about the vision you had?"

"The vision?" That put him off. John didn't want to get into it.

"Yes. You know…when you ate the container of fruit."

"Aw yes, the magic fruit." He allowed the choice of words to stimulate his weird sense of humor. "The more you eat, the more you toot."

"Pardon?"

"Never mind. Better you don't know." He grew serious. "Allie, why do you want to hear about my vision?"

"I think it will make me happy. I'm curious. I have had the visions too."

"I'm not sure about the happy part," he said. "It didn't make me feel that way."

"How *did* it make you feel?"

John wasn't sure how to describe it. "Confused. Disconcerted. Maybe a little melancholy. Does that help?"

"Not really."

"Are you sure you want to hear about it?"

Even in the dim lighting, John could see her nodding. "Tell me."

John ran one last mental diagnostic to confirm that he was ready to relive the whole thing. The results were to the positive side of the scale by the smallest of margins.

"All right, Sigmund. Maybe you can explain its meaning to me when I'm done."

"I'll try."

John gathered himself.

Her voice came softly through the darkness. "Tell me."

John paused to gather his thoughts.

"I found myself standing on a sandy beach. It was calm; the waves were almost indistinguishable, barely lapping the shore. The water was a gorgeous shade of blue, and the sand was almost pure white. It was beautiful.

"I turned around and saw that I wasn't alone. The sand transitioned to grass, and on it, in the distance, I could see children playing. There were a lot of them, spread across the horizon. I could hear their voices. And laughter, I think. They all seemed happy. I couldn't discern any yelling or fighting at all.

"I decided to investigate. At first, I didn't think there were any adults among them, which even in my vision, I found to be unusual and out of place. Who was looking after them? Then, I saw a man in the distance, and my impression was that he saw me at the same time. He started walking towards me, and I felt a little nervous about it. As he approached, I could see that he was a big dude—like a football lineman or body builder. I wasn't exactly afraid, but he exuded some degree of authority. It also seemed obvious that this guy could kick my ass if he wanted to, pardon my French."

Allie giggled in response.

"Anyway, he comes up to me and I can see he looks puzzled. He asks me what I'm doing there. Since I don't have a clue, I can't answer. Then, I hear this sound. It's one of the kids in the distance, and he's squealing. Not screaming, like when you get hurt or scared; more like the sound of a kid who sees a big gift under the Christmas tree and realizes his name is on it.

"I look towards the sound and I see this little guy running towards us. Man, he's moving, his little legs pumping like you wouldn't believe. Now the big guy looks at me like he knows what's going on, and takes a couple steps back. I, on the other hand, have no clue what's happening.

"The little guy runs right up to me, slamming into my leg. He's looking up, smiling this huge smile, not even breathing heavy after that long run. Then he holds out his hands and I know what he wants, so I pick him up. He looks at me with these gorgeous blue eyes. He's smiling like he's been waiting to meet me his whole life and this moment is the greatest thing that ever happened to him...and I don't know what to say or how to react because I have no idea who he is or what's happening. Then I hear a voice."

John stopped talking, having reached the point that made him avoid recounting the vision. He hated losing control and had taken himself to the brink of that very thing. He paused to get a handle on his feelings.

"John? Are you all right?"

He nodded, then gave a one word response. "Yes." It was plain that the opposite was true.

"You heard a voice?"

John took a purposeful breath, collecting himself. "Yeah."

He was hanging by a thread. Allie nudged him along. "What did it say?"

When John was ready to continue, he spoke slowly, measuring his own reaction as the words flowed out. "It said, 'Abby, get down.'"

"So, Abby was the little boy?"

"Yeah. I thought that was weird for a boy's name, but that was in the background of my mind. What really hit me at the time was that I recognized the voice."

"Who was it?"

He teetered on the edge of emotional control.

"It was my mom." Even as the final word came out of his mouth, he knew he had lost it. He sobbed, embarrassed to be doing it in front of her. "Sorry," he blubbered as quietly as he could, not wanting Kemina to come out to investigate all the commotion.

Allie put her arm around John's shoulder, hugging him. "It's all right."

"Not really," he responded, now a little defiant and belligerent. "It might be all right if I understood any of this, but I don't."

"Did you wake up then?"

"No. That's another thing. I don't think I was asleep at all. I could see clearly, I could hear every sound, I could feel the breeze on my arms; I could even smell things. The kid felt heavy when I lifted him, and I noticed he had small, subtle flecks in his iris. That's pretty detailed for a dream. Everything was Technicolor and three dimensional—just like real life."

"Then what happened?"

"I...turned towards the voice, and there she was. When she saw me, she gasped in surprise, putting her hand to her mouth. She was acting like she had seen a ghost, but from my perspective it was the other way around. She didn't look like I remembered her. She was a lot younger, like in the wedding pictures that I saw around the house when I was growing up. She was...beautiful."

Emotion overwhelmed him and he came close to losing it again. "Then the big guy was back, and he says to me "You've got to go". He wasn't snooty or demanding or threatening about it, but I could sense he wasn't kidding, so I made like I was going to set the little guy down again…"

"Abby," Allie corrected.

"Yeah. But, before I can do it, he puts one little hand on each side of my face, and kind of holds me there in the centre of his field of vision. He smiles and says, 'G'bye' in this cute little voice. Then he says…" John felt yet another wave of emotion wash over him. "He says, 'G'bye, Uncle John'." He lost it again, blubbering like a baby…or a fool which was closer to how he felt.

Allie processed the information. "You had a nephew?"

John shook his head, which worked only because speaking wasn't involved.

"So who was he?"

"I don't know. But…"

"John? What is it?"

John struggled to collect himself with a mighty effort. "He kind of reminded me of my dad."

Allie frowned. "How's that possible?"

"I don't know." There was frustration in his tone.

"What happened next?"

"I heard your voice."

That surprised her. "Mine?"

"Yes. You said 'John, can you hear me?' I could hear you then as clearly as I do now."

"I think I did say that. You were kind of in a trance or something. I wanted to make sure you were okay."

"I get it. Anyway, I put the kid down fast because it felt like something was going to happen. That was when everything there, everything I could see and hear and feel, just started to fade. It was like it got thinner, if that makes any sense. I heard mom say 'Goodbye, John', and then, I was back in your apartment. You were staring at me like my nose just fell off."

"Wow. John, that's awesome."

"I suppose. To tell you the truth, the memory of it has kind of been messing with me."

"Can I ask you a question?"

John gave her a look that was meant to convey what he didn't want to say. "One more?"

She nodded.

"Fine. What is it?"

"Do you have brothers or sisters?"

"I have a sister." He knew where she was going.

"Did she ever, you know, lose a baby or something?"

"You're trying to figure out if I could have a nephew?"

She nodded again.

"No. Not that I know of."

The room grew quiet.

"Is it possible?" she said.

John had already self-imposed that question. "I suppose. I left home before she did because I was a bit older. I was sort of estranged from the family for a while."

"What about your dad? Is he still alive?"

"Oh yeah. Living in southern Florida with a woman who's twenty years younger. We're not on good speaking terms." He sighed to release a buildup of unhappy thoughts. "I think we've reached the end of holding a magnifying glass on the inner workings of my life. Why don't you try to get back to sleep?"

"Thank you for sharing, John."

"Sure."

She stood up from the couch. "Are you okay? Do you feel like a snack or something?"

John furrowed his brows. "I hope after what we just talked about, you're not thinking of feeding me any more of that magic fruit. Are you?"

She hesitated way too long before answering. "No. Just asking."

"Go to bed, Allie. Get your rest."

He was thankful when she went.

John feared sleep would elude him for some time. The harder he tried to clear his mind, the more it filled with fleeting images, each one jolting him away from the peace needed to shut down his consciousness. He hunkered into position, staring at the ceiling.

CHAPTER 23

Specht recognized Dr. Redding immediately. It was a relief to finally see a medical professional ready to give them some attention. Now, if he only had good news.

"Good evening, agents. My apologies but your exact names escape me."

"Specht and Collins," Robert replied. "How are they, Doctor?"

"The same as all the other victims, which is both good and bad. They have suffered through a severe trial pain-wise, but are now on the road to recovery. If all goes as I expect, they should be up and about tomorrow. The only lasting effects will be some minor skin damage at the site of the wounds and the memory of the event itself."

Specht and Collins were both smiling, a reflection of relief.

"The prognosis is as good as we could have hoped for. Thank you, Doctor." Specht extended his hand which Redding shook.

"If you two could come up with a way of putting an end to these attacks, I'd be willing to call it even."

The two agents exchanged a quick glance. "That's next on our agenda."

"Very good." Redding consulted his watch. "I'm going to finish my rounds. Circumstances notwithstanding, it was nice to see you again. Goodnight."

They nodded and smiled, then huddled up after he walked out of the room.

"What's next?" Collins asked.

"I'm calling in. I think it's time for a more direct approach. And on a brighter note, I get to disturb the Director at home."

Collins rolled her eyes. "If you wait for another hour or so, you could probably wake him up."

Specht was pulling out his phone. "A good plan, partner. Too bad this is time sensitive."

"Try to talk him into doing something decisive. I want to see an end to this. Too many bugs and not enough criminals for me."

After the call, Specht was able to give Collins good news. An active response was now on the agenda.

Specht and Collins arrived at the Rivers' farm the next morning. Access was now restricted by a roadblock manned by military personnel. They maneuvered through the barriers and found the farmer himself. He had to be mollified regarding the bug eradication plan. After all, it's not every day that the military drops live ordinance on your corn field. All arrangements had now been made, and the chopper should be arriving at any moment.

Specht looked down at the dust on his usually pristine shoes, sighing in exasperation. "Crap."

"No," Collins said, "just dirt. You'll have to head over to the barnyard to find some of that." She finished her pronouncement with an artificially large grin.

Brent Rivers had dominated their agenda thus far. Keeping him calm and out of the way had proved to be a monumental task. Specht would have preferred to end their conversation quickly and get settled in to a prime viewing position for what was about to happen at the chasm, but he had his orders. The farmer had returned a second time for a fresh round of questions and concerns.

"You said the government will pay for any damages you cause, correct?"

Specht maintained a calm, neutral countenance. Frustration was not the sign of a professional. He had brought this issue up on an earlier conference call. His superior agreed to pay for any reasonable request for reimbursement pertaining to crop damage.

"That's right. There shouldn't be any damage caused by what we're doing today, but in the unlikely event it happens, we will cover any reasonable expenses."

Brent didn't look as thrilled as he could have. "And can you describe this process to me again? Exactly what are you going to do here?"

Specht looked at his partner, silently indicating it was her turn to respond. He was in need of a break. Also, he had seen the tall, pretty blond melt through the toughest demeanors many times before.

"The bugs are about to have a Vietnam experience of sorts, Brent. We're going to drop napalm into the crevasse. The controlled burn, magnified by the effect of being concentrated by the high walls, will utterly incinerate the bugs as well as any nests, eggs or larvae. Again, due to the effect of the walls, we anticipate little to no crop damage. Once things cool off, a detailed examination will occur. We are confident that the bug problem will be eliminated, but our team will confirm it before we leave." She finished with a dimple-accentuated smile.

Brent was still frowning, but seemed to find a degree of control over his frustration. "Well, I hope so. I can only imagine what my neighbors must be thinking about all of this." He turned towards the road. Having it off limits to traffic due to a small, military blockade was weird enough before adding a bombing run. Uniformed soldiers with weapons apparent stood on guard. Any frustration on his neighbor's part would no doubt lead to awkward encounters where he would be apologizing for something he didn't want in the first place. "I'll just be glad to get this over with."

The faint sound of helicopter blades slicing through the air reached their ears.

"It sounds like you won't have long to wait," Collins said cheerfully.

"Let's hope it ends up being good news when this is all over." Brent strode off towards the house to update his wife who had wisely stayed away from the morning's proceedings.

"Son of a bitch!"

Collins was shocked. Her partner never swore or used bad language. She turned her eyes skyward as the chopper flew overhead. It was not a military bird at all. Painted on the sides were the call letters for a television news station.

Specht had his phone out. "They'll get in the way and slow this whole process down, if not postponing it altogether."

"How did they know this was happening?" Collins asked. The question was rhetorical—Specht was already dialing the director to talk to about this new problem and couldn't respond.

The conversation which followed was short. Specht hung up with a sour expression. "Apparently the agency gave them permission. They agreed to maintain a safe distance away. Sounds like someone invited them to film this. Crazy bastards."

"I get it," Collins said. "Let's show the world that we're taking decisive action. Smacks of politics, doesn't it?"

Specht frowned. "That's one sure way to screw things up."

A deeper sound drew their attention. The unmistakable silhouette of an Apache attack chopper flew into view.

"Now it gets interesting," Specht said. "Let's hope the other copter stays clear."

"We're not going to be able to see anything from here, are we?" Collins lamented.

"Don't worry. Apparently, we'll be able to see the whole thing on the evening news."

The Apache was hovering in position with the target clearly visible.

"Albany control, Delta three-one-one Echo."

"Three-one-one Echo, Albany control."

"Target acquired, requesting weapons hot."

"Weapons hot, verified. Happy hunting, three-one-one Echo."

The pilot turned to the co-pilot, grinning from ear to ear. Live fire was extremely rare and he was pumped. "More like shooting fish in a barrel."

"Let's light it up," the co-pilot replied.

The chopper moved forward, nose pointing downward.

"Initiating firing sequence." The pilot launched a missile, then five more sequentially, effectively covering the entire chasm. Once completed, he banked the chopper hard left and away from the results of the explosions.

The reverb of dull thuds announced the moments of detonation. Flames and black smoke immediately billowed out of the chasm in massive quantities.

"Ooo-whee!" The co-pilot was obviously enjoying the show. "Nice shooting, partner."

"It's a stationary target the size of a battleship, but I'll take the compliment. Let's clear the area."

"Roger that," the co-pilot said as they banked away.

"Now that's a sign of progress." Specht smiled as he watched the smoke rising on the horizon.

"They do know how to blow things up," Collins conceded. "Should we be worried about pissed off survivors?"

Specht shook his head. "I wouldn't think so. Napalm goes from room temperature to incineration point in the blink of an eye. Those things might hold their own against a fly swatter, but not modern ordnance."

"That's a relief." Collins still had a look of concern.

"They won't be able to examine the damage until it cools off. We might as well head back into town and retain our rooms. I believe we have one more day in Barrington."

"Great. I love the rustic ambience," Collins said.

"All in a day's work," Specht replied as he started towards their car. He wanted to get away before Rivers came out with more questions.

Collins fell in beside him. "I'm going to need a bigger overnight bag."

Specht snorted. "Just do what I do and leave all the makeup at home."

When Specht and Collins walked out of the motel office, they noticed a young couple standing in a manner that basically blocked their path.

"Are you the agents?" the girl asked.

Both had their training kick in and were immediately on high alert. Collins made sure her hand was unimpeded in case she needed to pull out her weapon.

Specht took lead. "Can we help you?"

The girl was smiling now. "I'm Brandisha Young and this is Charles Wheeler. We both work for the USGS."

Specht made the connection. "You're the ones who discovered this whole mess."

Brandisha nodded. "Yes. That was a day I'll never forget."

Now in work mode, Specht had a myriad of questions pop into his mind. "Why are you here? More importantly, how did you find us?"

"Our boss called your boss. He gave us permission and helped to track you down."

"He helped you track us to this very spot?" Collins still looked leery.

"We were sent to Barrington, which was no surprise. He just gave us this location about five minutes ago. He's tracking you by your phones."

Specht made an internal note to remember to speak with his superior about this little incident. "That answers one question. I still don't get why you were sent here in the first place."

"We weren't," Brandisha said. "We came of our own accord."

Specht waited for more. "There are still some blanks we need you to fill in."

"The bombing of the crevasse was all the talk on the news," she said. "Charles and I heard about it and we have some information to share that might be valuable."

"You're too late," Collins retorted. "The fireworks are over."

Brandisha shook her head. "We didn't come for that."

"Actually, I kind of wanted to see it," Charles interjected.

"We came," Brandisha continued after giving him a critical look, "to warn you about what you're going to find when you examine the crevasse."

"There won't be anything but ashes," Collins said.

Specht held up his hand. "Hold on. What exactly are you talking about, Brandisha?"

"When I went in, I discovered an opening in the wall on the south side."

Specht was no geologist. "What do you mean? What kind of opening?"

"It was a cave, based on what little I could see. I basically just poked my head in so I really couldn't determine many details. But it was big and I think that's where the bugs originated from."

Specht raised his eyebrows. "A cave? Inside a newly formed crevasse? Is that normal?"

"No," Brandisha answered without hesitation. "But it is definitely there. And I suspect it will have been at least partially sheltered from the effects of the bombing. Whoever goes down there should use extreme caution. You do not want to get stung by those things."

Collins couldn't help herself. "What was it like? We keep hearing about epic pain."

Both Brandisha and Charles looked grim. "It's hard to find words sufficient to describe it," Brandisha answered. "But I've had some time to reflect on it. Imagine there was a lion or tiger big enough to fit your entire body in its mouth. Now imagine it's chewing on you with everything that entails. Now, further imagine you're fully conscious and can feel every bit of it. And it never stops. It just keeps chewing and chewing. A few seconds seems like an hour. When I finally got to the hospital, I swear it seemed like it had been two weeks since I got stung. It had been two hours."

Collins looked horrified. "That's not going to help me sleep."

"You asked for it," Specht said. And then, "Is there anything else you two have to tell us?"

Brandisha and Charles exchanged a quick glance. "I don't think so," she said.

"In that case, thank you for sharing. I'm going to contact my superior and pass on the information. I'll make sure the incursion team knows what to expect."

"Good," Brandisha said. Both young people looked relieved.

"Then I'm going to excuse myself. I have to make a call."

CHAPTER 24

Saturday proved to be an eventful day for Barrington and its residents. John was destined to miss it.

He got up early, grabbing a piece of toast with Dream Tree jam before heading out. Allie moped around the kitchen, watching him with a forlorn expression on her face.

"When will you be back?" She had asked the same question several times.

"I'm not sure, Allie." The answer was also the same. "It depends on how everything goes when I get there."

"Less than a week?"

"I still can't say."

Kemina breezed into the kitchen, fresh from her morning routine. "So, you are ready to leave?"

"I am. I figure I'll drive nonstop and get home in time for a late supper."

"Your wife will be expecting you?" Kemina asked.

"I texted her that I was coming back but didn't give her any details. Maybe I'll just show up at her boyfriend's house, knock on the door wearing nothing but a big bow and yell "Surprise!" when somebody opens the door."

Kemina smiled a little. "Yes, that should help you sort things out."

John stood, taking his plate to the sink. "Look, I've got to run."

An awkward silence fell over the room.

"Thanks for putting up with me. You guys have been great." He meant it. It was hard to imagine how things would have turned out if they hadn't crossed paths.

"Don't forget anything," Kemina responded in a business-like fashion.

"That shouldn't be a problem." All of his possessions were in a bag sitting beside the door.

As he turned to leave, there seemed to be some sort of gravitational pull working against him. He made it to the door, picked up his bag and turned to face them for the last time. "Ciao."

Allie ran out of the room.

"Aw, crap. I'm sorry."

Kemina nodded. "I know. I will talk to her."

"Thanks." John walked out, feeling a little sad and guilty. The gravitational pull lessened as he stepped out the door and he walked with purpose towards his car.

When Specht and Collins arrived at the crevasse, a team of military personnel was already suited up.

Specht, curious, walked right up and surprised one of them by grabbing the material and giving it a good feel. "Seems tougher than a bee suit."

The wearer gave a muffled laugh. "Yes, sir. No stingers are going to penetrate this."

He nodded in response, keeping any doubts to himself. "Good luck down there."

"We need to get a couple of those suits," Collins said as they walked towards a large black panel van that was functioning as the mobile control for this operation. "You should ask the director."

"If you want the answer to be yes, you do it."

A couple of armed guards stiffened their posture as the agents approached, but a voice from inside the open rear door called them off.

"Let them through. I'm expecting them."

The guards stepped aside. Specht was the first to poke his head inside the van. A myriad display of electronic equipment covered one side of the interior. A tall but slim, grey-haired man had taken up residence in the only visible chair and seemed busy adjusting various knobs and switches.

"Come in, both of you. There's a couple folding chairs straight ahead. Set them up wherever you deem suitable."

Specht looked around, trying to make sense out of the controls. "I'm Specht, this is Collins. Thanks for letting us sit in."

The man was still adjusting. "Call me Ghost. That's what these guys do."

Specht was confused. "What happened to name, rank, and serial number?"

"I'm not traditional military. A changing world requires new ways of doing business. That's where I come in."

Specht chewed on the response and found it unsatisfying. "Fine. Although, Ghost is going to feel really weird coming out of my mouth."

Collins slid her chair in place beside Specht. "How about an alternative? We could make up a fun acronym to call him, like B.I.T.C.H. You know, *Boys I'm Taking Charge Here*. Or I could think up something more vulgar. We could make a game of it. They do it in the military all the time."

Specht ignored her suggestion. Collins could become snarky when a person immediately rubbed her the wrong way. "Does the new way of doing things include insect control?"

"If it is a possible threat to our national security," Ghost replied.

Specht hadn't thought of it in such broad terms.

Three monitors flickered and came on. Helmet cameras gave full color views of whatever the person wearing them was seeing.

"Alpha team, cameras are on and clear. Proceed when ready."

"Roger that, control. Team is moving out."

Ghost turned part-way around. "We expected this to be straightforward until we got the bad news about the cave."

Specht had pondered the potential consequences it could have on the effectiveness of the bombing, but didn't have enough hard information to even formulate an answer. Collins, paranoid about being stung, said, "Do you have a backup plan if the bugs are still in the cave?"

Ghost turned back to the controls. "I always have a backup plan. It's a major component of my job." He neglected to elaborate, however.

The troops were walking briskly, their movement making the camera images dizzying to watch. "Control, we are now beginning our descent."

"Roger, team. Stay tight, stay focused."

"What about the bugs outside the crevasse?" Specht asked. "It seems like they were expanding outward at a fast rate."

"That's the second phase of this operation," Ghost said. "We'll eliminate them as well. After catching a few for testing first, of course."

The speaker squawked. "Control, we've got about four inches of charred remains on the ground. Fun to walk on, but so far, no signs of life. Everything is burnt to a crisp."

"I read you, Alpha team. That's good news. Continue forward progress."

Specht and Collins strained to see the monitors. The picture showed a dark, dull environment.

"Control, Alpha team requesting an EMD reading, over."

"Roger that," Ghost said. "Proceed."

"What's an EMD?" Collins asked.

"Electronic Motion Detector. It can read the slightest movement for up to one hundred yards. It's a great way to avoid otherwise unseen surprises." The smug tone of Ghost's reply suggested he had invented it himself, although that wasn't the case.

"Control, EMD reading is negative, say again, negative. There's nothing flying, crawling or otherwise moving down here except for us."

"Roger that. Good news. Proceed to tunnel opening."

Specht turned to his partner. "All going according to plan."

Collins had been hoping for this outcome. "So far, at least."

Specht smiled. "Still a little concerned, are you? Ghost, can you share what the backup plan is if there are still live bugs in the tunnel?"

He considered his answer. "I don't see why not. The team is carrying cyanide canisters. If anything is moving in the cave, we're going to gas it."

"Cyanide kills bugs?" Collins said.

"Extremely well," Ghost replied. "Anything that breathes, that stuff will kill."

Collins released a long breath. "That's good news. At least under the circumstances."

Ghost smiled and it gave him a creepy look. "Not a fan of bugs, Collins?"

"Not a fan of pain on that level," she said.

Once again, the radio crackled to life. "Control, we have eyes on the cave entrance. Repeat, we can see the entrance, over."

All three in the van refocused on the screens. "Ok, team. We have a view of it on the monitors. Proceed slowly."

"Roger that."

The opening came into view on the monitors, filling the screen as they walked closer. Inside was pitch black.

Ghost keyed his mike. "Peters, move into lead position and fire up that light."

"Roger," a new voice replied. Specht didn't know what kind of light was being used, but the entrance to the cave suddenly lit up like it was under the noon-day sun.

"Control, we're in position. Request permission to enter cave."

"Affirmative," Ghost said. "Proceed with caution."

As the team moved in, the cave's interior was illuminated by the powerful beam.

"Yuck," Collins said.

The floor wasn't level, but slanted downward. The area was larger than any of them had expected. Under the sweeping ray of light, both stalactites and stalagmites were visible. No other meaningful details could be seen on the screen. The overall look was dark and dreary.

"Control, this is bigger than we anticipated. From our vantage point, it appears to extend indefinitely."

"Roger that. What kind of traction do you have? Is it safe to proceed further in?"

"Traction is decent. As long as it stays dry and the slope doesn't get any steeper, we can move safely."

"Roger that. Team proceed."

Specht looked at his partner and saw an expression of concern. "How are you feeling about this, Collins?"

"Glad I'm not down there. I'll feel better once the team gets safely out."

The movement on all monitors suddenly stopped.

"What's happening, team?" Ghost asked.

A high-pitched squeal was discernable. "Uh, Control—are you hearing this?"

"Be more specific," Ghost snapped.

"The EMD is picking something up."

"Again, be more specific! I need complete information from you in order to make good decisions. Remember your training."

"There's some slight movement ahead of us. It's at the limit of the sensor, approximately one hundred yards straight ahead."

"Light it up," Ghost snarled.

Under the glaring beam, nothing was at first visible. Then Collins jammed her finger almost into the closest screen. "Right there! See it?"

Several insects, barely discernable at that distance, fluttered into view.

"Control, movement is intensifying, over."

Ghost did what he was paid to do—make quick decisions. "Team, pull out. Repeat, pull out immediately."

"Control, Roger that."

A new voice came across the speaker. "Here they come!"

Two of the monitors showed nothing of interest, but the third was focused perfectly to catch the action. A cloud of bugs exploded out of the depths and swarmed towards them.

"Get out!" Ghost screamed. "Now!"

The response was garbled, but the erratic movement now showing on the screens indicated that they were on the move.

Specht put his hand on Ghost's shoulder. "Get those two guards in here stat. Close the doors and all the windows. Those things will be coming and we don't have suits on."

"Shit!" Ghost yelled. "Things go FUBAR and I lose my mind." He turned towards the open door at the back of the van. "You two get in here. Now!"

Inspired by the serious tone of his voice, the guards came on the run.

Collins addressed the men as soon as they entered. "Would one of you mind closing that door? I'd rather not experience the most painful sting in the world."

With that thought as motivation, the door was quickly closed.

CHAPTER 25

It meant a long day's drive, but John was determined to get home, so he pressed onward long after the initial feeling of adventure had dissipated into monotony. At least his back felt better than during the earlier *Running from Reality* portion of his trip.

He made the final turn onto his street just as the sun was about to sink below the horizon. He wavered between congratulating himself and feeling weirded-out by being there. A wave of nostalgia washed over him as the house came into view.

John pulled into the driveway, fighting a mild sensation like he was stopping at a stranger's home and had no business being there. He stepped out of the car, looking around.

The grass had been cut. The property still had a "lived-in" look. He knew the credit for that was due to Theresa's management skills.

"More like *micro-management* skills," he mumbled as he shut the car door. He wanted to get inside, eliminating the possibility that a neighbor might see him and saunter over for some casual conversation that would have to include all the juicy details about what was going on between him and his now estranged wife. He inserted his key, pleased that it still fit (the possibility that she had changed the locks occurred to him). He opened the door and stepped inside.

It shut behind him, the latch snickering into place. A thunderous silence fell around him, leaving John feeling alone and out of place. He needed to inject some life into this house. The first remedy was to turn on some lights.

"Okay," he said, his voice echoing, "that would be a start."

He clicked the nearest switch and started walked through, comparing recent memory to current reality. The house was now sparsely furnished, which came as no surprise. But there was still a little food in the cupboards, a television in the den, and bedding on the king-size mattress that sat on the bedroom floor. In contrast to calling his car home or sleeping on a stranger's couch, this should seem like heaven.

He turned on the television, adjusted the volume so that it would give some background noise to the downstairs portion of the house (artificial life was better than none at all), and then set his sights on finding something suitable for supper. *Suitable* transitioned into *edible*, and a feast consisting of canned tomato soup and a frozen microwaveable burrito (not even in the same stratosphere as his recent introduction to *real* Mexican food), materialized. John quickly reached the dreaded *what now* portion of his evening. He picked up his phone, punching in Theresa's number.

She answered on the third ring. "Hi." It was all he could think to say.

"John?"

"Yeah. I'm home."

"Oh? You're at the house?"

"Just got here a short while ago."

There was a temporary silence over the phone. And then, "So, what's your plan?"

Her response seemed to catch him off guard. "My plan? What plan?"

"Are you staying for a while?" There was a hint of irritation in her tone. It was subtle; a mere suggestion of things to come.

They had exchanged less than thirty seconds of introductory small talk, and John was already getting miffed. He didn't owe her any insight into his life strategy, such as it now was.

"Depends. I'll be here for a few days at least, or so I would imagine."

Somebody was speaking to her in the background. It was a male voice (hooray!). John heard the muffled sound of a palm being pressed against the phone, and Theresa saying "It's John" in a fashion she may have considered to be discreet.

"I'd have dropped the stuff off sooner if I'd known," she replied in that smarmy fashion that always set John's teeth on edge.

The translation was child's play; John was fluent in innuendo. *If you'd communicate a little, you inconsiderate jerk, I could have delivered the paperwork earlier so I didn't have to come over and see your ugly face.*

"Tomorrow will be fine." He kept his answer succinct. The less he played with the gun, the less chance it might go off.

"Any time in particular?" *How can I avoid seeing you?*

"No. I might pick up some groceries, but other than that, I'll be around."

"I'll bring over all the papers you need to sign sometime in the morning."

"Just slide them under the door if I'm not here."

To his surprise, that didn't seem to fly. "We have things to talk about, John, especially if you are planning on going on another of your disappearing acts. I need to know how to proceed if you're going to dump the responsibility of managing everything on me again."

John struggled not to return fire. She was right, after all. He thought of the perfect manicured lawn.

"John?"

"Okay," he said. "Fair enough. I'll try to come up with some answers."

"I'll see you in the morning, then."

That was the send-off signal. They had endured a short conversation without telling each other to drop dead. He wasn't quite sure how to end the call, wavering between the opposite extremes of "love you", (still true, but not applicable), and "I hope you die in a fiery wreck" (not true, but more reflective of how he felt at the moment). He decided to compromise.

"Goodnight."

John hung up, reassessing his situation. He meandered off through the house in an attempt to find something (*anything*) that could entertain him until bedtime arrived. In this, he was destined to fail.

Inside the van, the monitors showed nothing but bugs. The close-up view was horrifying—heads, wings, stingers—all magnified in exquisite detail as they crawled over the camera lens.

"Control, we've been overwhelmed. I can't see to walk."

"Are the suits working?" Ghost asked. "Are you being stung?"

"Negative. They're trying, but the material must be too tough for them to penetrate."

"Good. Can you confirm how much air you have left?"

"That's going to be thirty minutes approximately."

That answer put Ghost in a bind. "Don't, repeat, do not deploy the cyanide canisters. I need some degree of certainty that you'll be able to exit first."

Collins had been doing research for her own benefit on the lives and behaviors of stinging insects. "Your team needs to be motionless. That's what triggers the bugs to think they are no longer a menace. Have them sit down and go silent."

Ghost wasn't big on getting advice, but having them stumble around without being able to see was going to be extremely dangerous anyway.

"Team, if you are safe for the moment, I advise you find a comfortable position and go motionless. Sit if you can. Don't move or talk if you can avoid it. The insects will lose interest if they think you've been neutralized."

"Roger that."

Collins, looking forward past the driver's seat, saw a bug land on the windshield. It was frighteningly large. "This is a stupid question as this point, but you didn't leave any windows down, did you?"

There was an intense moment of silence as Ghost searched his recent memory. "No. They're all shut."

More bugs were landing on the glass. The sound of their stingers hitting the windshield was discernable.

"That's rather good news," Collins said, trying to sound casual.

Specht had always been bothered by confined spaces. He reminded himself how fortunate they were to be somewhere safe. "Anybody bring a deck of cards?"

Kemina closed the back door of the restaurant, locked it, and breathed a sigh of relief. It had been a busy day—good for the bottom line but not for an understaffed kitchen. She had been run off her feet. She wanted nothing more than a long soak in a warm tub. It hadn't taken long to get used to John carrying most of the weight for cooking and food prep. She would be facing a hard decision about replacing him if he didn't come back.

It had been some time since she had to walk home and the distance seemed longer than she remembered. Finally, she found herself turning onto the street where her apartment was located. Two boys were sauntering down the sidewalk on the opposite side. She heard them laughing but had no particular interest beyond that.

"Can I have a taco?" one of them yelled, followed by more raucous laughter.

She took the obscure comment as some sort of compliment regarding the current level of success that the restaurant was enjoying. She might have turned, giving the boys a friendly wave, if she hadn't been so tired. Her goal was in sight, so she trudged along.

"Allie is a slut!"

The words were screamed so loudly, there could be no doubt that Kemina would hear them. As far as that went, everybody in a two block radius could have heard them. She stopped, turning to look towards the boys while her blood went ice cold. They pointed at her, laughing.

Why would they have screamed something so inappropriate? It was clear enough that the unwanted comment was directed at her. Who were these boys? Had they just come from the direction of the apartment?

Thinking back to the incident out in the country, she grew concerned about her daughter's well-being. She resumed walking with a purpose. The boys continued yelling obscure references about common Mexican foods, laughing as if the rowdy gibberish was the height of hilarity. This was the first time anyone had been mean to her since moving to Barrington. The feeling wasn't very nice. She hoped this would turn out to be a one-time aberration.

"Allie?" She walked into the apartment, relieved to close the door against the outside world.

"In my room." The tone of her voice seemed neutral.

Kemina opened her door, walking in. Allie flinched when she entered, looking at her with defiant, red-rimmed eyes.

"Mama! Why would you walk in on me like that?"

This was no time for inconsequential sparring, as far as Kemina was concerned. "Are you all right, little one?"

"Yes!" Her response was strained and unappreciative.

"Who were those boys?"

The life went out of her expression, replaced by a blend of sadness and resignation. "What boys?"

"You know what boys. Allie, what is going on?"

"Nothing." A polygraph wasn't necessary to know she was lying.

Kemina walked in and sat on the bed beside her. "Allie, tell me. I am your mother. I want to help."

Allie looked frustrated and embarrassed. "There's nothing you can do," she said.

"I can listen. Tell me."

Allie looked at the floor. "It's…"

"Tell me."

Her defenses crumbled, eyes filling with tears. "Oh, mama!" They embraced, Allie releasing a build-up of emotion.

Kemina sat at the kitchen table, cradling a mug of tea as it grew cold. It was one of the rare moments when she had no plan of action to follow.

She had encouraged Allie to talk, listening as her tale of woe unfolded. It had been hard to hear—worse than living through it herself. Her first emotional response was anger. She fought to keep it inside, not wanting Allie to feel that it was in any way directed at her.

Afterwards, it was frustration and helplessness that washed over her. If the cop who had visited them earlier was any indication, there would be no resolution through the local law enforcement community.

Why were those boys doing this? It made no sense. Allie would never do anything hurtful or deserving of such treatment. It couldn't be in retaliation for anything she had said…she was quiet and reserved, with no inclination towards meanness. For the boys to have the nerve to yell hurtful things at her, an adult, was inconceivable. But it had happened, giving credence to the notion that it could happen again. Kemina thought back to the eggs thrown against the front window of her restaurant and wondered if they had been responsible.

Just when things appeared to be getting better, John left and this happened. No rhyme or reason to it. Just a problem initiated by a couple of kids who apparently didn't know any better. So, why couldn't she think of a way out of it? She moped and pondered while the tea continued to cool.

CHAPTER 26

A painfully tedious hour had gone by, and the bugs had finally disappeared from camera view. Neither were there any on the windshield of the van.

"Team, this is Control," Ghost said quietly. "Just listen and don't respond. From our vantage point, it looks like the bugs have moved away. But that's up here, and that's our view from inside the van. You may be able to see something we can't. If you feel it is safe to do so, please respond. You can speak softly if you prefer. We can hear you regardless. If you feel there is still an imminent threat, do not, I repeat, do not respond. Control is standing by."

For a stressful moment, there was nothing but silence.

"Control, this is team leader. Stand by."

Silence now raised more concerning questions in their minds.

"Team leader, I just rolled over. We've been motionless and on our stomachs. I can't see any signs of them, but it's extremely dark. How do you feel about using the light, over?"

"Negative, team leader. Can you see the entrance at all from your vantage point?"

Grunting sounds announced his movements. "Roger. We're close to it now. It shouldn't take more than a few seconds to get back into the actual crevasse. What are our orders?"

"Team, get on your feet slowly. Try not to make any sudden moves. Walk carefully out of the entrance and give me an update as soon as you are clear of the cave, over."

Long seconds ticked away slowly.

"Team leader, we are all clear. There are no signs of the bugs."

"Great. Listen carefully. Dispense the canisters now in case there are any stragglers, then get out of there. We'll see you at the top. Be careful. If the bugs reappear, get out of the cave and then back down on the ground. I'll call in for reinforcements if that's the case."

"Roger that."

Ghost looked at the two guards seated uncomfortably on the floor. "Let's get that door open and see if there are still any of them around."

The two got awkwardly to their feet.

"Leave your guns in here. They won't help with this threat and I don't want you accidentally firing off a shot in a panic. Roll up some printer paper if you want an appropriate weapon."

A cap with Army Reserve embroidered on it caught their attention. "Mind if I borrow that?" one asked.

Ghost shrugged. "Closest thing to a flyswatter that's within reach, I suppose. Here." He picked it up and extended it to the waiting hand. "Proceed slowly. Take lots of time to look around as you go."

One of them released the door latch and swung it open. They both stepped outside.

"How's it look, men?" Ghost asked.

"Nothing yet," came the terse reply. They moved away from the relative security of the van. After thirty seconds or so, they moved back closer. "Sir, no signs."

"I can see the incursion team," the other said, pointing in the direction of the crevasse.

"Good news," Ghost said. "Let's get everybody in a vehicle as quickly as possible. I'm going to radio in about our experience and find out what the next step is going to be."

Collins couldn't have been happier about the apparent lack of bugs. It did raise a disconcerting question, though. "I wonder where they all went?"

When Barrington got a Walmart, there were many people who saw it as a sort of status symbol. Not that it made the city seem high class, but simply that it had grown to a size where it could support such a venture. The independent business owners were less enamored.

Tina Colson didn't care about any behind-the-scene politics affecting the retail industry; she was only concerned about the groceries in her cart and the new top she had purchased which had been on a rack of bargain clothes marked down to a price that was almost a steal. She parked the cart in the store entranceway, confident she could carry her bags just fine without it. As she turned and faced the big sliding doors, movement caught her attention. A huge bug landed on the outside of the glass and began to crawl upwards. Tina never really liked bugs anyway, and the sheer size of this one creeped her out. She caught the attention of a complete stranger who seemed to be wondering what she was staring at so intently.

"Have you ever seen a bug like that one before?" she asked.

The man jumped back in revulsion. "No! What is it?"

A small group of customers approached from outside, and as they did so, the door automatically slid open. The bug was disturbed to the point that it flew off the glass and then in through the entranceway.

Tina squealed in horror. "Stay away from me!" she screamed.

Other shoppers now spotted it. They moved away from it as best they could.

"There's another one!" someone shouted. A full-blown panic ensued. The bird-sized bugs were circling just below the drop ceiling, more entering by the second. Tina could see people in the parking lot running, covering their heads as best they could. Someone, not far from where Tina stood, screeched loudly and dropped twitching to the floor.

More screaming ensued and people ran hectically in all directions, trying to get away. Tina, at a loss as to what she should do, looked back towards the doors. The glass was now covered with bugs.

John's next day was filled with few accomplishments. Somehow, he had envisioned a busy schedule full of issues that needed his attention. What he got was a handful of papers to be signed and a brief but tense conversation with Theresa on the front step. Her reluctance to enter the house was another confirmation of the decrepit state of their former relationship. That was followed by a long day with no specific agenda to follow.

It was his house, his yard, his neighborhood…all the places and things that made up the entirety of his life up until a short time ago. Now it all felt foreign and empty. It was like looking at a loved one in a casket. You knew it was them, and yet, the life that made them who they were was gone.

He had to decide what tomorrow would bring. Perhaps this old life was dead—but he wasn't. He felt better than he had in years. He was ready to have a focus again. The question was—what would it be?

It was late afternoon when Kemina called. John was driving at the time. He had made a few preliminary decisions about his future and was acting on his new plan. Her voice lacked the usual, uncompromising resilience that John had come to expect.

"Hello, plumber man," she said.

"Hi," he responded. "Is that the sound of excitement in your voice?"

"Yes, it is very exciting here."

"How bad is it? You sound a tad melancholy."

"That is hard to say. John, I am sorry for calling. I promised myself I wouldn't bother you."

"Something happen?"

"Oh no. Just looking forward to another day at the restaurant. A busy day."

"That's not exactly unexpected."

There was a moment of hesitation. "Hard work is the beginning of a good business plan."

John forced his eyes to stay on the road. He was violating his rule (and the state's law) about not talking on the phone while driving. "Not to mention the finest Mexican cuisine in the entire state. Word must be getting around."

"John, I feel awkward asking this, but do you have any idea if or when you might be coming back to Barrington?"

"Looking for another set of hands?"

"I know this is bad timing for you," she said. "I don't want my problem to become your problem. You have your own life to worry about."

"Yeah, but in all honesty, it's not much of a life. I signed the papers for listing the house and gave my ex authorization to sell all my remaining stuff. That left me staring out the window of a home that won't be mine much longer, scratching my head, wondering what I'm supposed to do with myself."

"I have work if you will take it. You can stay with us as long as you want. You decide."

"I already have."

"And what have you decided?"

"I'm coming back to Barrington."

"Are you sure?"

"As sure as I can be."

Kemina felt her burden lift. "We will be glad to see you."

"I won't be late. I'll drive straight through."

"I will make you something for supper."

"No, you've got your hands full. I'll make something myself, or get take-out from one of the other places in town."

"Traitor! You will do no such thing. I will have something waiting. Stop talking and watch the road."

That was more like it. "Right. See you later on."

When Kemina hung up, she was smiling.

Both of them were waiting when John arrived. Allie, throwing all reservation to the wind, ran up and hugged him. He reciprocated with genuine affection.

"Hi, kiddo."

"I'm so glad you're back."

"Don't set your expectations too high. I tend to become annoying once I've been around too long."

"No you won't." Allie gave him a warm smile as she disengaged.

"Hello, handy man."

John nodded. "I see you survived the day."

She shrugged. "Of course. What else could I do? I hope you're hungry."

"You ignored my suggestion and made supper?"

"I run a restaurant. Why do you act like me making food is a surprise?"

"Because I'm a man," he said, "and I'm always wrong."

"Sit down. Everything is ready."

Allie sprang into action. "I'll serve it. Momma, sit down."

John contemplated how good it felt to be there before turning his attention to what Allie was placing in front of him. As always, it turned out to be delicious.

"Thanks for this," John said.

"It's nice to have you back." Kemina smiled through a wave of exhaustion.

It was late and they were both tired. It had been a long day. John relaxed on the couch while Kemina had a shower. Allie went off to bed.

Kemina walked out of the bathroom, clad in her terrycloth robe.

"Well," John said, "is it full speed ahead tomorrow now that you have reinforcements?"

Kemina managed a tired smile. "Yes, as always. And we will have a great day."

"Good." John tried to suppress a yawn and lost the battle. Silence fell over them.

"I have a question I would like you to answer," Kemina said. "But I also need some sleep. How can I incorporate the two?"

John battled through his weariness and missed any possible implication. "Is it a question about me?"

"Yes."

John straightened himself. "Let's have it. Otherwise it will keep me up tonight."

"You must not be as tired as I am," she responded.

"Spit it out. Let's get it over with."

"You came back. I'm glad."

"I did. But that's not a question," John said.

"I know." She looked around as if assessing something about the room. What she was actually doing was checking to make sure all the blinds were closed.

John interpreted it as a stalling tactic. "You're not usually this hesitant. Come on—ask me so we can pack it in for the day."

Her eyes met his. "I need to know what your plans are. Are you staying, John? Or do you even know yourself? Because when you are gone, I will need more help. If you are going to leave, please tell me so I can make arrangements."

"That wasn't the emotional plea I was expecting."

"That wasn't the answer I was hoping for."

John could imagine the need for her to know. "Kemina, the truth is…I'm still not sure." He let his eyes wander around the room while he collected his thoughts. "When I went home, I was surprised how dead it felt to me. It seemed like I was a stranger there. I recognized everything but none of it felt intimate; kind of like recognizing things from pictures in a travel brochure when you go on vacation. I was in my own home, but it felt like a mausoleum. When I drove away to come back here, do you know what I felt?"

She shook her head. "No."

"Relief."

She smiled softly. "Instead of a direct answer, everything you just said is open to interpretation."

He smiled. "I know you need an answer. And I need to have a life. I need to feel at home in a place full of acceptance and opportunity. That much is easy to figure. The hard part is to know where."

"Can you commit to anything? One week perhaps? Two? A month?"

The longer he stayed, the more difficult his leaving was going to be for all of them. The stumbling block was that he didn't feel clear committed to either option. One thing he did know—the next time he left would be permanent. He managed a feeble shake of his head, followed by a shrug of his shoulders.

"I see."

His mind had gone blank. "Sorry. I think my brain is asleep."

"Then let us go to bed."

John stood, fighting what seemed to be excessive gravity pushing against him. "Sounds good to me," he said, missing the importance of the inclusive language she had used.

"I don't think you are getting the message," Kemina said. "Maybe this will help." With one deft move, she undid the sash that was holding the front of the robe together. A moment later, it was gaping open. She was wearing nothing underneath.

John actually took a step back. "Oops, you've got a serious clothing malfunction going on there." He started to look away, but she took a step closer, pulling the robe wide open as she did.

"Get in here with me," she whispered, her voice husky.

John hesitated, unsure. In that moment, she enveloped him. Kemina leaned in and pressed her lips against the side of his neck. "It is warm, no?" She kissed him again. "And soft." One more kiss followed. "Take me, plumber man. Do as you wish."

John didn't make a conscious decision, but his hands started moving, seemingly of their own accord. Kemina's soon followed example.

"There. It seems you are not too tired for what I have in mind after all."

Any fleeting misgivings were trampled by a sudden onslaught of lustful desire. His hands now explored her with reckless abandon, fully familiarizing themselves with places he wouldn't have allowed himself to even imagine a few short moments ago.

"Come to bed, plumber man," she gasped. "I have one more job for you tonight."

They moved, slowly, awkwardly—still entangled and groping as they went. Getting through the doorway while thus engaged was a trick, but the urge for more made it happen.

John's day was about to end in a much better fashion than it had started.

 Specht no sooner got off the phone than there was a soft knock on his room door. "It's open."

Collins entered, a look of concern on her face. Specht assumed it was because they were spending another night in Barrington. He was wrong.

"What, no coffee?" He gestured towards the small chair and desk combo in front of the sole window. "Have a seat."

She remained standing. "You need to see this." Her tone was dead serious.

"See what?"

She started to step back outside. "Follow me."

Confused, he stepped out into the cooling night air. "Well?"

Collins pointed to his left. He refocused his eyes and saw flashing lights. Lots of them.

"Remember how we were wondering where all those bugs went after swarming the team in the cave?"

"Don't tell me they came here. Not in town."

She nodded. "At least according to some random guy I just talked to in the parking lot. Apparently a lot of people got stung. They have the downtown area blocked off for now."

Questions appeared and fluttered through Specht's mind. "This is getting serious."

"He said the hospital is overwhelmed. They're only allowing emergency cases in."

"I wonder if headquarters knows about this?" Specht said.

"I wonder if Ghost and his team got recalled?" Collins added.

Specht stepped back inside. "I'm calling this in. And you might not want to stand around outside, under the circumstances."

"They're inactive after dark, remember?"

Specht took a step out the door and pointed to a light on the edge of the parking lot. One huge bug flew against the light, like a fly against a window pane. "Maybe it's not dark enough."

Collins literally pushed him back inside and slammed the room door shut. "I'm not liking this assignment," she gasped.

Despite circumstances, Specht couldn't help but smile. "What happened to *all in a day's work?*"

CHAPTER 27

"Allie. I'm glad you're up, little one."

"Hello, Momma." She walked over, exchanging hugs.

"I was afraid you were going to be late this morning."

Allie's countenance darkened at the mere insinuation of going to school. "No, I am ready. I'm never late, Momma."

Kemina looked at her daughter who seemed perched between childhood and maturity. "I know. You're a good girl. Now, if only we can get the third person in the house to get up on time, everything will be in order." Kemina raised her voice. "Isn't that right, John?"

John was hoping to stay in Kemina's bedroom until Allie left for school. He didn't want to see the expression on her face when he did the walk of shame right in front of her. Being summoned eliminated any chance of avoiding that.

"If you say so." He came shuffling out, looking sheepish. Allie, who wasn't yet fluent in all the subtle nuances of an adult relationship, seemed to interpret the fact that he had spent the night in the bedroom as a good thing. She sported a big smile.

"Good morning, John," she said.

"Hey kiddo. Don't you have school today?"

"I'm just leaving. I'll see you later on."

Kemina walked with her to the doorway. "Don't forget your lunch."

"I've got it." They kissed, and Allie went off. Her mother stood on the step watching her go. She was also watching for any signs of those boys. Why should she have to feel apprehension about something as basic as her daughter's safety in a place like Barrington, Vermont? Avoiding that was one of the reasons she moved here in the first place.

"Coffee?" John asked.

"No, coffee disgusts me."

"Great response. Now I can't wait to have some."

She walked over, joining him at the counter. She slid her arm around his lower back as he was filling the brewer. "You've been to this place where Allie gets fruit before, yes?"

It was a dramatic turn in the conversation. "Fruit?"

"Yes. The gooseberries that she used to make the jam."

"Oh, that fruit. Once. Allie talked me into it."

"It is deep in the woods?"

"Not too far," John responded, focused on his task.

"What kind of bush do these berries grow on anyway? Are you sure they are called gooseberries?"

"They don't grow on a bush, they grow on a tree."

"A tree? What kind?"

"I have no idea. I've never seen or tasted anything like them before."

Kemina was trying to envision it. "So, how do you pick the berries off the tree? Just reach up from the ground?"

"No, they're way too high for that." Once the words were out of his mouth, the problem materialized. It was too late to take it back now.

"How high?" Her tone was suspicious.

John closed the lid on the coffee maker. "You're not going to like the answer."

"You just said they were high."

"Well..."

"How many feet?"

John was going to come off looking bad in this, and there was no way to avoid it. "I don't know. Maybe...twenty?"

"Twenty?" Her voice rose.

"Yes. Or maybe a little more."

"More?" Her voice rose higher.

"I guess. I'm not very good at estimating."

"How did you get the berries that were twenty feet or more off the ground?"

He was trapped. "Allie climbed up and picked them."

"She did what?"

"She picked them and threw them down. I gathered them up."

"You let her climb up this high to pick berries?"

"It was her idea. She said she'd done it before."

"You did not think, as an adult, that you should stop her? What if she fell?"

He felt like he was on the witness stand, being tripped up by a good lawyer. He sported a visage of guilt. "She seemed very confident."

"What were you planning to tell me if she fell out of the tree and died?"

Her arm was still holding him in place, keeping him in her personal space.

"Uh...sorry, I guess."

"Sorry? You stupid ass!"

"Now, now—no need to resort to foul language."

She shook her head. "No more berries for jam. Not these berries. No more trips to the woods. We can make jam out of something else if Allie wants to make more."

Kemina didn't know about John's now functional back and how it seemed to create a viable argument in favor of continued usage. "I wonder if we can have a little talk about these berries."

"No." She removed her arm, walking towards the refrigerator. "They are no longer welcome in my house. Allie is to have nothing to do with them. I cannot believe that between the two of you neither was smart enough to know this was a bad idea."

"Kemina, sit with me for a minute."

"Why? You think some sort of propaganda will change my mind?" She fully intended to nullify any argument in favor of returning to the tree.

"Do you still have any of the jam here at the apartment?"

She was reaching for orange juice, the refrigerator door open. "Yes, there is quite a bit left. Why?"

"Bring one out and sit down. Please."

She fumed as she retrieved it, setting it on the table with a loud clang. He wondered how close she'd come to breaking the glass.

"Here! It is the last jar you will ever see in this apartment."

"You don't like being challenged, do you?" he said.

"There is nothing to discuss when it comes to putting my child in danger."

"Okay, look. I have a simple challenge for you. If you do it, I will accept and follow whatever decision you make about the berries."

"I have already decided."

"Seriously? Last night with the open robe, and now we can't even have a civil discussion?"

She sighed. "You won't change my mind. This is a waste of time."

"That's fine. I won't try to change it. I just want you to do one thing before we consider the matter closed."

"What is it?"

"You see this jar of jam? I want you to eat half of it."

"Eat half? That is too much; it will make me sick."

"No, it won't."

"Half a jar?"

"Right now, here in front of me. If you do that, I will accept your decision."

She shook her head. "You can be a strange man." She stood up from the table.

"Hey," John interjected with concern, "where are you going?"

"To get a spoon and some cottage cheese to mix it in—if that fits with you and your odd proposal."

John looked relieved. "Sure. That works."

She returned to the table. "If this upsets my stomach, you are taking the blame."

"Don't worry about that," John said. "Just eat."

Her expression indicated she was dubious, but she started scooping the jam into the bowl of cottage cheese, mixing it together as she did.

"Make sure you get half. You're not there yet."

She dropped one more spoonful into the mixture. "That is half and don't tell me otherwise."

"All right. Close enough. Now eat up."

She found the everyday act of eating to be uncomfortable and awkward with someone's eyes glued to her every move.

"Do you have to do that?" She returned his intent gaze with a dirty look.

"I do."

The amount was far more than she wanted, but if it brought this discussion to an end, then so be it.

John watched as she ate and then washed down the last bite with a swig of orange juice.

"There," she announced. "I am finished, and so is this argument. It is as you agreed."

John was still staring. "How do you feel? Okay?"

She was growing suspicious. "I feel fine." In truth, she felt a little strange but didn't want to give him any satisfaction. "Why? Have you put something in this jam?"

"No. Nothing at all. Allie made the jam by herself."

"Then why would you ask me that?"

John hesitated before answering. "Are you sure you're okay?"

"John?" She gave him a look that was transitioning from mild concern to full-blown helplessness. "What is happening to me?"

He put a hand on her shoulder for both support and balance. "It's okay. You're fine. Just relax."

"I feel strange." She did. It started as a kind of mild dizziness, but now it was like the world was shrinking away from her. Was this what dying felt like? "I'm fading away, John!"

John was saying something. She couldn't make it out even though he was right in front of her. Why couldn't she hear him? She no longer controlled her own body. She couldn't stand or even move her arm. Her kitchen was fading fast. Terrified, she was helpless to resist. Her eyes grew wide, her head tipped upwards as if there was something on the ceiling that she wanted to see, then her expression glazed over and she was gone.

A bright light caused Kemina to squint. She looked away from it and found herself standing in what seemed to be an enormous garden. The ground was dark and rich, recently tilled, and weedless. Growing out of it were rows of vegetables, still in the development stage, all deep green and flourishing. It was beautiful and peaceful. She felt no alarm at being in this unexplained place.

She looked around, noticing a man bent over in one of the rows. She couldn't tell what he was doing, but based on his dress and the color of his skin, she concluded that wherever this was, they too used Mexicans for field work. That was when he lifted his head, making eye contact.

Kemina gasped. She felt as if everything in her entire existence had just changed in an instant. It couldn't be true.

He was reacting the same way. Some small tool in his hand fell to the ground unheeded. He began to walk towards her, his facial expression incredulous.

"Kemina?" His voice, which she immediately recognized, somehow carried the distance between them. She'd heard it many thousands of times before. It was forever engrained in her heart and her mind.

"Miguel?" She posed it as a question. She was too astonished to believe her eyes.

"Is it you?" He was drawing near, slowing his approach to a more cautious pace.

She saw his rugged good looks, his piercing dark eyes and the small scar on his right cheek. There could be no doubt. She looked into his eyes as he drew near, sensing the very essence of the man she had loved. She put a hand over her mouth, bursting into tears.

He stopped in front of her. Kemina could recognize his unique smell. All her doubts and defenses melted away.

"How is this possible?" he asked just before she grabbed him in a powerful embrace.

They held each other for a long time, each sobbing and crying tears of the highest joy.

He held her at arm's length, taking a long look. "How can you be here? It's not your time."

She smiled. "I don't care what time it is. I'll never let you leave me again."

He was confused. "Do you know where you are?"

"Where I always should have been…with you, my love."

"What about Allie?"

For those few moments, she had forgotten about her daughter for the first time since the day she had been born. "Allie?"

"Did she come with you?"

"No." Kemina was now confused. "I don't think so."

He had a more knowing look on his face, as if he'd figured it all out. "I love you so much. But you have to go."

Panic set in. "No, I will stay. I won't go!"

He nodded, stepping back away from her. "You must. But don't worry, I'll wait for you. Everything will be ready."

"I can't leave you."

Now this world started to fade away, just like her kitchen had.

"I'll be here for you."

She reached for him but it was too far now. She couldn't close the gap.

"No!"

It all became chaos, one world fading away as another replaced it.

Kemina moaned, trying to move. John held her just enough to make sure she didn't fall out of the chair.

"No!" she yelled, startling John.

He tightened his grip as life came back into her eyes. "Kemina, it's all right."

Snapping out of it, she stood up abruptly, knocking over her chair.

"Kemina, it's me. You're in your kitchen. You're safe. It's okay."

She made eye contact. "Oh my God." Her voice was shaky and so was she.

John picked up the chair. "Here, sit down until you get settled."

"Don't touch me. I'm all right."

John hadn't expected that reaction. "Fine. But sit, please. I don't want you to fall over."

"I won't." She had shared her bed with this man only hours ago. Now her husband had visited her in a vision. And her vision was…so real. How could she have disrespected his memory that way?

"If you say so." John seemed unwilling to pull completely away.

She put her hand to her forehead. "Oh my God."

There was nothing for John to do but wait.

"Did you know this was going to happen?" Her voice was antagonistic, her eyes hard and defiant.

"It's hard to say since I don't know what *this* is. You just stared off into the distance for a couple minutes—that's all. Do you want to tell me about it?"

"No!" Her response was quick and hard as steel.

"Okay. No problem."

"I have to go to the restaurant. There is still work to do."

John started to rise. "Fine. Let's go."

She held up her hand. "No."

"You don't want a ride?"

"I'll walk. It is a beautiful day."

"Don't you want me to come in at all? I thought you needed my help."

"No." The look on his face indicated that further explanation was required. "Not today. I have to wait for the order to come in, and plan the specials for the rest of the week. You can have the day off."

John's feelings were obviously hurt at this point. "If that's what you want."

"Yes." She walked to the door without picking up anything along the way. She opened it, hesitating briefly. "You cannot sleep in my bed again."

John recoiled in silent surprise.

"As a matter of fact, it would be better if you left and didn't come back." She then walked out, shutting the door behind her, leaving John stunned and motionless at the table.

John was beyond discouraged. If his relationship with Kemina was over, then he had nothing left. First his marriage, and now this. Was he that repugnant to women? How did things change so abruptly?

He sat trance-like, trying to keep his mind blank, giving himself time to calm down. Thoughts, of the unpleasant variety, filtered in regardless.

His first inclination was to jump in his car and leave. He could continue his magical journey, and consider his stay in Barrington part of the larger experience. That way he wouldn't have to deal with another angry woman who wanted him out of her life. He had enough of that for one lifetime already. At least he would be leaving with his back feeling good. But he knew he would hurt Allie if he disappeared without explanation. Even if it did come down to that, he wanted to see her and say goodbye first.

He could go to the restaurant against Kemina's wishes and force her to talk to him about this dramatic change in attitude. The problem was how strong her sudden disdain for him seemed; that idea appeared destined to fail.

Sitting at the table all day doing nothing was abhorrent and unacceptable. Stay or go...the two remaining scenarios ran through his mind like rabid animals, snapping and biting at each other until he couldn't take it anymore. He mumbled an obscenity and stood from his chair. If she no longer wanted him, fine—he would leave. He grabbed his few things and headed out to the car.

CHAPTER 28

Brad Merritt and Lonnie Attwater had both left their respective classrooms at a predetermined time, for the supposed reason of using the washroom. In reality, they had recently taken up smoking and needed to partake. Brad felt it made them seem even cooler and tougher. It also presented, in his mind, a legitimate reason for getting out of class, even if only for a few short minutes. He had just caught a glimpse of Allie as she disappeared into the girl's washroom.

Brad grabbed Lonnie by the arm, stopping him in his tracks.

Apparently Lonnie felt the grip was a bit excessive. "Hey, asshole, let go."

"Shut up, dick breath!" Brad hissed. "Did you see taco girl down there?"

"No."

"She just went in the can."

"Yeah?"

"Come on. We have to be fast."

Lonnie managed to follow his companion in a brisk walk down the hall.

"We both go in. You put your big foot against the door so nobody can open it. I'll do the rest."

"The rest of what?"

"You'll see. Just shut up. Come on, douche bag."

"But I want a smoke."

Brad shook his head. "You're so fucking stupid."

The daily order arrived early, and Kemina had just finished putting everything in its proper place. At least things in the restaurant were now properly organized. The back door opened and John walked in.

"There you are." He walked over, hoping she wouldn't turn and walk away. He decided to get right to the point. "Look, I don't know what happened earlier, but you made it clear you were no longer comfortable with me around. If that's the case, then I won't stay. I can't. Do you understand?"

She did, of course. But she gave no indication either way.

"You can't even speak to me?"

Her expression was not softening. "What do you want me to say?"

"How about this...what happened back at the apartment?"

She shook her head, saying nothing.

"Was it something about me? Was I part of it?"

"No."

"Then why did it make you so cold towards me? Why do I feel like you want me to disappear as fast as possible?"

Kemina relapsed into silence.

"I thought we were drawing close," John continued. "I thought you wanted me here, according to your own words and actions." He looked around as if to find the answer floating somewhere in the room, frustrated by her lack of response. "If that's not true, I'll get in my car and go. My things are packed and ready. So, I have to ask—is that what you want?"

She started to tear up. John fought through his frustration and waited for a response. She had to say *something*. But the moments went by and she stayed silent and aloof.

"Fine," John snapped. "I won't inflict myself upon you any longer. Goodbye."

"I saw my husband." She stifled a sob.

John felt his anger melt as understanding slowly dawned. "Your husband?" She had never spoken of him in any detail before.

"Yes."

John needed more. "Kemina, I've had the visions too. They seem very real."

"It *was* real!" She snapped like a sleeping dog that had been kicked. "I was there! I saw him. We spoke. He held me. I could feel him, see him, even smell him. It was real! We held each other for the first time since he passed…and it was only minutes after I got out of bed with you!" She snuffled, sobbing.

There it was, clear and laid out. She invited him into her bed only hours before her husband made an appearance. No wonder she now held him in such low esteem. And he was the one who had insisted that she eat the jam.

"Oh. Kemina, I'm sorry."

She waved at him like she was swatting at a fly.

"I think I understand."

She looked up, eyes teary. "I wanted to stay with him. I told him I wouldn't leave."

John tried to tread lightly. "What did he say to you?"

"He said…he'd be waiting for me when it was my time."

John nodded. He had no response that seemed appropriate.

She looked at him, any signs of softening now absent. Her eyes flashed with defiance. "Did that fruit do this to me?"

John hesitated, formulating his answer.

"Did you know this was going to happen?" Her voice was raised.

"I…"

"Answer me! For God's sake, just tell the truth!"

"Kemina, I…wasn't sure what would happen."

She narrowed her eyes. There was no trust in them. "Have you had visions?"

No doubt the expression on his face had already given it away. "Yes. Twice."

"After eating the fruit?"

"Yes."

She curled her lip. "You bastard." She hissed it at him.

"I didn't know for sure…"

"Why would you do this to me?"

He tried to formulate a legitimate defense. "I wanted you to know why the fruit was important."

"You couldn't trust me enough to tell me about what it would do first?"

He remained silent.

She grew quiet. "I think you should go."

Maybe she was right. Allie had tricked him, but she was just a girl. He should have explained the possible side-effects before encouraging Kemina to eat that much. He should have known better. "If that's what you want."

"It is." She spun around, walking out of the kitchen.

All other options evaporated. John turned, walking out of the restaurant for the last time.

The washroom door made a subtle squeak as it opened. *So much for being alone*, Allie lamented. Supressed laughter with a distinct masculine timbre echoed off the tile walls, and Allie felt a chill. More than one person was entering, and they didn't sound like girls at all. Worse, they sounded familiar.

"Hold it shut," a voice hissed, followed by more laughter. All doubt was gone—it was her usual tormentors. But here, in the girl's washroom...how was that possible? Did they not respect any barriers at all?

"Hello...anybody in here?" The squeaky tone was exaggerated to sound like a female voice. It wasn't even close.

Allie's eyes swung to the deadbolt lock on the door to her stall. It was shut (thank God) but would that keep her safe? Not really, she supposed, as fear took a good grip, stealing her ability to think. She hadn't felt safe at all of late, and this incident was going to make that even worse. She couldn't imagine any option for escape—they had her trapped.

A soft clicking sound got her attention. She looked up to find the source. A phone was being held above the stall. A photo had just been taken. That crossed a barrier that even fear couldn't deny and she reacted without thought.

"Hey!" she yelled with conviction, leaping up, yanking her clothes into normal position as she did so.

Now there was the sound of movement, sprinkled with more laughter. "Got it!" somebody declared and the hallway door banged shut.

She opened the stall, stepping out. She was alone.

What now? Unused adrenalin gave her a bad case of the shakes. She washed her hands, while her mind was elsewhere. Should she tell her teacher about this? Would that help or make things worse? She decided it would be worse.

The door swung open again, and Allie jumped back. It was a girl from another class.

"Hey, were those two morons just in here?"

Allie was trying to compose herself. How should she answer? "They just stepped inside the door."

"They can't come in here," the girl responded with defiance that Allie wished she had.

"They were trying to be funny," Allie said.

"I'm going to the office. I'm telling somebody."

Allie imagined that she would get blamed for that, and could imagine what the retaliation might consist of. "No!"

"Why not? Those two are idiots. Why protect them?"

"They just…it was nothing."

The girl gave Allie a funny look. "Don't be afraid of them."

That's easy for you to say, Allie thought. *They're not urinating on your front step.*

"It's okay. I'm fine." Allie walked out feeling anything but fine. At least they weren't waiting in the hallway.

Why wasn't she unaffected by their presence like this girl? What was it that made her feel like she was vulnerable to their meanness? She remembered the police officer that had visited the apartment. He had blamed her for even speaking about how they were treating her and warned her to stop.

Apparently this was all part of her American educational experience.

Specht was sleeping soundly when his phone rang. The number identified as his boss, and despite his grogginess, he was immediately annoyed.

"Specht here."

"This is Edwards."

"Good morning, sir."

Pleasantries were not typical for their conversations and this call was no exception. "There's been yet another incident with the bugs. I want you two to get there as soon as possible. I need info and lots of it."

"All right. What are the details?"

"More nests have been found. This time they're approximately ten miles from Barrington. An apple orchard is infected with these things. Reports are that there are as many as twenty nests in the trees. Some workers were attacked. The bugs are spreading and multiplying at an alarming rate. Interview everyone you can and put together a report ASAP. Send it to me as soon as it's done. Understand?"

"Where exactly?"

"I'm sending you directions now."

"We're on it."

"Don't even stop for coffee," Edwards said just before hanging up.

"Fascinating," Specht said as he recalled the conversation for Collins.

"The bugs?" Collins said.

"No. That he could think there's any chance I won't stop for coffee."

She smiled. "Then get me a peppermint tea while you're at it."

Specht grimaced at the thought as he drove out onto the street.

CHAPTER 29

When Principal Quinn walked in, motioning for the teacher to come over to the doorway, Allie paid no attention. She wasn't as easily distracted from her work as some of the other students. Besides, she was getting the hang of this new mathematics. She found geometry interesting now that she understood the basics.

"Allie?"

She looked up in surprise.

"Principal Quinn wants to talk to you."

The other kids all made an 'ooo' sound as if to insinuate that she must be in some sort of trouble. Allie slowly stood up, and then walked to the door, perplexed.

"Don't pay any attention to us. Please carry on." Principal Quinn stepped aside, letting Allie walk into the hallway before reclosing the classroom door.

"This way, Allie. We need to have a little talk in my office."

"Am I in trouble?" she blurted out, not knowing what other explanation made any sense.

"We'll talk in my office," he reiterated in a business-like tone.

Allie did not find any comfort in his words. She racked her brain for possible reasons why this would be happening, coming up with nothing. She had never gone looking for trouble. She overlooked the reality that trouble sometimes went looking for her.

"Right in here, Allie. Take a seat if you please."

She sat, stiff and upright, hands folded in her lap, looking up at the administrator with an expression of anguish.

"Sorry to pull you out in front of everybody like that, but this is time sensitive." Principal Quinn also took a seat. He stared at Allie in a way that made her feel even more uncomfortable. "Allie, have you been having trouble with any of our students here?"

"Trouble?"

She was white as a ghost and trembling. The principal, reading her reaction, committed to go as easy on her as possible. "Yes. Has anybody been teasing you or bullying you in any way?"

Her face turned red but that was her only response.

"It's okay, Allie. You're not in any trouble. But we have very strict rules governing how I respond to confirmed cases of bullying. So, I need you to be honest with me."

She nodded but said nothing.

"Your teacher says that you are very well behaved and that you never have conflict with the other kids in your class. But this school is bigger than one classroom, isn't it? Have you had any trouble with kids from the other classes?"

"I…"

"Has anyone been saying things to you that are inappropriate?"

Her mouth opened but no words came out.

He wasn't new to this. He was already formulating a picture, even with her lack of response. Here she was, relatively new to the community; a quiet girl who gave the appearance that she might just roll over and absorb any abuse without fighting back. Perhaps afraid to rock the boat. Perhaps cognizant of not having a lot of friends on her side. Perhaps not wanting to escalate an already bad situation. However, he needed her cooperation in order to take action. It was going to hurt her a little, but that was better than allowing the problem to progress, if it did indeed exist. He was certain that it did.

"Allie, do you spend much time on the internet?"

It was another unexpected question. "I guess. I use it to help with homework sometimes."

Maybe a little too studious as well, he noted. What the other kids would consider a nerd, or whatever the current lingo was for that designation. It was a shame that academic achievement could be considered a bad thing by the very kids who would need their education to survive in this changing world. *Be nice to the nerds, you might be working for one someday.*

"Allie, can you stand up and come over to this side of my desk? I want to show you something on my computer."

Puzzled, she obeyed without question.

"Now Allie, I don't want you to get upset. I want you to know that we're going to take care of this. But I need you to be realistic about what's going on here. I'm going to need your help, okay?"

Still not knowing where he was going with this, she felt she had no other alternative but to agree. "Yes, all right."

He clicked his mouse, bringing up a page from one of the prevalent social sites. The photo in the middle of the screen was what grabbed her attention in an instant. It was a photo of her in the girl's washroom. She was seated on the toilet. She was looking up with surprise written all over face. Shame overwhelmed her like a tsunami wave. She started to tear up.

"This was just brought to my attention. A student alerted a teacher about it. Apparently it was just posted. What can you tell me about this? Who took the photo?"

She seemed incapable of talking. He reached for a tissue and handed it to her, implying that it was all right to let her emotions out. Allie managed to keep a fragile grip on herself, but couldn't stop from crying just a little.

"Do you know who took this, Allie?"

She knew, all right. But the truth was, she hadn't seen anybody. "I just saw a hand."

He nodded. At least she was talking.

"Did you hear voices? Do you know if it was one person alone, or were there others?"

"I...think there were two."

"Even though you didn't see them, do you have any idea who it might have been?" Quinn already had an idea, but needed confirmation.

"I can't say for sure."

"Fair enough. You didn't see them, so you don't know for sure. Answer me this, Allie; who do you *think* it was?"

This was the threshold she was afraid to cross. What was she to do now? Her emotions and logic argued. She met the principal's eyes, setting herself to respond.

Once the floodgates opened, everything poured out. Principal Quinn, sensing the magnitude of the scenario, called in his secretary to witness the statement and take notes. By the end, his secretary was upset, and he was furious. This was unacceptable, and it was about to come to an abrupt end. He would see to it.

Having put Allie through what he considered to be more than enough emotional turmoil for one day, he offered the option of going home rather than returning to class. Terrified more than ever of running into the boys who had been after her, she took him up on the offer. After she had left his office, he was quick to move the process along.

"I want Merritt and Attwater called down, now. And Catherine?"

"Yes?"

"Phone the police."

His secretary raised her eyebrows. "Are you sure?"

"Damn right I am."

Merritt and Attwater sat outside the office awaiting their audience with the principal. Brad maintained an arrogant *I don't give a shit* look on his face, while Lonnie looked dumbfounded.

"What'd we do?" Lonnie said.

"The fuck'd I know?" Brad replied with a scowl.

The principal's door opened. "You two come in here." His voice was clipped and terse.

"Sit down." It wasn't a request—it was an order. They complied with stiff movements, as if they were forcing themselves

"I see no point in drawing this out. Did you two go into the girl's washroom earlier this week?"

There was dawning recognition in their expressions.

"Why would we piss in there?" Brad sneered.

The principal's face darkened. "Did you follow Allie Vargas into the girl's washroom and take a photograph of her while she sat on the toilet?"

In the midst of a situation that should have been bristling with obvious pitfalls for them, the word 'toilet' somehow made them both smile.

"Might I suggest," the principal said in an icy tone, "that the two of you start taking this very seriously. You need to think about what you're about to say. Your futures here at this school depend upon it."

"Big deal," Brad responded. "It was just a joke. Let her go back to Mexico if she doesn't like it."

His arrogance set Principal Quinn's teeth on edge. He forced himself to remain calm. What he wanted to do, deep down in his heart of hearts, was to close his laptop, pick it up and smash this hopeless dullard over the head with it on the slim chance that it might knock some sense into him. He opened the side door of his office.

"Would you come in please?"

Constable Moody appeared, putting a smile on Brad's face. In contrast, the cop's face was grim.

"Catherine has briefed you on why you were called, I assume."

He nodded.

Quinn's attention swung back to Brad Merritt. "Hand over your phone." He extended his hand.

Brad looked at his uncle.

"Give it to him," Moody said in a strained voice, with no hint of sympathy in it.

Brad's anger boiled over. "The hell I will!"

Both adults stood in position, not changing their posture or facial expression one iota. Brad was trapped, with no control over what was happening. He reached into his pocket.

"Assholes!" He flung it towards the desk. It careened off the computer, falling on the floor.

"That's quite enough!" Principal Quinn snapped. He stooped, picking up the phone. "What's your password?"

Brad stared in disbelief. "Fuck you."

His uncle grabbed him by the shoulder. It was by no means gentle. "Tell him or I'll get our IT guy to figure it out down at the station and we'll have a good look at everything you have on there."

Brad looked at his protector in disbelief. His uncle returned the stare, unflinching.

Brad lowered his voice. "*fuckyou*. That's the password. No spaces or capitals."

That figures, Quinn thought to himself. He unlocked it, immediately going to the photo folder. The one he was interested in was the last one taken. He opened it up, showing it to Constable Moody.

"This one is posted. It was Brad who took it. He didn't even try to hide it."

Moody sighed, looking at his nephew. "What were you thinking?"

Brad had another anger attack in response. "Who cares? She's just an alien! You can't see her snatch or anything. Big deal!"

Lonnie grinned at the vulgar euphemism.

"Oh, it is a big deal, Mr. Merritt," the principal responded, his voice now eerily calm. "You are in violation of our bullying and harassment policy. It is a zero tolerance policy. Do you know what that means?"

Brad, despite his desire to be associated with his tough-guy persona, didn't enjoy looking like he was stupid.

"It means I can't do it again."

"It means you won't be given an opportunity to do it again. It is my recommendation that you be expelled as per Board Policy 127, subsection 13. Anyone found to be guilty of repeated bullying or harassment can no longer attend our institution."

"What? Are you kidding?" Brad looked genuinely stressed.

Quinn shook his head, feeling only a little uncomfortable that he was enjoying this. "No. This incident, along with the affected student's statement, and the file we have on you for prior infringements, places you in violation. I'm going to be calling your grandmother as your legal guardian as soon as we finish here. You will have to make arrangements to attend school elsewhere."

Brad, for once, had nothing to say. He sat in stunned silence. Quinn wasn't surprised at his reaction. It reflected how he had been raised. A lifetime of experiencing nothing but enabling behavior from all the adults in his life had led him to believe that he would never see any consequences for how he acted.

Quinn swung his attention to Lonnie. "Do you understand what is happening here, Mr. Attwater?"

"Uh, Brad got suspended?"

"You're part of this incident just the same. You will also be expelled." Quinn could almost feel sorry for this kid who was clearly having trouble understanding this whole process. Almost.

Moody was looking uncomfortable, but Quinn found that he didn't really care about that. This wasn't finished yet.

"I will escort you to your lockers. I want you to take everything with you. Once you walk out the door, you can never return here again. I would suggest that you don't even try. A trespassing order is going to be made out and sent to you by registered mail. I would also insist that you have no further contact with Allie or her mother. I am going to suggest to them that they also seek a restraining order to make any such actions on your part illegal."

Quinn looked at Moody with stern eyes. "Can I speak to you alone for a moment?"

"Of course." His tone was in contradiction to his words. Quinn imagined that he couldn't wait for this to end.

"Follow me."

Quinn led him out to another small, unused office, shutting the door behind him once they had both entered.

"I know you're Brad's uncle. I also know, based on what Allie told me, that you have already talked to her and her mother about a previous incident. Is this true?"

"I did speak to them, yes."

"They both felt upset and intimidated by your visit. They also both felt you were siding with your nephew."

Moody's collar seemed to be getting tight. "Based on the evidence presented, there was some doubt about the veracity of her claims."

"You felt she was lying?"

"I…felt that by not reporting the incident, they gave me reason not to take their version at face value."

The principal stared while Moody squirmed. "Would you have reacted the same way if the accused had been anyone besides your nephew?"

That was apparently too direct. "Hey, if your daughter was assaulted, would you just ignore it like it never happened? My concerns were legitimate."

His response earned him more of the steady, direct gaze. "Do you have any concerns about *this* incident or my response to it?"

Quinn had intentionally backed him into a corner.

"No. The evidence seems clear."

"You will follow through in a professional manner?" The insinuation was insulting, but a confrontation was not going to be a good thing for Moody and he knew it.

"Yes. As a matter of fact, I think I will hand this case over to one of our other officers. That eliminates any chance of impropriety, and makes life a lot simpler for me."

Quinn nodded. "I understand. Thank you for your professionalism in this matter. I have no doubt this is a difficult situation for you."

Moody didn't have anything else to say.

"Very well. Let's get this finished."

They left the room together.

CHAPTER 30

Allie felt, under the circumstances, a request to get picked up was reasonable. She stood in a quiet corner of the hallway, dialling John's number. News about any bug related danger hadn't made its way to the school yet, so Allie was unaware of any threat. The phone rang several times before it was answered.

"Hello?"

"Hi John. It's Allie."

"Oh, hi Allie."

His voice was subdued, almost disinterested. This surprised her. "John, are you at the restaurant?"

John was in fact on the road, heading away from Barrington to a destination he hadn't figured out yet. "No, Allie. I'm on the road, actually."

"Oh. Are you far?"

A moment filled with only road noise. Then, "I'm not sure how to answer that. Is there something you need?"

"Yes. I was sent home from school. I was wondering if I could get a ride."

"Why did they send you home?"

"I can't really tell you over the phone."

"You didn't do something that you got in trouble for?"

The phone was quiet for a moment. "No, nothing like that. I'll tell you in the car." Allie, not knowing what had happened to Brad and Lonnie, still didn't feel safe in the school.

"Sorry, kiddo," John said. "I wish I could help, but that's not possible."

"John, where are you? Is something going on?"

"I'm glad you called. I want to tell you something. You need to know this." He gave a succinct account of the fact that he was forever leaving. When he concluded, there was no immediate response. "Are you still there?"

"Yes." Her quiet voice was brimming with emotion.

"Allie, I'm so sorry."

"Goodbye, John." She hung up, barely finishing the call before breaking down.

John looked at the home screen of his phone to confirm the call had ended. "Damn."

Those in the political realm feel pressures unique to their positions. Motivation is predictable—self-preservation for them (and their party) is always at the top of the list while integrity gets demoted to a place of little importance.

Vermont's Governor had been getting regular updates on the bug situation in the Barrington area for the last twenty-four hours. Despite the military's attempt to put an end to the problem (and the assurances they gave him that they would), it seemed things had escalated into an out-of-control phase. Worse yet, the media now turned its focus towards Barrington, essentially declaring it the *disaster du jour*. That meant extensive coverage, elevating the importance of this latest end-of-the-world-as-we-know-it scenario to the top spot in people's minds. It also meant it was time for him to take action.

In a decisive move, the governor declared a lock-down status for Barrington and mobilized the National Guard. Then, realizing the media attention could work to his advantage, he called the White House to discuss federal funding to assist with the issue, and set up an in-person visit to the area with a high-ranking member of the President's cabinet, a decision that the media would shout to the world.

With no real reason to do so, John was making good time. For the first time today, eating had finally made it to the top of his priority list. He pulled off the interstate to find a place where he could grab some food. He was heading towards home because he couldn't come up with any other idea, but he had no idea what he would do when he got there. Both his short, medium and long-term futures were nothing more than a chaotic blur.

He had no desire to eat somewhere unknown, so he started looking for a familiar chain. The city limit sign flew past, catching his attention.

"Plattsburgh? Why does that ring a bell?" The answer came to him in an instant. "Father Joe! Son of a bitch. What are the chances?"

Father Joseph McMillan had been the priest at the small Catholic Church he and Theresa had attended back in their brief religious phase. Father Joe had also married them.

"Well, I can't hold that against him," John said, now recalling why he remembered the name of this place. The priest had transferred from Pittsburgh to Plattsburgh, a joke too obvious for most of his members to miss. He wondered how hard it would be to find the church. A talk with Father Joe seemed appealing. Would he make time for him if he showed up unannounced? John remembered the words from his first fruit-induced dream.

"It's never a coincidence, John. It's all meant to be."

Not convinced of that by any means, John nevertheless made the decision to look up Father Joe.

"Father Joe?"

The man of God looked up from his notes, now spread in a messy smear across the top of his opulent desk. It was a ridiculous thing—huge and ornate. It looked like it belonged in the White House or perhaps a crime boss's office (not that there was any similarity between the two). It had been a gift when he arrived, so he had used it with thanks to the caring parishioners who had provided it.

"What is it, Claire?"

"There's someone here to see you. He doesn't have an appointment."

"Oh? What does he want?" He couldn't be a member or even an adherent without Claire knowing who he was.

"Just to say hello, Father Joe." A man's face materialised over his secretary's shoulder.

Joe squinted to sharpen his long-distance focus. "John? Is that you?" A smile broke across his face.

"In the flesh, if that's not too inappropriate to say."

"Well, I'll have you in the spirit soon enough. It's all right Claire; John is from my previous parish."

She stepped back to allow him entrance after a final suspicious glance. Convinced all was well, she returned to her work, leaving the two alone.

Father Joe got out from behind his desk with surprising speed and agility. He wasn't tall, but he was by no means a small man. John knew he had been a decent rugby player in his youth.

"John, good to see you!" He by-passed all reserved forms of greeting and instead, grabbed John in an embrace. It wasn't strong enough to dislocate any ribs, but it wasn't far from it.

"Hey, easy now. Remember how we had to keep reminding you that you don't know your own strength?" John said.

"It's good to see you, John, even if you are a bit of a pansy," Father Joe said. "So tell me; what in the world are you doing here in Plattsburgh?"

"It sounds corny, I know, but I was just passing through," John said, as Joe pulled back for a better look at his old friend.

"John, don't be cute with me. Nobody just passes through Plattsburgh."

"I was on the interstate and needed to grab a bite. I pulled off, not even realizing where I was, and saw the city sign. Of course, I thought of you. You know…Pittsburgh/Plattsburgh. Who could forget that?"

"I've been trying," Father Joe said with a smile. "Well, come on in. Take a seat at the world's most ostentatious desk. Get comfortable while I take care of one quick thing."

John sat as directed. He had a lot to unload and he couldn't help wonder what the reaction to some of it might be.

The burly priest returned with a small glass in each hand. "Here you go. It's the best I can do on short notice."

John regarded the brown liquid with a bemused look. "Changing the definition of Holy Water somewhat?"

"Rationalize it any way you want. I consider the presence of whisky evidentiary to the question of whether God loves us or not." Father Joe lifted the glass in a big, hairy hand, draining it in one gulp as if there was no other way to do it.

"I'm more of a sipper, myself." John took a small sample.

"My goodness, what a surprise this is. Where to start, where to start? So, how is Theresa?"

John grimaced. "That's a bit of a long story."

Father Joe was no stranger to this type of reaction to a question regarding the status of one's marriage. He knew all too well what it meant. "Oh? How's that?"

"She moved out. She left me for another guy." No point in beating around the bush, John figured.

"No! John, I'm so sorry."

He shrugged in a "what are you going to do" manner. "She got tired of me being somewhat disabled. She also got tired of me not paying my share of the bills."

Father Joe looked distraught. "I don't think most couples realize how important finances are to a successful marriage. How long ago did this happen?"

"Not long. Maybe a month or so now."

"Any chance of reconciliation?"

John sighed. "I doubt it. Once Theresa makes up her mind about something, it's hard to get her to change."

"I seem to remember that, now that you mention it. Since you've brought it up, how is your back?"

"Believe it or not, it's good. Better than it's been in years."

"Excellent. You look comfortable enough sitting in that chair. Is this the result of some new treatment?"

"You could say that."

"Long term prognosis?"

"I'm not sure. I should go and talk to my doctor again. It's been awhile."

"I see. So, why were you on the interstate in my neck of the woods?"

John hadn't figured out how to transition from small talk to his recent adventures yet. "That's a long and strange story."

Father Joe, after giving John a bit of a stare, picked up the receiver to his office phone.

"Claire, could you hold all my calls? Yes, I remember; just cancel that one. Thank you." The phone hung up, the stare returned. "I just cleared my calendar for the rest of the day. Therefore, I have time to listen to *a long story*, as you put it."

"You might think I'm nuts by the time I finish."

"Who says I don't already?"

John came to a quick conclusion, hoping that it was the right one. If he couldn't trust this man, who could he trust? "All right. Where should I start?"

Father Joe propped two big forearms on his desktop, leaning forward in anticipation. "At the beginning, of course."

John laughed. "Your counsel is always invaluable."

"Stop farting around and proceed."

John cleared his throat and did just that.

150

CHAPTER 31

Entry to the orchard was blocked by a state trooper who remained safely ensconced inside his cruiser, even after Specht and Collins pulled up in their unmarked car. His reluctance to get out wasn't encouraging.

Specht, after exiting their car, looked around as best he could, hoping his old-man eyes could see any active bugs in their vicinity. "What do you think? Is it safe out here?"

Collins was also doing a visual scan. "Not according to that trooper."

"I suppose all those leafy green trees provide great cover."

Collins managed a wry smile. "Especially if they're planning an ambush."

Specht sighed. "I guess this is what I get paid for."

"I'm right beside you," Collins said. "They're paying me too."

Specht knew her fears and appreciated the courage she was displaying. "Keep your eagle eyes open."

As they approached the cruiser, Specht noticed two things that he deemed important. The first was the sight of large nests hanging from the trees. The second was the gestures of the trooper, obviously indicating that they should jump into his car. This they did with enthusiasm.

"Phew!" Specht slammed the door shut. He looked Collins over quickly, then satisfied that she was all right, turned his attention to the trooper who was regarding them over the back of the seat. "Police and FBI, hiding in a cruiser because of some bugs. It's a proud moment in law enforcement."

The trooper smiled but not from amusement. "The odd one flies by and bounces off the windshield or side window. I've seen their stingers from close distance. Hiding in here is not such a bad idea."

"Were you one of the first on site when this happened?" Specht asked.

"I was the first. I beat the paramedics by a few minutes."

"Perfect," Specht said. "Could you tell us in as much detail as possible what happened here?"

"Sure." The trooper re-adjusted his position to make it more comfortable to face partially backwards. He told a tale of disabled workers lying on the ground, harrowing close calls to both himself and other medical workers, and the signs of extreme pain on the faces of the victims.

"Do you have any idea what triggered the attack?" Specht asked.

"Not for certain," the trooper replied. "The victims couldn't speak. It seems it was simply proximity. They were sent in to do some work and got swarmed shortly after they arrived."

Specht released a long sigh. "Same M.O. as in the other attacks."

"You know what I find most disconcerting?" Collins asked.

Specht waited for an answer.

"How far and how fast they're spreading. If we're supposed to get a handle on this, we'd better do it fast. Do we have a direct contact with whoever is in charge of the National Guard response unit?"

Specht considered his response, and then picked up his phone. "Yeah, our boss. I'll report in. After that, I've got another idea."

John finished his narrative, now concerned by the expression on Father Joe's face. "Do you think I'm experiencing some kind of psychosis?"

Joe didn't answer, lost in thought. "Could you find this tree again, John?"

John hadn't expected that response. "I suppose so. I was only there once."

"You believe that eating this fruit resulted in your back being healed?"

John shrugged. "Maybe. Every time I ate some of the fruit, it felt better."

"Then you would have a vision?"

John thought about that. "When I ate a significant amount. Once I had just a taste and that didn't seem to bring on any effects at all."

Father Joe stood, walking over to the expansive book shelves along the back wall. He chose a large tome, sliding it out of its resting place.

"Why are you so interested in this tree?" John asked.

Joe repositioned himself at the desk. "Give me a minute before I answer that, John. Be patient if you would." He looked up from the now open pages. "Are you out of time?"

John shook his head. "No. I have nowhere to go."

"Good." Father Joe realized how that sounded as soon as it left his mouth. "Sorry. I don't mean that it's good that you have nowhere to go…"

John smiled. "I know what you meant."

Father Joe pulled a pair of reading glasses off of the desktop, slipping them on. He looked over them at John who looked quizzical. "Bear with me, all right?"

"Sure."

"Okay, let's see what the Gutenberg King James has to say." He cleared his throat. "And the Lord God said, Behold, the man is become as one of us, to know good and evil: and now, lest he put forth his hand, and take also of the tree of life, and eat, and live for ever (Genesis 3: 22 KJV). So he drove out the man; and he placed at the east of the garden of Eden Cherubims, and a flaming sword which turned every way, to keep the way of the tree of life (Genesis 3: 24 KJV)."

John squirmed. "You think the tree of life is growing in central Vermont? Does this mean I'm going to live forever?"

Father Joe looked over his glasses, tapping a sturdy finger several times on the desk before responding. "No. But after listening to your wild tale with a closed mouth and an open mind, I would think you could extend me the same privilege."

John felt his face turning red. "Of course. My apologies."

"Let's go from the very beginning to the very end." He flipped a thick portion of pages over, then fingered through the few that remained.

"Here we are. Listen up. "And he shewed me a pure river of water of life, clear as crystal, proceeding out of the throne of God and of the Lamb. In the midst of it, and on either side of the river, was there the tree of life, which bare twelve manner of fruits, and yielded her fruit every month: and the leaves of the tree were for the healing of the nations (Revelation 22: 1, 2 KJV)."

Father Joe peeled off his glasses, dropping them on the desk. "Well, what do you think?"

John blinked. "Keep in mind that I'm no biblical scholar."

Father Joe stood up and started to wander around the room. "Everyone who knows the story of Adam and Eve knows about the Tree of the Knowledge of Good and Evil and its forbidden fruit. But there's not much ever said about the Tree of Life."

John, who had been hoping for practical advice, wasn't thrilled with the direction the conversation had turned. "That's interesting."

Father Joe, who had spent his life counselling and trying to understand people, picked up on subtle nuances in speech patterns as well as anyone. John's sentiment was not genuine. "Is it?"

John, feeling like he had just been caught doing something wrong, wasn't sure how to respond. "Sort of."

Father Joe smiled. "At least you're being honest now, John."

"I don't mean to diminish the importance of your thoughts. I was hoping you were going to offer me some life changing advice, that's all."

Father Joe wasn't ready to be deterred. "Did you know that the original ancestor of modern aspirin was made from the bark of willow trees?"

"I remember hearing something to that effect."

"There are multitudes of medicines in use that are derived from plants. Researchers are combing what's left of the rainforests hoping to find more as we speak."

"You think this tree might have actual healing properties?" John asked.

"I wish your doctor had taken a before and after look at you. It would be most interesting to hear his or her opinion."

"I should have done that right away," John said. "It seemed easy to accept that I felt better—I was therefore lacking in motivation as far as medical visits are concerned. Why go to the doctor when you're feeling good?"

John could see that Father Joe was mulling something over in his mind. "John, I'm thinking of something as I consider your story. Perhaps I should say *someone*. It's crazy, but I can't help it. I have a woman in my congregation. She is thirty-eight years old, married and has two children. Linda is her name. Nice lady. Unfortunately, her family is going to lose her soon. She has terminal cancer."

John began to feel uncomfortable. "I'm sorry to hear that."

"We all are," he said. "It's a brain tumor. Her doctors and the hospitals have been mucking with it, medically speaking. I think they felt like they were obliged to do *something*. Most recently, they've decided to face reality, and sent her home to die." He paused, frowning.

"I've seen this before. I know she'll accept her fate at some point. But her family never will. They'll carry this burden with them every moment of every day for the rest of their lives. It will be a major roadblock to their faith. That's where I come in.

"All I have to do is say the right things that will make them feel okay with this. I'm supposed to perform the miracle of taking away the resentment, frustration and anger that comes from watching a nice lady, who just happens to also be their wife and mother, get slowly tortured to death by this damn disease."

He paused to calm himself. "John, I don't think I'm doing a very good job. I wouldn't be surprised after this is all over and they're walking away from the grave site, if they don't all tell God to piss off."

John was no stranger to the frustrations that life could send. He could identify.

"Thank you very much for taking the woman we loved and needed in this horrible and painful fashion, and by the way…please don't ever come back."

John, having no idea what to say, held his tongue.

"All I have to do is make them okay with all this. Doesn't sound too hard, does it?"

Another silence fell.

"Do you have any semblance of an idea why I'm so interested in this tree, John?"

The picture was becoming clearer. John was only slightly horrified. "Maybe."

"How long would it take to drive there and pick some of this magical fruit?"

John was beyond uncomfortable. "Father Joe, what if I'm wrong? What if I'm not healed at all? Or what if I am, but it had nothing to do with this tree? For all I know, eating it could make her worse or kill her."

"I don't know much, John," he said, "but I do know this. At this point, she would be willing to take the risk."

Returning to Barrington a third time felt like getting an arm that hadn't healed properly re-broken. John had zero desire for it. But there were other people in the world besides himself to give a shit about. Father Joe was on the list. Maybe this lady should be, as well.

"It would be around a four hour drive one way from here. Then we'd have to hike into the woods. The biggest problem would be that the fruit is at the very top of the tree. There's no chance either of us would be climbing up to get it."

"How did you get some in the first place?"

John knew that she would be his only hope of getting any on short notice. "Allie."

CHAPTER 32

Specht hung up the phone. He had made several calls in total.

"Well?" Collins asked.

She was antsy. They had been sitting in the cruiser long enough. Even with the threat of bugs in the immediate area, they were both more than ready to leave.

"Our old friend Ghost will be here in a few minutes. He said if we waited, he would make it worth our while."

"What's that supposed to mean?" Collins asked. "He's bringing cold beer and a meatball sub?"

"He said, and I quote, *I am become death, the destroyer of bugs*."

"I don't understand."

"It's originally from some Hindu writings," the trooper in the front seat injected. "Except for the bug part."

"And I was thinking it was a quote from one of the Die Hard movies," Collins said.

"It means," Specht replied, "that we get to watch some bugs die. Hopefully."

Collins got resettled. "Now that is something I'd pay money to see. Did he give you any details?"

Specht shook his head. "No. I think he likes the drama that comes from uncertainty."

The back seat flew open and Ghost jumped in. He regarded the looks of surprise all around the car and laughed with enthusiasm. He slammed the door shut, all the while giggling like a child. "You should see the expression on your faces," he gasped.

Collins meditated on how close she had come to punching him in the face. So far, only Specht had noticed that the trooper had started to pull his service weapon out.

"Doesn't the Department of Defense require psychological evaluations?" Collins asked.

"Oh, don't be like that," Ghost said between laughs. "You'll like me a lot better once the show starts."

"Next time," Specht said in an even tone, "you should consider the potential side-effects of unexpected actions." He gestured towards the front seat where the trooper was putting his weapon back in its holster.

"I could have predicted all your responses perfectly. Psychology is an important component to my job. Try to relax. A little trust would also be nice. Oh, and by the way, Trooper? You might want to back up by a few hundred feet or so."

The trooper's only reaction was to look puzzled.

"You're not dropping more bombs, are you?" Collins asked.

Ghost tried to look offended. "No, of course not. That would be wildly reckless. We're going to use chemical warfare this time."

That got the trooper's attention. The engine of the cruiser fired up and the car began to roll away from the orchard.

"Not too far," Ghost said. "I want to see the effects first-hand."

"Doesn't our health come into play?" Specht said, doubting the effectiveness of moving a short distance away.

"No worries. This formula is specifically designed to attack only the insect's respiration system. And it becomes inert as soon as it hits the ground. Besides, there's virtually no wind and these pilots are pin-point accurate."

"Multiple assurances from a government official and still I'm concerned," Collins said. "Go figure."

"Peel back a few more layers on this onion, and you'll find that we work for the same boss." Ghost only looked creepier when he smiled. He flashed off a big one.

"Onions stink and so does this." She tried to reciprocate with an artificial grin of her own.

"I hear something," Specht said, happy to interrupt.

"Here comes the show. Last chance to wave goodbye to the creepy crawly bugs." Ghost leaned over to get a better angle of view out the window.

Collins and Specht followed suit, craning their necks awkwardly.

"There!" Collins pointed at something on her side of the car.

An enormous plane flying dangerously low appeared on the horizon and quickly drew near.

"Hard to beat a B-52," Ghost said reverently. He lowered the car window and stuck out his head. "Don't mess with America!" he screamed.

"Put that window up!" Collins looked like she was going to faint.

Ghost gave her a strange look. "You're under the impression that this car will protect you from a chemical attack? You might as well drink it straight from the drum it came in."

"You said we'd be safe," Specht snarled.

"We are. Otherwise I'd be fifty clicks away. Being in the car has nothing to do with it. I suggested we back up primarily so this stuff wouldn't smear the windshield."

The plane flew past them and over the orchard. It was moving slowly, but that didn't stop the engine from thundering to the point of vibrating the car. In mere moments it covered the area and banked into a turn. Now the engines were really working, black smoke trailing behind them.

"God bless you, boys," Ghost said reverently. And then, "We'll wait for five minutes, and then take a leisurely stroll to assess the carnage."

Collins was by no means convinced that either the chemical or the bugs would pose no threat after that short period of time. "After you."

"As it should be," Ghost replied.

Specht was still looking out the window. "I can't wait to see this."

"That's long enough," Ghost proclaimed. He popped his door open. "Let's have a look."

Specht followed suit immediately. Collins, still leery, nonetheless felt the need to rid herself of the feeling of claustrophobia created by sitting too long in the car.

"Why do I feel like I'll be trying to explain this to my doctor ten years from now when I come down with some rare and terminal condition?"

Specht leaned in and lowered his voice. "He wouldn't be here unprotected if it wasn't safe to do so."

"That logic only works if we assume he's fully sane."

"Nothing wrong with my hearing," Ghost said as he took long strides towards the trees.

Collins had a good look and stopped in her tracks. "That's not good."

Huge leathery nests hung from the trees. There were dozens of them. She stayed rooted on the spot.

"Oh come on," Ghost snarled. "These frequent bouts of cowardice are becoming annoying."

"First of all," Collins replied in an icy tone, "a little respect and professional courtesy is the minimum standard I expect. Secondly, are you absolutely positive these things are at the very least incapacitated?"

He rolled his eyes. "Yes. Hold on." His eyes went downward, scanning the ground. "Here!" He took three steps forward, pointing as he went.

Collins walked over and had a look. A bug was in the grass, clearly in distress, but also still alive. It buzzed as it tried to get airborne. "It's still alive."

"Not for long," Ghost said. He stepped on it and ground his foot. The sound of crunching could be heard. "See?"

"Very convincing."

They continued to walk closer to the trees. More buzzing, twitching bugs were on the ground, hopefully beyond any chance of recovery.

"Not a good place for sandals," Collins observed.

Specht was staring at the closest hive. "If this chemical becomes inert when it hits the ground, how will it have any effect on the bugs in the nest?"

Ghost didn't seem to have any qualms about being there at all. "The mad scientists in our secret government lab hit a home run with this stuff. The slightest hint of it is fatal to bugs. Respiratory stress tests at one hundred percent lethality. So, you two ladies can keep your panties on. Why don't you go and give the owner the good news? I'll recon a bit more while you do so."

As they turned to leave (with no small amount of relief), Collins had a thought. "Is this wonderful chemical the final solution to the bug problem?"

Ghost didn't bother to turn around. "Sure looks that way."

Specht continued walking. "Come on, partner. Maybe we can go back to the office now."

Collins fell in stride. "Home has a nice ring to it." She took one last glance back towards Ghost as he strolled leisurely amongst the trees and hives. "I hope that pompous ass doesn't get stung."

Specht smiled. "I bet you do."

Father Joe had insisted on driving. John wasn't sure if that made backtracking any less painful, but here he was regardless. They were humming along the interstate in an oversized SUV that seemed like a ridiculous vehicle choice for a single individual.

"We have some time to kill, John," Joe said, as if implying that something needed to be done about it.

"You're right. I should try to have a snooze." John had no intention of falling asleep, but he wanted to throw up a roadblock to what Father Joe was about to suggest.

"You're young for needing an afternoon nap."

"I'm establishing an escape route to avoid whatever you're about to ask."

Joe chuckled. "So I figured."

Road noise was all that fell on his ears. John wondered why the conversation stopped and realized he was uncomfortable with the quiet interlude. "Well, go ahead. What's on your mind, Father Joe?"

"I want to hear more about the two visions you had," he said.

John had skimmed over them in their earlier talk, providing superficial details. "Why? They were just meaningless hallucinations."

"Do you believe that?"

John couldn't lie to the holy man. "I'm not sure what I believe about them, to be honest."

"Then tell me all, and I'll give you my expert opinion."

"What if the telling of them would make me feel uncomfortable?" Father Joe wouldn't let such a trivial obstacle get in the way, but John had to ask.

"Nonsense. Telling me will make you feel better. It's never healthy to keep something like that bottled up inside."

Perhaps he was right. John would be willing to let it out if it would dissipate, or better yet, disappear altogether. His memories of Barrington were now painful and confusing. "Fine. But if at any point you start laughing or making a twirling motion with your finger beside your head, I'm quitting."

"More than fair," Joe responded.

John cleared his throat, taking a moment to recall the details. He then recounted them from beginning to end

Father Joe nodded multiple times, but didn't interrupt. His face was a picture of concentration.

John couldn't think of any sort of flourish to end with. So instead, he said, "That's it."

"Hmm. Very interesting."

John turned away, staring out the window. "That's your expert opinion? I find that disconcerting."

"Never mind my interpretation for the moment. I have some questions for you."

"I was afraid of that," John said.

"I'll try not to drag this out. You know you always have the option of refusing to answer."

"Is that an option?"

"Sure. But it is a long walk back to Plattsburgh."

John smiled. "Fire away."

"I find this fascinating. I've had many people come to me over my career and tell me they've had some sort of vision. The problem is, the vision was exactly what they needed it to be, and that sets off a lot of alarm bells. Your visions, on the other hand, seem to fill you with uncertainty at best, mild dread at worst. You didn't seek them. You didn't anticipate them. You were quite reluctant to even speak of them. Now, although none of that is an inherently good thing for you, it adds legitimacy as far as I'm concerned. And John, I am a bit of an expert."

"Oh good—then tell me what they mean."

"We'll come to that. First of all, tell me about the man on the bench. Did you recognize him in any way?"

"I'd never seen him before."

"That's not what I asked."

"I didn't recognize him."

"So you don't know who he was?"

"No."

Body language indicated he was being entirely truthful. "He mentioned the tree?"

"Yes."

"And he told you to protect the girl. What do you think that means?"

John shook his head. "I haven't figured that one out yet."

"Do you think it was in reference to this girl you met? Allie?"

"I would have thought so, except that her mother just told me to get lost. I doubt I'll ever see her again."

"Except for today."

"I haven't called yet. Nothing is certain. Kemina may just say "no"."

"All right, let's skip over that for now. Let's talk about the second vision; the one where you're standing on the beach."

"That one was weird. It made no sense at all."

"You say that you saw your mother."

John let the memory flood over him. It filled him with a poignant yearning. "Yes. She came over to me after the little boy showed up. And the big muscle dude."

"You mentioned that the details were very realistic."

"Father Joe, it was identical to real life. I could smell things; I could hear subtle background sounds; I could feel the wind drift across my arms. The reality of it was blowing my mind."

"It wasn't like a typical dream."

"No. Nothing was out of focus or changing. I remember seeing some flecks of black in the iris of the little boy's eyes."

Father Joe nodded. "That is an unusual detail for a dream. Tell me about your mom."

This was the hard part. John steeled himself and determined to remain stoic. "Her appearance surprised me. She was young, Joe. She looked like how she was when she married my dad. I saw her like that in old wedding photos."

"Interesting."

"And her reaction when she saw me. It seemed so real; so genuine. She was shocked."

"Did she say anything to you?"

"No. That was when the Schwarzenegger look-alike told me to get lost."

"And the boy? Tell me again what he said."

John sighed. "He called me Uncle John."

"How did that make you feel?"

"I don't think I've ever been so shocked. Even compared to when Theresa told me she was leaving. It was completely unexpected. I just stood there with my mouth hanging open."

"That's when it ended?"

"Yeah. The whole thing just faded away and I was back in the apartment."

"And that's everything?"

John nodded. "I think so. Oh, wait. Did I mention this? Mom said the boy's name out loud."

Father Joe raised an eyebrow. "You don't say. What was it?"

"She called him Abby."

John noticed that Father Joe gave a little start.

"I thought that was a funny name for a boy," he said in conclusion.

"It's a variant of Abbott," Joe said.

"Oh. Why didn't I think of that?"

They drove along in silence for several minutes, both digesting the conversation until Father Joe glanced sideways at John, saying his name aloud. "John?"

"Yeah?"

"Did it strike you as funny that he called you "uncle"?"

"Very much so. But there were so many other things to be freaked out about that it just fell into line behind the rest of them. It was one of the details that made me think the whole thing was bogus."

"Why is that?"

"Because it offset the legitimate things. It called the authenticity of the rest of the vision into question."

"John, can I tell you something?"

John smiled in response. "If I said no, would it deter you in any way?"

"It might." His reply was serious.

"I was kidding. Please proceed."

Father Joe's forearm remained draped over the steering wheel as he began speaking. "In my capacity as a priest, it is not uncommon for people to swear me to confidentiality before telling me something. The same thing applies to confession, unless I hear someone admit to committing a serious crime. It is an aspect of my position that I take very seriously. I believe that people need to have someone in their life that they know they can trust. Without trust, I couldn't do my job."

"I understand," John said.

"I'm about to violate that trust. I want you to know that this is not an easy decision for me, nor is it something I do lightly."

John was at a loss as to where this was going, which led to fear about what his friend was going to say next. "Can I ask whose trust you are about to violate?"

John got a brief look in response. It was strained. "Your mother's."

John reacted as if slapped. "What secrets could my mother have had?"

"You're ignoring the essential component of a secret. If she had one, you would by definition be unaware of it."

"She had one?"

"One that we're going to consider, yes."

John felt cold. "Is it something terrible?"

Father Joe considered the answer. "Perhaps. But it doesn't make *her* look terrible, if that's what you're concerned about."

"Father, if you tell me that my mother was a murderer or had an affair, it's going to ruin my image of her. She was a good mother to me. I don't want that tarnished, okay? I've got enough garbage to deal with right now."

Father Joe nodded. "I understand. But I'm not sure how to alleviate your fears without spilling the beans. For what it's worth, I don't think what I am considering telling you would damage your image of your mother."

John already knew that he must hear it. Even with the risk, it couldn't be taken off the table now. "It's a good thing I trust you."

"I hope you still do when we're finished."

John prepared for a leap of faith. "Tell me, Father Joe."

CHAPTER 33

Kemina felt something was amiss as she walked into her apartment. Allie was sitting alone at the kitchen table and offered no greeting.

"Little one. Is something wrong?"

Allie turned to look at her mother but gave no other response. Her expression was hard to read.

"I heard about the school being closed. Did you have any trouble getting home?"

Confused by the statement, Allie immediately wondered if it had anything to do with the fallout from Brad and Lonnie getting into trouble. "Why was the school closed?"

"There are stinging bees in Barrington. Did your teacher not inform you?"

"I guess I got sent home before that," Allie said.

Kemina frowned. "But why?"

"What difference does it make?" Allie said, her voice monotone and subdued. And then, "I called John for a ride."

There it was. Kemina should have known. It had to happen sooner or later. "Oh. Did you…talk with him?"

"Did you send him away?" Now the voice was louder, emotional and accusatory in tone.

How to answer that? The circumstances could not be discussed. "Allie, I had to. Trust me."

"Trust you!" Allie jumped to her feet. "How can I ever trust you again? Why would you do such a thing?"

Kemina had precious little to say in response. "Allie, he was never going to stay forever."

"Yes he was!" Allie teared up. "He was going to stay, and I was going to have a father and we could be a whole family again."

Kemina felt herself getting emotional as well. "No. That was never going to happen."

"Yes! Yes it was!" Allie stormed off into her room, slamming the door shut behind her.

Kemina considered going after her, but decided a cooling off period was needed. She closed her eyes and took several deep breaths.

Kemina felt as miserable as her daughter, but empathy wouldn't put them on speaking terms. She wanted to open the door and check on her, but that seemed dangerous and counter-productive.

It was all coming apart. They were alone again. She was understaffed. So much happening—why did it all have to be bad?

Kemina knew the answer. It was her fault. She had made a series of bad decisions, each increasing the fallout as her life came crashing down.

Asking a strange man to come home. Encouraging this man to stay. Inviting this man into her bed. What had happened to the woman who was stoic and led by common sense?

It didn't even matter now. She couldn't undo what was already done. All that was left was to deal with the aftermath.

That damn tree and its hallucinogenic fruit. How many of their problems stemmed from it? The more she thought about it, the more she was convinced that the answer was all of them. If Allie hadn't been going out to visit it, she wouldn't have had the issue with those boys. She wouldn't have met John and brought him home. Kemina herself wouldn't have had that vision. Life, not that it had been perfect, would have continued to flow along as before.

She grew tired of sitting at the table feeling sorry for herself.

Father Joe squinted as the sun slid out from under a cloud. He flipped his visor down to mitigate the effects.

"When was the last time you talked to Dianne?"

"She called me around Christmas last year."

"That's a long time between calls for a brother and sister."

John had figured he was going to get some sort of lecture over that. "We're both busy. We're moving in different directions right now. She's giving every waking moment to her career."

"Hmm. So you don't call her because she's too busy?"

"Something like that."

"John, she had an abortion."

John sat upright with a start. "What!"

"A long time ago."

John had a blur of questions log jammed in his head. All he could do was stammer.

"But...I..."

"That was your mother's secret. It weighed on her."

"When? Why?"

"Dianne was quite young at the time."

John couldn't stop fighting his emotions. "I never knew."

"It bothered your mother for the rest of her life. She asked me for special dispensation."

"Oh, man."

"Well said. I feel much the same way."

"Did my dad know?"

"Yes. It was a difficult and controversial decision for all of them."

"Everybody but me." John wondered about the effect on the deterioration of his parents' relationship.

"I don't think anybody saw potential benefits to you by sharing the bad news."

"So, I wandered through my life unaware."

"If you mean that you were the only one in your family not carrying this burden, then yes."

John's initial response began to wane, replaced by a revelation. "So you think that the little boy in my vision actually was my nephew?"

"I don't know, John. Not by a long shot."

John flailed through his memories, grasping at imaginary straws. "Did they know if it was going to be a boy or girl?"

"Not as far as I know. I don't think they wanted that knowledge. It would have made things harder."

"I suppose."

"I can tell you this, however. By the way, this is the part that grabbed my attention, making me think that I should share this information with you. Your mother told me once that if Dianne had kept the baby and it had been a girl, she wanted it to be named Abigail."

"Or Abby for short," John said. "My maternal grandmother's name was Abigail."

The conversation took a brief respite. Father Joe was the one to break it.

"Now can you see why this tree is so intriguing to me, John? The visions...the healings...how they seem to tie in to what I know and believe about my faith?"

John processed before answering. "So you're telling me that you think this tree could be the same one that is mentioned in the bible?" He did a poor job of keeping the skepticism out of his voice.

"No, I'm not saying that. I don't see any way that could be true based on scripture let alone the scientific road blocks. But trees and plants can reproduce in various ways, can they not? As I already said—many of our medicines today are derived from plant sources. We read that it is possible that a tree could have healing properties, even to the point of extending our lives."

"I've eaten from this one. Should I expect to live forever then? Because if that's the case, I might have to change my long-term plans."

"No," Father Joe laughed. "I think you should plan on three score and ten; then factor in all the modifying variables, just like the rest of us."

"But my back seems to be healed."

Joe nodded. "Again, I wish you had gone to your doctor. It's hard to say what a lack of pain in the short term means. I hope you're right, but what if you're wrong? What if this fruit is just somehow dulling or masking the pain?"

"And what might it have done to the rest of me?"

"It is a most captivating thought. I wonder what your blood pressure is. Or your cholesterol levels, for that matter. If I recall, you had a liking for carbs."

John settled back down, staring out the window. "Abby."

Father Joe stole a sideways glance. "A big coincidence, wouldn't you say?"

"Maybe. Or maybe I heard my mom say it when I was a boy and remembered it subconsciously."

"So it was just a regular dream, you think? Even so, why would you apply it in this particular vision? Why not one of the hundreds of other names you heard bandied about in your home?"

"I don't know."

"It's not central to all of this, regardless. Why don't you try calling this girl and see if she can help us get some of this magical fruit?"

John was reluctant. The most likely scenario he envisioned was that Kemina would answer the phone and either hang up on him, or give him a piece of her mind before denying the request.

"I guess."

"You're not feeling comfortable with this, are you?"

"No. To say I didn't leave on good terms is an understatement."

"If things go south, hand me the phone. This was my idea, after all. Maybe I can convince her."

"You *can* be very convincing."

"No doubt why you're in this current situation."

"Point taken. If our conversation can take a brief respite, I'll get this over with." He pulled out his phone and punched in the number.

When her phone rang, Kemina was deep in a line of morose thoughts. She glanced at it, recognized John's number and was smitten with sudden onset paralysis. Dealing with him was too much at this already difficult moment. She stared at it blankly until it stopped. There was really nothing the two of them needed to say to each other anyway as far as she was concerned.

Kemina remained at the table, sitting motionless. The normal things that needed to be done seemed pointless. And all of them would now feel forced and awkward. She wanted to talk to Allie, to begin the process of healing over this painful episode in both of their lives, but at the same time dreading the first response Allie was likely to have. A period of time would have to elapse before they could exchange words in a civil manner.

Kemina wished herself into the future. If only she could skip this next week or so, and land in a time when reconciliation had already happened and normal life had returned. She sat at the table, dreading both the present and the future that was about to unfold.

Her phone rang again. She glared it, but was surprised to see a different, unknown number on the screen. Answering still seemed like an unwanted and unpleasant task. Even mundane conversation, such as the kind generated by a wrong number, felt intolerable. But it could be something to do with the restaurant. Steeling her reserve, she picked it up and pressed the answer button. "Hello?"

"Hi," a deep voice answered. "I'm calling for Kemina Vargas."

The voice was unfamiliar. "This is she speaking."

"I'm Father Joseph McMillan. I wonder if I could have a moment of your time?"

A priest? Kemina was completely at a loss to understand the potential nature of the call. She had attended church locally when time allowed, but had never heard this name before. Nonetheless, she would not be impolite to a man of faith. "Of course. How can I help you?"

"If you can indulge me with a little patience and understanding, I think I can make this call as succinct as possible."

"Yes, I'm listening."

"As a man of the cloth, I would be remiss if I was anything but completely open and truthful from the onset of our conversation, wouldn't you agree?"

The point of the call grew even murkier. "I don't recognize your name. Can you tell me the reason for this call?"

"That would be the next step. Might I beg your indulgence to the extent that you don't hang up on me until I finish what I have to say?"

More confusion arose. "Why would I hang up on you? Especially if you are a priest."

"Because I'm John's priest."

Kemina was stunned. John ran to his priest this quickly?

"Are you still there?"

She really wanted to hang up the phone. It was a near thing. "I'm here." Her voice lacked all interest or enthusiasm.

"I'm not calling to talk to you about John or any aspect of your relationship, past or present. I'm not going to berate you to change your mind about reconciliation or anything along those lines. As a matter of fact, this call really isn't about John at all."

That seemed extremely unlikely to Kemina. "Then how can I help you?"

"I have a parishioner who is very ill. I think it is possible, even though I can't offer substantive evidence to support the idea, that the fruit your daughter found in the woods may be able to help her."

Kemina recoiled away from the phone. That damn fruit again! "That fruit is evil! You should stay away from it."

"Did you know that it might have healed, or at least partially mitigated the effects of John's bad back?"

She did not. They had never had any conversation about it. "That fruit," she hissed, "is the reason John is no longer welcome in my home."

"I think I understand. I'm not asking for that to change. I would like to have some of this fruit, but will need the assistance of your daughter for a short time in order to get some."

That was too much. Kemina had reached her breaking point. "Because of that fruit, my daughter won't even talk to me!" She hung up and threw the phone across the room.

CHAPTER 34

Joe pulled the phone away from his ear and regarded it critically.

"Let me guess," John said. "She hung up."

Joe set the phone down on the console. "With gusto."

The SUV continued to roll along.

"So now what?" John asked.

Joe looked speculative, like he was still working that out. "I say we continue on. I'll try to talk to her in person."

"And if that doesn't work?"

"Then we will have had a nice drive together."

John's stress level had been climbing with every mile they drew closer to Barrington. "As far as I know, she doesn't have any weapons in the house."

Joe turned with a smile on his face. "So?"

John turned his attention back outside. "At least the odds of her actually killing us go down somewhat."

Allie, brimming with frustration and angst, decided to go to the one place where she could be alone and hopefully find some peace. The screen in her bedroom window was easy enough to remove. She climbed out and walked to the street, keeping low so she couldn't be seen by her mother. The brief statement about bees didn't even adhere to her memory in the midst of everything else that was happening. She started walking briskly, almost hoping in a strange way that she ran into Brad and Lonnie. She was in a fine mood to deal with them now.

Father Joe hung up the phone after Kemina didn't answer, hoping he hadn't initiated something that would turn out to be no more than a wild goose chase. "How much further?"

John consulted a mileage marker as it zipped past. "Not that far. How fast are you driving, anyway?"

"Time flies when you're having fun, John. You know what a delight I am to be around."

"Everyone knows about that. You're going to want exit 58, Montpelier."

"I'll keep an eye open."

"Father Joe?"

"What is it, John?"

"What if I can't get the girl to come? Then what do we do?"

The big man grunted. He was ready to get out and stretch. "Hmm. Well, we'll go anyway. Have a nice walk in the northern woods, enjoy the scenery, and have a look at the thing. Maybe we can find some of this magical fruit on the ground."

"Okay."

"You're staring at me, John. Why?"

"Would you try it?"

"Hmm?"

"Would you eat some of the fruit if we find any?"

"Do you think this is a personal quest for my benefit?"

John shrugged. "I don't know. Just curious."

"I don't think so. As far as I'm aware, my health is decent for a guy who's carrying around a few extra pounds. Besides, my life is in God's hands."

"And the visions?"

"John, they scare me a little bit. Suppose they're real in some way. Maybe I'd learn something about myself or my life that I don't want to know."

"Tell me about it."

"A little too personal, eh? Sorry. I'll tell you what, though, John. If we get some fruit, I might have somebody look at it. You know, analyze it."

John nodded. "I considered that. I know a guy who works at an agricultural college in the lab."

"That's a start."

"What about the lady from your church? The one who is sick?"

Father Joe nodded. "Unofficially...I'd offer her some. No promises, no guarantees."

"Would she try it?"

"In her situation? My heavens, yes. She'd try anything."

After a brief comparison, John decided to stop feeling bad about his life situation. It was becoming a tedious backdrop anyway. "Don't miss that turnoff."

Enough time had elapsed. Kemina braced herself and walked to the closed door. She started with a soft tap. "Allie?"

Not a sound in response.

"Allie, can I come in?" Kemina knew the door didn't lock, but wanted permission regardless.

"Little one, please. We need to talk."

Still absolute silence.

"Allie, I'm coming in." She turned the knob and swung the door open slowly, peering into the room as she did so. Allie was nowhere to be seen.

"Allie?" Surely she wasn't hiding under the bed. That would be too childish for her daughter. That was when Kemina saw the screen lying on the blanket.

"Allie?" Her voice reflected full-blown panic. Where had Allie gone in her emotionally distraught state? And worse yet...what about the bees?

"How about some directions?"

"See the traffic lights coming up? You'll want to turn right three blocks after we reach them. The street you want is called Mansfield Avenue." They had reached Barrington and John's stress levels were climbing dramatically.

"I can do that. Then what?"

"Drive straight. Just before town ends, you'll see a small apartment building on the left. Pull over and park on the side of the road while I run in."

Joe continued to drive along.

"John, a thought occurs to me."

"Do you wish to share with me?"

"Since you and this lady have had a very recent emotional run in, how about I go to the door instead of you?"

"You?"

"Why not? I deal with people every day, often while they are under duress of some sort. She may have an immediate bad reaction once she sees you, and that might be hard to undo. Let me try to break the ice and introduce her to our mission. If I fail…I can bear the brunt of her anger. What do you say?"

"Works for me." John looked with some degree of dismay at the police cruiser parked on the edge of the front lawn. "I wonder what that's all about. Pull over here."

Father Joe stopped, putting the car in park. "You weren't expecting trouble, were you?"

"No. Not at all."

Father Joe shut off the engine. "She wouldn't have caller ID'd you and called the police to make a complaint?"

"I don't think so."

"I only ask, because if she did, this would be a bad time to make an unannounced appearance."

"Father Joseph?"

"What, John?" he replied.

"Kemina handles knives for a living. Be careful."

Officer Moody had taken the call about the missing girl. He was as thrilled as Kemina was to see that he was the one who responded. If only his shift had ended just an hour sooner, he would have been off duty and home safe.

Moody hadn't gotten far with his preliminary investigation. The woman was borderline hysterical on top of exhibiting discernable distrust in him. That he understood. Maybe he had it coming. Nonetheless, he just wanted to get this wrapped up and go home.

"Ma'am, I need you to relax. You need to give me clear answers to my questions in order for me to help you. Understand? Just take a few deep breaths and try to calm down, if for no other reason than for your daughter's sake."

She nodded quickly, hyperactive and not really processing what he said.

"Okay, good. Now, you went into your daughter's room and found that she was gone and the screen was out of the window, correct?"

"We had a fight. She was angry. She isn't thinking clearly." Kemina sobbed as she caught her breath. "I told her about the bees but she didn't listen. What if she gets stung? I heard the news. Will it kill her? If so, it will be my fault!" Now she completely broke down.

Moody knew all about the bugs as far as the issue they created. But he didn't know anything about the bugs themselves. "Ma'am, that's not likely to happen. Look at it this way—the sooner we find her, the safer she will be. Can you please try to answer a few more questions? If you don't know the exact answer, that's fine. Just tell me what you do know, all right?"

Once again, she responded with fast nods of her head. This time, it was accompanied by intermittent sobs.

"Okay, good. Now, where would Allie go when she isn't at home? Maybe a friend's house?"

Now the head was shaking just as fast as the previous nods. "No. She doesn't have any friends. That's my fault too. We should have never come here!"

Moody kept his expression stoic and dealt with his frustration internally. "None at all? Nobody she hung around with ever?"

Kemina regrouped slightly. "There is one girl. They talk at school."

"Do you have a name?"

"Yes," Kemina replied. "It's, uh, Zoey. Zoey Chandler."

Moody nodded. Now he was getting somewhere. "I know the family. I'll head over there and check to see if she is there or has been in contact recently."

"But what if she isn't?" Kemina was still far from settled.

"It won't take me long to check. Before I go, can you think of anywhere else?"

Kemina looked haunted. She had a growing feeling of impending doom and had no idea why. "I..." She started sobbing again. "No, nowhere else."

Moody knew that under normal circumstances, the police wouldn't even consider her to be officially missing so soon after she had last been seen. But between the bees and the fact that Moody didn't want to give any appearance of disinterest, he would be happy enough to find the girl. Maybe it would add some integrity to his status in their eyes.

"All right. I'm going to run over there right now. I'll let you know what I find out. If you think of anything else that could be of importance, or if Allie returns, call the station immediately. All right?"

Kemina sobbed and nodded.

Moody exited the house with no small amount of relief and made a straight line for his cruiser, an endeavor destined to fail. A stocky man wearing a clerical collar effectively blocked the sidewalk.

"Excuse me, Officer, but is everything all right?"

"Yes, Father. Well, a girl has gone missing but only a short time ago. If it wasn't for the bugs, we wouldn't even be investigating it yet." Moody made his way past by walking on the grass.

"Bugs?"

"You didn't hear about the temporary shutdown?"

"Can't say as I have," he responded.

"You shouldn't even be outside." If he had more time, Moody may have allowed the conversation to continue. As it was, he hopped in his cruiser and sped off.

Puzzled, Father Joe continued up the walkway. He knocked with vigor on the outer screen door.

A woman materialized almost immediately, desperate longing for good news painted across her face. It faded when she realized she had no idea who this man was.

"Hello. Are you Kemina?"

"Who are you?" she asked. "Do you have news about Allie?"

"Unfortunately, no. I am Father Joseph. We talked on the phone earlier."

Dawning crept into her eyes, followed by a darkened countenance.

Father Joe had inserted himself into emotionally charged situations before, and he was not afraid. "May I come in for a moment?"

"This is a very bad time," she responded.

"I'd like to talk about Allie."

The name of her daughter was like a key that opened the door of reluctance, even though she really didn't fully understand the implication.

"Allie?" She reached for the door and unlatched it.

Father Joe stepped in, careful not to invade her space. "Yes. Actually, she's why I'm here."

The outside light coming through the door darkened and John appeared.

"What happened to Allie?" he asked.

Kemina had an ocean of conflicting emotions suddenly overwhelm the dam which was holding them back. She burst into tears. "John, she's gone!"

CHAPTER 35

Specht pulled back onto the road and left the orchard. "Tune to the local police frequency on the radio, will you?" he said.

Collins reached for the controls. "This chemical seems to have worked, but what about the bugs in town? They can't spray there."

Specht began to accelerate. "I don't know. Ghost was both boastfully arrogant and painfully evasive. If I had to guess, I would say they haven't figured that out yet."

Collins frowned. "So much for permanent resolution. When are we ever going to get to go home again?"

"As soon as Barrington is safe," Specht said.

"We're just on the sidelines, watching it all unfold," Collins lamented. "And we don't know anything about bugs. I question our effectiveness to the point of wondering how to justify our continued presence. I feel like we're at a point where we're getting in the way."

Specht nodded slowly. "I agree. Even our reports are laced with uncertainties and huge gaps in information."

Collins finished tuning the radio and it immediately crackled to life.

"Control, Car Four."

"Go ahead, Car Four."

"Regarding missing person, she was not at the Chandler residence. I'm returning to 422 Mansfield to talk with her mother again. Is anyone else available to assist? I'd like to wrap this up before dark, especially with the bug issue."

"Car Four will be on active duty in fifty minutes. I can send them to the residence, over."

"Okay, Roger that. If the status of the search changes, I'll let you know."

"Ten-four."

The radio went silent. Specht looked briefly at Collins while he drove. "You want to do something more meaningful than chasing bugs?"

Collins already had her mind made up. "Like finding a lost girl?"

"Bring up 422 Chandler on your GPS," Specht said as he accelerated.

The more Moody questioned Kemina about other possible places where Allie could be, the more hysterical she became. Father Joe tried to interject several times, only making the situation worse. John stood near the doorway, trying not to get caught up in the chaos.

Incredibly, two more people showed up, claiming to be from the FBI. Their presence didn't make sense and added to the confusion.

John started to tune out the noise and that's when it happened. In the midst of the chaos, commotion and stress, John felt himself fading away from the scene. He grew peaceful as he was transported to a very different place. The bedlam faded, and a quiet, pastoral scene reappeared.

"*It's the tree, John.*" The handsome young man was before him once again, giving his cryptic proclamation.

"*Protect the girl.*"

The mental fog was clearing. John knew what the words meant! The thought hit him like a bolt of lightning. He screamed with such enthusiasm, that even in the midst of the unfolding fracas, they all fell silent, giving him their undivided attention. "Quiet!" In a non-sequitur of unfathomable magnitude, John broke into a happy smile. "I know where she is."

The room remained completely silent.

"How can you know?" Kemina walked towards him, a frantic blend of hope and despair smeared across her tear-stained face.

"She went to the Dream Tree."

Kemina stood mute. She offered no argument. Of late, everything had been revolving around the tree.

"What tree?" Moody demanded.

John turned his attention to the officer. "It's a bit of a long story. Can I tell you on the way?"

Moody shook his head. "I can't bring you with me. Just tell me where it is. I know the area well—I'll find it."

"It's in the middle of a forest. You'd never find it."

"Come on," Specht said. "We're wasting time. You can ride in my car."

Before Moody could respond, Kemina interjected. "I'm going as well! She's my daughter."

Moody held up his hands. "Out of the question. It could be dangerous for all we know. You might slow us down and impede this entire process. For your daughter's sake, you must stay home."

"But I can't just sit here waiting! Please let me go."

Moody pointed at John. "Only him, and only because he knows the way. Let's go."

"We'll bring her back," John said as he walked towards the door.

The group exited and the apartment was instantly and uncomfortably quiet.

"May I make a suggestion?" Father Joe asked.

Kemina swung her eyes his way, almost like she'd forgotten he was there. "I don't know what to do."

A woman of action, Joe thought. *She needs to be preoccupied.* "I understand you run a restaurant here in Barrington. I have a suggestion if you are interested."

She looked baffled. "I don't understand. Casa Comida is closed. And I can't think about other things until Allie is safely home."

"I know John well. He won't let them come back without her. What I was thinking was that they all, including Allie, might be hungry when they return. Perhaps having them meet up at the restaurant would be nicer than here in the apartment. It would be a crowded affair in this space. And think of what a fine gesture it would be to provide the rescuers with a small token of your appreciation. John tells me it is the finest Mexican food in the entire country."

Her mouth started to move, but no words came out.

"I can drive you. My car is parked out front. It would be my pleasure."

"But…"

"I'll text John and let him know for all of them to meet us there. I know my way around a kitchen. I would be honored if you would allow me to help in the preparation."

"I suppose…"

"Besides, I'd love to hear your story. You know—how you and Allie came to be here and start the restaurant."

Kemina sighed. "I suppose standing here won't help Allie. Unless she comes home on her own."

"Does she have a key?" Joe asked.

Kemina nodded.

"It won't be hard to find her here if she does return. I think it would be helpful for both of us to stay occupied for the next little while. Besides, I'm new to this town. I wouldn't have a clue where to go on my own."

"I guess." Kemina still didn't seem committed to the idea.

"Splendid!" Joe exclaimed. "In that case, please follow me."

"Let me grab my keys."

Joe started moving slowly towards the doorway, unwilling to give up the momentum he had just achieved. Keeping her busy would be helpful in maintaining her peace of mind, and building some trust might help convince her to let Allie help them get some fruit. Besides, he was keen to try some of this food John had been raving about.

Specht started rolling but needed more information before he could proceed far. This entire scenario had unfolded very quickly. "Where is this tree located?"

"In a small forest just outside of town. Drive straight ahead. I'll give you directions as we go."

"I'm Specht by the way, in case you missed our introductions back at the house."

"I'm John."

The blond lady turned towards them. "I'm Collins. John, I hope you don't mind if I ask a question, but there's still a lot I don't understand about what's happening here. Who exactly are you? I mean, what's your relationship with the family?"

"I'm a friend," John said. "And I know Allie well. She's a great kid."

"How old is she?" Collins continued.

"Thirteen," John answered.

"Has she run away before?" Collins asked.

John didn't know the answer. "I'm honestly not sure, but I would say it seems out of character for her. She has been to the tree a number of times before; that much I know."

"What's the attraction?" Specht asked, genuinely curious. "Doesn't sound like a typical hang out spot for a teenager."

"That's a hard question to answer in twenty words or less," John said.

Collins looked over her shoulder. "Is the question of any importance as far as finding the girl is concerned?"

John didn't want to open the floodgates as far as the tree's more unusual traits were concerned. He needed to say something that wouldn't spark a lot of intrigue and follow up questions. "It's not out of the question that she might have climbed it."

Neither Specht nor Collins liked the sound of that. If the girl had fallen, it would account for her not returning home.

John leaned forward, pointing. "The road turns to gravel but keep following it. Our target is a grouping of trees at the back of a field. That's where it is."

Specht started to accelerate. "You called it Dream Tree earlier. Why?"

John used the easy answer. "That's what Allie calls it."

"Do you know the reason?"

John squirmed. "The fruit is edible." It was hardly a concise answer, but John hoped that it would somehow suffice. If the conversation about the tree got any deeper, things would get weird. "And quite delicious. I suppose you could say it was dreamy."

"A fruit tree?" Collins said. "So what are we talking about—apple, pear, peach...?"

"I've actually never seen anything like it before. I don't know what it's called."

"It's early in the season for it to bear fruit," Specht added.

John hadn't thought of that. "I guess you're right. It never crossed my mind."

Specht had heard enough. They needed to refocus on the task at hand. "Let's find that girl. John, can you update where I'm heading?"

Allie never reached the Dream Tree. It was her intended target, but it had been rendered unapproachable. She had been walking briskly through the mulch, her mind focused on the many strange things that had just exploded in her previously uninteresting life. The loss of John had hit her the hardest. Allie needed to eat some fruit and experience the peace it would give her. Maybe she could start to work things out with a little help from the tree. A giant bug flew past her, the sound of its heavy wings loud enough to grab her attention and set off an internal alarm. She froze in place, eyes wide and all senses on full alert. She was back in the moment now.

The bug was freakish in both size and coloration, and even without the warning issued back at the school, Allie would have instinctively known that this thing was trouble. It had made a tight turn and was clearly intent on flying back directly towards her. She could only imagine one reason for that. And she had nothing to use to defend herself. A long dead branch lay on the ground beside her. She leaned down, snapped off the end of it and then held it low, arms cocked and ready.

The bug seemed either confident or stupid in its aggression as it flew in a straight line towards her face. This was a one shot chance, Allie thought before forcing herself to refocus. She remembered the story about the troops who were told to wait until they could see the whites of their enemies' eyes before opening fire. She knew her timing and her aim had to be exact.

Now! She swung as hard as she could and was rewarded with a hit. One small twig actually snapped under the weight and momentum of the bug, but the slightly thicker branch held. The impact knocked the bug into the leaves where it buzzed angrily as it tried to right itself and get back airborne. That was an option Allie decided to remove. She stepped on it despite her light shoes, grinding it into the ground with all her strength, then lifting her foot and looking at it in disgust.

While she stood observing the remnants of the bug, another noise reached her ears. It too was a buzzing sound, but rather than close and acute, it was distant and soft. She turned her eyes towards the Dream Tree and beheld a horror.

The tree was swarming with bugs. A dark, swirling cloud had completely enveloped it. Bare tips of some branches were visible and gave voice to what was happening. The bugs were stripping it of everything green.

"Why?" Allie uttered in anguish. The magnitude of her own vulnerable situation then occurred to her. There were thousands of bugs within a few seconds of flying time from her and she was standing in the open. Slowly, she stepped behind the nearest tree trunk.

Brad and Lonnie had been on their way to Allie's apartment when they saw her walk out to the sidewalk and turn to go out of town. Brad in particular was furious about being kicked out of school because of some foreigner who had no business living in Barrington in the first place. It was true that he had been told to stay away from her, but he was thinking even less clearly than usual. He wasn't sure what they were going to do to her, but he had a message to convey. Maybe when they were done, she would move back to Mexico. That should resolve his problems.

Delighted with this unexpected opportunity, the two had followed her out into the country. Here she would be isolated and they would be free to exact any kind of revenge that they wanted. They almost rushed her several times, but patience paid off big time. When she walked back into the trees, it was almost like she was intentionally giving herself to them.

They crouched in the corn, staying partially hidden. Why she hadn't turned and seen them was a mystery to Brad. He didn't know about her distracted state. All he knew was she had gone to a place where she would be unseen and unheard from the rest of the world. This was going to be good.

CHAPTER 36

Allie heard the sound of leaves being disturbed by a heavy source—a source that didn't seem to be concerned about alerting the bugs.

"Hey, Mexicano girl."

She couldn't believe it. The thought that she had to worry about these two dolts appearing here never occurred to her. As bad as their presence was, it wasn't what painted the look of fear on her face.

"Quiet!" she hissed.

Brad had slowed his approach to a more methodical pace. They had her now. If she ran, that might even be more fun. He fantasized about laughing as he caught up to her and pushed her down. Then the real fun would start.

"What did you say to me?"

"The bugs will see you." Her voice was a whisper.

"Nice try." Brad turned to his accomplice. Lonnie was staring off into another direction. "Are you hearing this bullshit?"

Lonnie was standing transfixed. Brad followed his line of sight and what was left of the Dream Tree came into view. The sight of it was unlike anything he had seen in his life. "What the hell is that?" Brad asked.

Allie had little doubt that they would draw the attention of the bugs in some blundering, unthinking way. She slowly started walking towards the direction of the road while Brad and Lonnie's attention was on the tree. She kept the tree trunk between her line of sight and the bugs as best she could.

"That's a lot of bugs," Lonnie said.

Brad was thinking the same thing. "Are those the bees they were talking about at school?"

Lonnie didn't know. He continued to be mesmerized by the sight of them.

Brad grabbed him to get his attention. "Come on. Let's drag her to a safer place and do what we came to do."

The spell of the bugs was broken. Lonnie turned and looked at Allie. Brad had been talking about the various things he planned to do and Lonnie was intrigued by some of them. "Okay. Let's do it."

Brad swaggered over to where Allie now stood. "You gonna go where we tell you, or do we have to drag you?"

Allie's eyes were wide. "Are you crazy? Hide before they see you."

Brad laughed. "I'm not afraid of some bugs." He turned and looked at the swarming mass. "Kiss my ass!" he screamed. He smiled and worked on a nonchalant appearance. "See? Besides, you've got bigger problems."

Lonnie turned and ran, his feet crunching loudly through the dry leaves.

"Hey!" Brad yelled. "Get back here!"

Brad might have been too dull to know what that meant, but Allie wasn't. She looked around wildly for any kind of hiding place. She raced off as fast as she could towards the first thing that caught her eye.

"Damn it! Stop or I'll pound you!" Brad took off in close pursuit.

"Run!" Allie screamed. "They're coming!"

Brad initially assumed her words were some sort of attempt to distract him. The urgency in her voice created a twinge of doubt. He glanced over his shoulder and felt fear overtake him. A cloud of bugs, large and freakish looking, was flying directly towards him. "Oh shit!"

Allie had noticed a large tree that had somehow fallen over. It lay on its side, the top branches somewhat compressed on top of each other, forming a rough shelter. Although no longer green, the leaves were still in large part attached to the branches. Allie dropped to the ground and scampered into the pile while Brad ran past, screaming and crying. Allie grabbed handfuls of leave litter and covered herself as best she could. Her good fortune was Brad's demise. He drew the bugs past her as they continued to overtake him.

Brad felt a bug land on his head and he swatted it frantically out of his hair. This effort further slowed him, and another bug stung him on his left shoulder. The pain was phenomenal, like he had been struck by a car. Shrieking, he fell to the ground and was enveloped by the swarm. Multiple stings occurred all over his twitching body, and the pain, unfortunately for Brad, was indescribable. He would agonize over the memory of this moment for the rest of his life.

Allie lay under the leaves, trying to remain unmoving, listening to the tortured sounds coming from Brad. She found sympathy for her tormentor in her heart, and fear for what might happen to her once he had been sufficiently disabled. She had no idea how she was going to get out of this mess.

She regretted running away. She regretted her anger towards her mother and the breakup of the relationship with John. Worst of all, she regretted that no one knew she was here.

"This is it," John announced. "Pull over."

The two cars stopped and everyone quickly exited the vehicles.

"What now?" Moody seemed anxious to assert some sort of control over the situation.

"A short walk through the field," John said. "The tree we're looking for is in those woods beyond."

"Lead us, John," Collins said. They had no time to waste on this cop who seemed determined to start some sort of macho pissing contest. They could find the girl first, and then he could beat his chest or take credit or do whatever made him feel better about himself.

John started into the corn. "Follow the rows straight back. It's way easier than trying to cross through them. We'll make a small adjustment when we come out."

They walked with purpose down the rows, brushing the long green leaves out of the way. John couldn't wait to find Allie and return her safely to Kemina.

He didn't expect a mending of their relationship, but at least he would feel better about himself than the last time he left.

"Who's that?" Collins asked, her eyes still the sharpest of the group.

Someone had exited the trees and was running in the field towards them.

Moody took a few moments to confirm his initial reaction. He knew who the boy was.

"Lonnie! Over here!"

Specht held up his hand. "Everybody stop. Let's wait until we sort this out before advancing any further."

The boy reached them, gasping for air.

"Where's Brad?" Moody asked. Everyone noticed Allie was no longer his first priority.

Lonnie looked back towards the forest. "The bugs. They chased us."

John recognized the boy and had an unrepressed feeling of unease that wasn't solely because of the bugs. "Who else is in there? Is Allie there too?"

Lonnie nodded, eyes wide and mouth gaping, gulping deep breaths of air. "Yeah."

Specht and Collins were the only two of the group that had seen these things in action and knew what the results would be.

"Hold on," Specht said. "These things are extremely dangerous and aggressive. If a person gets stung even once, they are instantly incapacitated. It's too dangerous for us to go any further."

John couldn't believe what he had just heard. "Allie is in there. We can't leave her there. She's only a child and she's completely unprotected."

"And so is…my nephew," Moody pleaded.

That revelation drew a long, hard look from John. Their previous interaction, when viewed through this new lens, became even more reprehensible. He knew resolution would have to wait. Moody would pay the price for his biased and personal attack on Allie, but not now. "I'm going after her. You all suit yourself."

"John," Collins said, her voice calm and measured, "you really don't want to get stung by these things. Even one sting and we've got another victim to rescue. You'll be no help to Allie if that happens, trust me."

John had a message replaying in his head—a remnant of brighter times spent with this special family that he would soon leave and break all ties with. It was also a gift from the very tree he was now about to see. *A great danger will come. Protect the girl.* "I'm going. The rest of you can put together a plan B or something like that. Go back to the cars for safety."

"I'm coming too." Moody stepped up and stood beside John. "Maybe we can help each other."

John still felt loathing for this man, but had to respect his courage. "Okay. I have two suggestions. First, let's spread out. That way we can cover more ground in terms of finding the kids and we will present slightly smaller targets for the bugs to hone in on. Second, and I know this will seem counterintuitive, let's move slowly and try to stay behind cover. Once they know we're here, it's game over."

"The wind should be in our favor. It won't blow our scent in their direction."

"Now you're thinking," John said.

They started walking towards the trees and the uncertainty of what awaited them.

Kemina unlocked the back door of Casa Comida and switched on the light.

"Follow me. I will get you seated at a table first. Then you can see a menu."

"Nonsense," Joe said. "A coffee would be wonderful, and anything beyond that is excessive." He meant it, but didn't entirely discount the value of keeping her busy at this stressful and uncertain time. "If food is going to be prepared, you decide what and when based on your convenience." Joe was certain from what little he already knew about her that she would ignore his statement.

"Follow me." She led him through the kitchen into the dining area.

Father Joe slowed as they emerged, looking around in appreciation. "Say, this is nice. I love the way you've decorated."

"Thank you. Now, have a seat. You can sit here at the back so we don't draw attention from passers-by. I don't want people trying the door or knocking on the window. Get comfortable while I grab a menu."

"My pleasure."

She returned in a moment and set the menu before him. "While you look at this, I'll put on coffee."

"Thank you so much." Father Joe sat, noting that the chairs were comfortable. "What a wonderful place this is."

"Thank you," Kemina said from the counter.

"Listen, why don't you sit for a minute?" Joe asked. "You've had a very trying day."

"Oh no. Cooking for you will be a pleasure for me."

"Not even for a few minutes between tasks? I'd love to hear about how you came to own this beautiful place. You must have quite an interesting story to tell."

She shrugged. "It is not something you would enjoy. Just life unfolding. You must hear these stories every day."

"Not at all. I can't imagine anything that would make me happier. I have a few questions as well, if you would be so kind as to accommodate me."

He had made it seem that *she* was doing *him* a favor if she agreed to open up. She knew what he was doing, but her defences started to collapse regardless. "Perhaps a few minutes."

Joe pushed out the chair beside him. "Very good. Why don't you sit here? That way we won't have to yell at each other across the table

She sat, but looked uncomfortable.

"First of all, what was your inspiration for this decor? I love it! Is it based on something specific or did you come up with it yourself?"

She paused to formulate her response.

Joe leaned in closer. "The plants are a great touch. It gives it such a natural, fresh feeling. It seems almost like I'll be dining al fresco. Was that what you were going for?"

She smiled. "You are too kind. It is a look that I enjoy. I like plants. They don't do well in the apartment, so I grow them here."

Kemina picked up the menu and handed it off to Father Joe's now extended hand.

"Thank you," he said, turning his attention back to verbal distraction. "So you're telling me these are all real?"

"Oh yes. These kinds are easy to care for. It takes no skill on my part."

Father Joe was looking at her in rapt attention, as if her every word was important. He could have been holding an audience with a celebrity. He closed the menu and set it on the table. "Excellent! Listen, why don't you make me whatever you think would be appropriate. I'm not familiar with most of the items on here anyway. I guess I really don't know what real Mexican food is. I trust you enough to let you choose."

"Hmm. Well, I have done most of the prep work for tomorrow's special. Would you like to try that?"

Father Joe beamed. "Yes! I can hardly wait."

Kemina stood and headed towards the counter. "Here, you can start with coffee. It is ready now."

Joe really was excited to test her cooking. In truth, he was starving. "So, Kemina, tell me how you ended up in Barrington."

Kemina returned with the pot, looking a little more relaxed. As she poured, she commenced talking.

CHAPTER 37

John and Moody entered through the trees a good distance apart. They could still see each other so as to communicate with gestures if necessary and not lose complete contact. Their mutual fear of the bugs was apparent by their slow and furtive movements.

"All right, Allie," John whispered to himself. "Where are you?" He experienced a moment of panic when the surroundings looked completely unfamiliar. He had only been here once before and the now setting sun was presenting more evidence of its decline inside the trees. It was already gloomy and that would soon transition to darkness. There wasn't time to waste. He thought they were moving in the right general direction and so he continued his slow progression.

If noise wasn't a concern for alerting the bugs, he'd have been yelling by now. He stopped and listened, hoping Moody wouldn't read too much into the pause. The last thing he wanted was for the cop to yell at him. Hearing nothing but soft, natural sounds of the forest, he continued walking. All senses were being strained to the limit, but so far no signs of the bugs. Imagining Kemina's joy and relief when he returned Allie safe and sound was enough motivation to keep him going.

Kemina read aloud from the menu insert. "Tomorrow's special is beef tenderloin with shiitake mushroom and Swiss chard stuffing. Oh, and of course, my special guajillo sauce."

Father Joe blinked in surprise. "What is that?"

"The most delicious thing ever. That's all you need to know."

"Sounds great, but complicated."

"No, not at all. I've already made up the sauce and the stuffing."

He was very tempted. "Do you think you'd be short tomorrow if we used some now?"

Kemina actually smiled. "No. I always make extra. I will put it on now."

"How long will it take?"

"Forty-five minutes."

"Perfect! Thank you so much. I can't tell you how excited I am."

"It also includes appetizers and soup. I have done some prep work on them as well."

Joe shook his head. "Oh no. That's asking way too much. Please don't go to all that trouble."

"The entire meal comes together as one. It is not a problem."

Here was a woman who was not easily swayed, Joe thought as Kemina disappeared into the kitchen. It was a good trait for someone leading an independent life.

John had come to a complete stop. He was convinced that he was lost. There was no sign of the Dream Tree and he began to fear that they had somehow walked past it. With little else in mind as far as a plan was concerned, he resumed a slow walk, hoping desperately for a sign of the tree.

From his vantage point, Moody had a clearer line of sight. He had never seen the Dream Tree before, but was instinctively sure this was it. The massive tree was covered with bugs, both on it and swarming around. He froze, terrified. And worse, he had no idea how to warn John without drawing attention to himself.

Kemina had served the soup and at Joe's urging was recounting the past decade of her life, nearing the point where she had lost her husband.

"You say this is mushroom soup with sautéed apples?" Joe said when Kemina paused to collect her thoughts. "I've never heard of it before, but I must say, it is heavenly."

"Thank you," Kemina said.

"So, Kemina," Joe managed in the brief respite between spoonfuls, "you were telling me about your life in Mexico. Please continue."

She stood. "In a minute. I must tend to the main course. I think you will be ready for it soon." She noticed and appreciated the gusto with which he was eating the soup.

John had stopped again. He managed to spot Moody and noticed he was stopped as well. The officer made a subtle gesture and John refocused in that direction. The Dream Tree came into focus. And it was swarming with bugs.

John's heart sank. If Allie had blundered into the proximity of the swarm, her fate might not be the happy ending he had been wishing for. How much danger was he in now? Were they already too close?

"John!"

His name hadn't been yelled or even said at a normal tone of voice. It was a strained whisper. But he had heard it distinctly. And the voice who called it was very familiar.

"Allie?" He swivelled his head slowly, feeling too exposed.

A small hand emerged from under a tangle of branches at the end of a fallen tree. "In here," the subdued voice said.

She's all right! John thought to himself. He took slow, cautious steps in her direction.

"Allie?"

"John, I'm under here. Crawl in before you get stung. The bugs are everywhere."

Sufficiently motivated, John dropped to his knees and crawled under the nearest branch. "Where are you?" he whispered.

"Under the leaves. It's a good hiding spot."

John plowed into the litter, slithering himself under it as best he could.

"John, you're back." Her voice carried emotion.

"Don't read too much into it. I'm pretty sure at this point that I'm losing my mind."

"I'm glad you're here," she said.

"By *here*, do you mean lying under a pile of leaves in the middle of a forest, waiting as the sun sets and praying I don't get stung by a swarm of bees? If so, I might have to respectfully disagree."

Allie managed a small giggle. Having John there made her feel infinitely better. "You know what I mean."

"Yes. I'm glad to be with you too. But you know what would make this all seem so much better?"

"No, what?"

John decided to be completely honest. "A plan." He had momentarily forgotten about Moody.

Moody lost sight of John. He had no idea what to do, so he opted for taking several slow steps backwards. Putting some distance between himself and the bugs seemed like a great idea. That was when he heard a sound like a human crying softly.

"Brad?"

He remained perfectly still, trying not to make a sound. He heard it again and refocused. There! The boy lay on the ground, motionless. Moody ran to him, making too much noise and drawing too much attention.

"Brad! Are you all right?" He crouched down and rolled the boy over. He didn't like what he saw. The expression on Brad's face was undiluted terror, his eyes wide and bulging. But he couldn't make an intelligible sound. All that came out was moaning and whimpering.

"Brad, talk to me. Are you hurt? Did you get stung?"

His lips moved but no discernable response came from them. Moody pulled his walkie-talkie out of its clip. "Base, this is Moody. Come in!"

The first bug to reach him discovered that the base of Moody's neck was exposed and made a great target. Moody felt like he had been speared. Uttering a choking cry, he toppled over onto the ground. More bugs followed the example of the first. The time of his torturing had begun.

"How are we going to get out of this, John?"

That was all he had been thinking about, but so far to no avail. "There are others that came with me, Allie. Police and FBI. They know we're here. Let's just stay still and quiet. They'll have a plan. And we're all right for now. This hiding place of yours is brilliant."

"Not really. It's the only thing I could think of on short notice."

"Why did you run away, if you don't mind me asking?"

It was quiet for too long. Then, "Because Mama sent you away."

"Oh." John wondered how to proceed without making a bad scenario even worse. "Allie, sometimes adult relationships can get really complicated. That's what happened here. Don't be too hard on your mom. She did what she felt she had to do."

Allie sniffled. "I thought it was going to be a happy ending. I thought it was all meant to be."

I've heard that part before, John thought to himself, recalling his vision. "I think it is, Allie. But sometimes it doesn't make sense to us. Hold on, ride out the storm as best you can and see what happens when you come out the other side."

"John?"

"What is it, Allie?"

"That's stupid."

Lying on the ground, waiting to be stung into a state of perpetual pain, John softly laughed.

Collins turned to Specht, frustration easily visible on her face. "It's been too long. Something bad has happened."

"It's getting dark. We know they go dormant once night falls. In a short while, we'll go in after them."

"What about help? Shouldn't we call for paramedics?"

Specht hated the idea of admitting to himself that all those people now lay in a state of torture while he waited safely in his car. Based on all other known contact with the bugs, that was the most likely scenario.

"Radio the Barrington Police. Tell them where Moody is and suggest an ambulance should be sent. They may have questions—try to answer them as best you can. I'm going to call Ghost and see if he's in the neighborhood. He may want to get in on this. By the time we sort through that, it should be dark enough. We'll grab some lights and look for them ourselves."

"We don't know where the tree is."

Specht looked over the seat. "This young man does."

Lonnie looked horrified over the suggestion. "Don't make me go back there," he pleaded.

Specht picked up his phone. "Then give us directions. We'll find it on our own. Don't worry."

Sure, Collins thought. *Just look for the bodies.*

"Look at this!" Joe exclaimed as he observed the steaming plate now before him. He shook his head in disbelief. "I don't suppose you could be talked into moving this fine eating establishment to Plattsburgh. You would have one faithful customer, I could guarantee that."

Kemina set a glass filled with pinkish liquid before him. "This may not be suitable for a man of the cloth. It's called Mexican Snakebite."

She waited for a response, but Father Joe had already picked it up.

"John can drive us back if it comes down to that." Joe took a sip. "Delightful! Kemina, it's perfect."

She smiled, bowing in acknowledgement of the compliment. "I have one more task and then I will join you."

She retreated back to the kitchen. Father Joe had no problem entertaining himself by enjoying this previously unknown version of Mexican food. When Kemina returned, his preoccupation with the meal made her feel more comfortable.

"Please, continue. You were telling me about your husband."

Either he was enjoying the meal, or he was a fine actor. Kemina chose to believe the former. She took a small sip of her own Snakebite before resuming her conversation.

CHAPTER 38

John had never had a creepier feeling. The forest was growing darker by the minute and he had no idea how they were going to get out of here safely. The air was getting cooler and he wished for a jacket or sweater. It was going to be a long night, but at least neither of them would be alone. He wondered if the bugs would settle down into the leaves for shelter over the night time period. He shuddered at the thought.

"John?"

"What is it, Allie?"

"Thank you for saving me."

John almost wished it was true. His self-respect could use a boost. "You were safe when I got here. If anything, you saved me."

"No. I was too scared to stay here by myself. I was going to jump up and run."

"Oh." John mulled over the possible consequences of her doing that. "Look, don't worry about it. We both seem to be safe for now. Somebody will come looking for us—we have to stay calm and quiet. Think you can manage that?"

"I can now that you're here."

John couldn't help but smile. "Good. I can do it with you here also. Thanks for the company."

"John?"

"Yes, Allie?"

"Are you really leaving forever?"

John didn't know if he should answer her question or try to deflect it and talk about something more uplifting.

"John?"

She's not a child, John thought. She deserves an answer. "Yes, it looks that way."

"Why? It was working so well before. What changed?"

"Oh boy. I'm not sure how to answer that."

"With the truth."

Ouch. John tried not to squirm and make extra noise in the leaves. "Okay. Fair enough. Allie, I screwed up. I thought I was being smart and I encouraged your mother to eat the Dream Tree jam. A lot of it, as a matter of fact. It affected her, Allie. She had a vision."

"Do you know what it was?"

"Yes. She told me that she saw your father. And in the vision, he seemed real to her."

"Really? Why is that a bad thing? Shouldn't it make her happy?"

"Allie, this is where it gets complicated. I think that your mom and I were...starting to fall for each other. Do you understand?"

"You were falling in love?"

"Something was happening between us. And when your mom saw your dad, it felt to her like she was being unfaithful to him. I think that's why she felt that I had to leave."

"Oh."

It grew quiet except for the night sounds of the forest.

"John!" Allie's voice had changed in tone. There was a degree of urgency in it.

"What is it?" he whispered in response.

"I hear somebody."

John hadn't heard anything. Too much of their own talking, perhaps. He strained his ears and was rewarded with a faint snippet of distant conversation. He couldn't make out the words, but he was sure it was a human voice.

"I hear it too. Allie, don't move yet. Let's wait and see if they get closer."

"What if they don't?"

"Let's go with a little faith on this one, shall we? Give it a minute or two and we'll see what happens."

They settled in for the longest two minutes of their lives.

Joe looked at his plate with absolute astonishment. "I'm a fool. I must admit it. I have lived my life thinking that Mexican food was tacos and the like. How can I have missed all of this? Oh, I have so much to make up for."

Kemina smiled. "I'm glad you like it."

"Please continue with your story. I'm finding it fascinating."

Kemina was finding herself both comforted and comfortable around this man. She refocused and resumed talking.

Amazing how the summary of one's entire life can be recounted in a matter of minutes, Kemina thought. She had all but reached the end of her tale, having just told the story of her fruit-induced vision. She broke down crying as she talked about seeing her husband, then sending John away after it ended.

Joe pondered. It was quite a tale. His curiosity and interest in the tree were even more pronounced now. But of more immediate concern was how to respond to this vulnerable lady.

"Kemina, do you think the vision was real?"

She nodded. "Yes." It was a quiet, subdued voice.

The level of detail was incredible. It matched John's experiences.

"Are you unhappy that it happened?"

She looked surprised at the question. "No. It was so wonderful to see him again."

"Not to dig up the most personal aspects of this, but you say that you and John spent the previous night together?"

She lowered her head in shame. "Yes. I...seduced him. It wasn't even his idea."

"Was your husband upset or angry?"

She looked back up. "What?"

"In the vision. Did he chastise you? Did he challenge you about it?"

"No..."

"The two of you shared an embrace?"

"Yes."

"Why wasn't he upset?"

"I...maybe there wasn't time for it to come up."

"Did he seem tense or distant?"

"No. He ran right over when he saw me."

"But not in an angry or confrontational way?"

She seemed a touch indignant. "No. He was never like that. He was a kind, gentle man."

"There you have it."

"Have what?" she said with a blank stare.

"He didn't know about it."

She hesitated. "Well, it had only just happened."

Father Joe shook his head. "No. You have missed the point."

"What point?"

"Kemina, *if* your vision was real, and your husband is in heaven, then he is separated from anything that happens in this world. He didn't know because he couldn't know. There could have been a nuclear war down here and he wouldn't have known about it. You see?"

Uncertainty painted itself across her face.

"Your relationship with him in this world has already unfolded and cannot be changed by anything you now do. Traditional marriage vows say *till death do us part*. You've fulfilled, and been released from, your vows and responsibilities. So has your husband. He will be up there biding his time, waiting for you to join him regardless of what happens here."

She sighed in response.

"Kemina, you've been through a lot. You can allow yourself to feel tired or sad. It's not a sign of weakness, you know."

"No. There is too much to do. I cannot stop or even slow down. Allie's life and future depends on me."

"Hmm. Can I ask you something rather personal?"

"You worry about that now after what we've just talked about?" Then, she nodded.

"Do you make a good living with the restaurant?"

"It has been getting better. We are busier now."

"I'm not surprised. Keep making food like this and you should do well. You've been here a year; it will take more time to get a reputation established."

"People can be reluctant to try something new," she said.

Joe nodded. "Especially in a smaller town. Most businesses have been operated by the same person or family for decades, and everybody knows them. That goes for restaurants as well, although my experience is that they tend to be a little more transient. I hate to say it, but the failure rate appears to be quite high. However, it seems that you have gotten over the initial hurdles and are now being accepted here in Barrington and subsequently on your way to long-term success."

He doesn't know about the eggs thrown against the window, Kemina thought. "I hope you're right."

"Allie! John!" Collins, unencumbered by her fear of bugs because darkness had fallen, proceeded with her usual confidence through the creepy forest. This was something she had never done after dark before. A repeat seemed unlikely.

John knew the voice. "Let's chance it, Allie. Follow me." The two of them emerged from under the tree, brushing off leaves and litter as they went. The beam of a powerful light washed over them.

"They're over here!" Collins announced, happy to see them moving. Somehow, they hadn't gotten stung.

John waved them over. "Are we glad to see you," he said, squinting under the glare of the light.

"Sorry." Collins lowered her beam when she realized she was blinding them. "And you must be Allie. What a pretty girl you are. We're so glad to see you both moving about."

Allie was very uncomfortable about the lights, the movement and the noise they were generating. "Shouldn't we get out of here?" she whispered.

"The bugs are not nocturnal," Collins was happy to share. "They basically go to sleep after night falls."

"Thank God," John said as Allie smiled a weak smile in appreciation of the news.

"No stings, obviously," Specht added. "How did you manage that?"

John smiled. "Allie is the brains of the outfit. She hid herself under a fallen branch and covered herself with leaves. I just followed her example."

Collins wondered why so simple a ploy would have worked so well. They still knew so little about these bugs. "Where are Moody and this other boy?"

"I don't know," John said. "He was maybe a hundred feet to my right as I was walking in. I lost sight of him when Allie grabbed my attention."

"I think Brad got stung," Allie added. "I heard it happen."

Collins swung her light around but initially saw nothing of interest. "There's an ambulance on the way. We need to find them."

"Do you two feel up to helping us?" Specht asked.

Allie, who had every reason to feel loathe to offer assistance to her antagonist, never hesitated. "Yes. I can show you the general direction Brad went."

Collins put a hand on Allie's shoulder. "Good girl. You come with me."

Specht nodded to John. "You stick close to me. We'll spread out a little and cover more ground that way."

"Lead the way, Allie," Collins suggested. "I'll be right here beside you."

"I think he went this way," Allie said.

"Watch your footing," John warned. "Twisting an ankle would be downright embarrassing considering the other dangers out here."

They moved steadily forward.

"There!" Allie pointed and Collins was surprised. This girl might have even better eyesight than she did.

They increased speed to a slow jog. Both Collins and Specht recognized the symptoms of a sting. John and Allie, newcomers to the horrors of the bugs, were shocked by what they saw.

Brad was looking upward, his eyes wide except for some swelling caused by a facial sting. His lips moved slightly, but only soft squeals and moans came out. The emotion his eyes conveyed would haunt them all for the rest of their lives.

"Help me to roll Moody over," Specht said to Collins as he knelt beside the prone officer. Between the two of them, they got him on his back. His face showed similar anguish.

"We need to speed this along," Specht said. "Send out another call. Officer down."

Collins pulled the portable radio free from its clip.

Allie turned to John as this was transpiring. "Will they be all right?"

John wanted to be encouraging, but didn't like what he was seeing. "Let's hope so."

CHAPTER 39

Kemina stared towards the front window of the restaurant with no real purpose in mind. She snapped upright like someone had slapped her.

"What is it?" Joe asked out of concern. And then he heard it too. An ambulance roared past, its siren shrieking.

"It's Allie!" she gasped. "They've found her."

Two police cruisers blasted past in close pursuit of the medical team. Joe could hear more sirens. It could have been for any number of different reasons, but the timing was suspicious. The hair went up on his arms.

"Come with me. We'll follow them."

The two literally ran out of the restaurant.

Specht stayed with the victims while Collins, John and Allie walked out to the car. When emergency responders began to arrive, Collins escorted them back to where Brad and Moody were, leaving John and Allie to rest safely in the back seat.

Soon there were an ambulance, two police cruisers and several fire trucks parked in a tight grouping, lights flashing blue and red. When Pastor Joe pulled up in his SUV, neither John nor Allie even noticed because of the chaos. At least, that was, until Kemina literally ran past them. Allie popped her door open.

"Momma!"

Kemina stopped in her tracks. She turned slowly around, unsure of whether the voice was real or some figment of her imagination. Then they made eye contact.

"Allie!" she shrieked and ran towards her. She gathered her daughter up in a bear hug. "You're all right!"

The embrace lasted for some time. John, despite much residual turmoil in his life that would still have to be dealt with, was enjoying the moment. When they finally disengaged, Kemina bent down and peered into the car.

"She's safe," John said. "She didn't get stung."

"Thank you," Kemina replied simply. She gave him a look that John couldn't discern, then straightened up and returned to hugging Allie.

Almost immediately, another person peered in through the open door. John didn't recognize him, but he didn't look like an EMT.

"I don't know you," he said. "I don't know any of you people. Where are Specht and Collins?"

"They're in the woods. They discovered a couple of victims back there."

The man nodded slowly. "Victims of what, exactly?"

"Insect stings," John said, wondering how this odd person had materialized in this place which had never hosted a gathering of any kind before.

"So that's where the little pricks went to hide."

John assumed he was referencing the bugs. "That's right. There's a tree back there that's literally covered with them."

The man looked in the direction of the trees. "We'll see about that," he said cryptically. He straightened up and walked off at a fast pace.

The encounter wasn't the strangest thing that had happened to John on this day, or even in the last hour for that matter. He easily forgot about the visitor and refocused on how glad he was to be safe.

Ghost was headed back to the forest, striding briskly and making a call as he went. Night strikes were well within the capabilities of the assets he had been given control over. With luck, all of them would have gathered in this one place; poor strategic planning on their part. He would see to it that these bugs would have a very bad night.

Once the initial joy of being reunited faded a little, Allie set about the business of negotiating the terms of what her relationship with her mother was going to be going forward. Kemina, usually unbending in all circumstances, was now open to debate. Once things were settled, she climbed into the car and sat in the seat beside John. He looked at her in mild surprise and obvious uncertainty.

"John…"

He waited, not knowing where this conversation was about to go. He noticed Allie standing close by, acting the role of encourager or possibly peace-keeper, depending on how this was going to unfold. Either way, she was positioned to hear every word and Kemina didn't object.

"I'm sorry."

John raised his eyebrows. Allie cleared her throat so that it could be easily heard.

"I'm sorry for how this all ended. I apologize for how badly I treated you. It was more my fault than yours."

John nodded. "Apology accepted. But I certainly played a role in initiating the negative stuff."

Allie reached in and poked her mother on the shoulder. "There's more."

The prodding was obvious and John knew Kemina was being forced. "No, don't worry about it. This is as close to a happy ending as we're going to get."

"John, you have saved Allie twice now. I can't imagine what may have happened to her without you. How you came to be such a guardian angel, I don't know. But you did. Thank you."

"Saving Allie might be the best thing I've ever done in my life. You have no idea how welcome you are."

Allie leaned in. "John, where are you spending the night?"

John's mouth started to move on its own until his mind caught up and realized he had no idea what the answer was. But what Allie seemed to be pushing for was something that was not going to happen. This was no fairy tale and there would be no perfect ending.

"I'll have to ask Father Joe. He's the driver."

Kemina, under Allie's withering gaze, forced herself to speak. "You can both stay with us. Allie and I will share my room. That leaves Allie's room and the couch for you two."

John was uncomfortable just thinking about it. "If we stay, I think we'll get a room in town at a motel."

Allie looked downcast. "Are you sure, John?"

"I am. But I do have one favor to ask while everyone is feeling so benevolent."

They both looked at him, waiting for the question.

After dropping Allie and Kemina off at the apartment and saying their awkward goodbyes, Joe started the arduous process of driving back to Plattsburgh. They were some distance down the interstate before any conversation was initiated. John was feeling deflated. He fully expected that he would never see Allie or Kemina again, despite the somewhat forced congeniality between them as he was leaving.

"When you showed up at my office, I didn't think for a moment you were about to take me on the adventure of a lifetime," Joe said.

John found a way to smile. "You spent most of your day biding your time with a stranger, waiting for us to return."

"I'm experiencing some details vicariously, and what of it? This was all too good to miss, regardless. I must profess that I don't understand most of it, though. I am sorry that I missed the tree."

"Which was the reason for going back in the first place," John said.

Joe nodded. "That's all right, John. We cannot always control circumstances, or how they impact our day to day existence."

John reached into the back seat, extricating his jacket. "I'm the poster child for that philosophy." He pulled a plastic container out of the inside pocket.

Joe gave John a hard look while somehow maintaining proper position on the highway. "Please tell me what you've got there."

Now John was grinning broadly. It felt good to be happy. Sometimes he wondered if he was forgetting what that was like. "The tree was unreachable tonight, but Allie's magic jam wasn't. Most of it got thrown away, but she had a container hidden in the back of the fridge. It's yours to use as you see fit."

Father Joe forced his concentration to stay on driving. "So the actual fruit is what this is made from?"

"Right. The jam is just as potent and I can personally vouch for that."

"The same fruit that caused visions and healed your back?"

"According to our current working theory, yes."

Father Joe's mind was whirling. "How much of it would someone have to eat in order to initiate this healing process?"

John shrugged. "I have no idea. This is not going to be based on any sort of precise science…you understand that?"

"I do."

"Then, if it was me, I would suggest eating all in this container. Every bite. The more the merrier."

Father Joe nodded. "It will never be any fresher than it is right now."

"I can't think of a valid rebuttal," John said.

"Do you suppose you could manage one more adventure before this day is done?"

John knew this night was already a wash as far as sleeping was concerned. "Could you come up with one that might have a happier tone to it?"

Joe nodded. "That's precisely the plan."

John actually fell asleep on the interstate. He didn't awaken until Father Joe's SUV had stopped in the driveway of a small, suburban home.

Everything looks dark, was John's first thought. He squinted at the digital time display on the dashboard. It was three in the morning. He'd been sleeping for hours.

"Did you call?" John said. "Are they expecting us?"

"I did not. I couldn't think of a way of explaining this over the phone."

John got it. *Hi, I'm stopping by with some magic fruit. Can you wait up for me?*

Joe undid his seat beat. "Ready for this?"

John had a nagging doubt. "What if it doesn't work? I mean, my case is a long way from definitive proof."

"You can be a bit of a killjoy, John."

"Sounds like something Theresa would say."

"Think positive thoughts, John. Now is not the time for negativity. Come on."

John exited the SUV, pausing to breathe in a lungful of cool, night air. Father Joe walked up to the door like he had every right to be there. Perhaps it was a side-effect of a lifetime of building relationships with people, John thought, wishing he had that kind of courage and self-confidence.

Joe started with a gentle rap. When that got no results, he graduated to a louder knock. A light came on before he had to resort to ringing the doorbell. A bleary-eyed young man whose face was covered with a discernable veneer of sadness swung the door open.

"Father Joseph?" His voice conveyed confusion.

"Hello Daniel. I apologize for this late intrusion. This fine gentleman with me is John, an old friend of mine."

He nodded in greeting, looking even more confused. "Hello."

"Hi." John was feeling uncomfortable and nervous.

Father Joe put his hand on the man's shoulder. "Is Linda sleeping?"

He shook his head. "She's in bed, but it's hard to say. She's in and out a lot these days."

"I know this is unusual, but I wonder if we might see her."

He seemed to struggle with the request. "Sure. I guess." He stepped back out of the doorway. "Come in."

"We'll be quiet, won't we, John? We don't want to wake up the children."

"Absolutely." John said his response in a whisper.

"She's in here." They followed him down a hallway and into a small room where a hospital bed dominated the space.

That's not a good sign, John thought.

"Honey?"

A weak voice responded. "Who is it? Is someone here?"

"Yes. It's Father Joe." He left it at that, not knowing how to announce or explain John's presence.

"Father Joe?"

Joe stepped forward, into her field of view. "Hello Linda."

"Hi."

He sought, found and held her hand. "I apologize for this unannounced visit so late."

"That's okay."

She sounds awful, John thought. Her sentences seemed to max out at three words in length, as if that was all she had strength for.

"I brought someone with me. My friend John here."

Neither she nor her husband had a response.

"I also brought you something. It's like…a sort of natural medicine."

The room remained quiet.

"Oh?" Linda gave a weak reply.

"It's edible. A type of fruit that has…great nutritional value. We have some that was made into jam. I know that sounds like a poor reason to stop by in the middle of the night, but I believe it might help you to feel better."

Spoken like a man who has learned to measure his words, John noted.

"John, I don't suppose you could summarize what eating the fruit has done for you?"

The request was a total surprise. John didn't know that he would be responding to such a request in front of such a unique and vulnerable audience. All eyes swung in his direction.

"Oh. Ah…sure. Why not?" He cleared his throat. "I was having problems with my back. Severe problems. I couldn't work or do much of anything for that matter. I was told surgery was the only option but even that wouldn't fix the problem—just alleviate some of the pain. So, I tried this fruit when it was recommended to me by a friend. It …seems to have cured me. Or, at least, I feel way better. I haven't seen a doctor yet, so I don't know if the effects will be permanent or not. But I feel good. Completely back to normal, really."

Now the husband was becoming somewhat engaged. "You think it could help her?"

Joe held out his big hands. "We aren't certain. But I believe there is at least a possibility. Would you be willing to try it?"

"I can't eat much," the sick woman croaked. "But I could try a little."

Joe smiled. "Excellent." His gaze swung back to John. "What do you need to prepare it, John?"

He had the container in his hands. "Nothing really. Just a spoon."

"We walked past the kitchen on the way here," Daniel said. "Help yourself to anything you need."

So that's how it's going to be, John thought. *This guy probably will ask Joe if I'm crazy while I'm out of the room.* "Okay. I'll be right back."

The kitchen layout was typical enough. John had little trouble finding what he needed. It felt odd going through a stranger's kitchen in the middle of the night.

"Are you a burglar?"

The voice startled John and he almost dropped the important container he was holding. A small girl was watching him rustle through the drawer.

"Hi. No, I'm not a burglar. I'm John. I came with Father Joe for a quick visit."

"Okay."

Now what? "Your dad is up if you want to see him."

She didn't budge, but continued to stare.

"I'm just making a little food for your mom to eat."

"Okay."

The agreeable little urchin was stuck to the spot like glue. With all other options eluding him, he resumed his rooting through the drawer. Once a small spoon was in his hand, he popped open the container lid. The unique smell was recognizable. John realized that he would like to eat some himself. He fought off the urge, finishing his business.

"I'm going back to your mom's room now."

She nodded. As he took his first step, it became apparent she was going to follow. That was fine. She could be dad's problem.

"Here we go," John announced as he stepped back in to the room.

"Lucy," her father said. "What are you doing up?"

John took an obligatory stab at being apologetic. "I tried to be quiet."

"Come here, sweetie." The father scooped her up in his arms.

"Hi mommy," she said from her high vantage point.

"Hi," came the strained response.

Father Joe stepped in, taking control. "John, are you ready?"

"I am. It looks and smells good; just the way it's supposed to."

"Perfect. Linda, do you feel like trying a bite?"

She clearly didn't, but made an effort regardless. She struggled to get into a more upright position. "Maybe one. Dan, can you raise the bed up?" She was lying too flat, a position that wasn't conducive to eating.

He grabbed the small controller with his free hand. "Can you do it, Lucy?"

She snatched it from him. The head of the bed started to rise. It was obvious she had done this before.

Giving her a chance to be involved, John thought. *How sad that she would lose her mom at such a young age. She may not remember her at all by the time she grows up.*

"Okay, sweetie. That's enough."

Now what? John wondered. He stood there holding the plastic container in his hands.

"She probably can't hold that," her husband explained. "She might need a little help."

If John had been uncomfortable before, it was now exponentially worse. Father Joe intervened.

"Here, John. I can manage." He took the container and spoon, to John's great relief. "Say, this does smell rather good. Maybe I'll sample it myself if there's any left."

"I'm sure there will be," Linda said.

"Here," Joe said as if he did this sort of thing every day. "Let's start with a small one, shall we?" He offered the spoonful. She took it in, wincing as she stretched her mouth to receive it.

"Good girl. How was that?"

She held up a finger.

"My apologies," Joe offered. "I didn't mean to rush you." She swallowed. It seemed to be a bit of a process. "Well, what do you think?"

She smiled a little. It was polite and perfunctory. Both Joe and John were hoping for more. Much more.

"It was nice. Thank you."

"Linda, we believe the effects are in large part predicated by the amount you take in. The more, the better."

Her husband assumed a concerned look. "She may have trouble swallowing. The doctor said not to force it."

John was looking at her for any small sign of improvement.

"One more?" Joe asked. "Just a little one?"

"All right. One more." She scrunched up her facial expression and it became all too apparent that this would be the last bite.

He held the spoon, filled a little higher this time, extending it. She managed to get it in, but once again, there was a moment of struggle before she swallowed.

"That was a good effort, Linda," Joe said, his hopes of a miracle fading. She looked up at him, uncertainty now replacing weariness and pain as the predominant expression on her face.

Her husband recognized the change. "Honey, are you all right?"

"I'm fine." Despite her assurance, she gave every appearance to the contrary. "I just feel...funny."

John stepped forward, enthusiasm growing despite his weariness. "That happened to me too. Don't worry. It's a normal reaction. It means the fruit is working." Or at least that was what he hoped it meant. That had been his experience. God help them all if it had the opposite effect, killing her right here in front of her family.

She squirmed, readjusting her position on the bed. She flexed her hands. "Here, hand me that bowl, Father Joe. I think I can manage it."

Now there was a subdued excitement awakening around the room.

"Here you are." He extended it.

Her hands were shaking but usable.

John, calm and stoic on the outside, was suppressing a street riot of emotion. He wanted this to be a miracle for the sake of this woman and her family. Truth be told, he wanted it for himself as well.

"Let me know when I get to the point where you think I'm overindulging," she said. Her voice was a little stronger.

She managed a spoonful on her own. A small amount of jam fell onto the front of her nightgown, but no one reacted. She swallowed. A look of some concern came over her.

"Honey, what is it?" Dan stepped forward, ready to take the bowl away if she offered it.

She blinked as if to clear her vision. "I don't know. It's hard to describe."

"Are you in pain?" His voice was soft, but laden with subtle apprehension.

"No. It's like…I'm waking up." She looked around the room at random things. "It's as if everything is coming back into focus. It all seems so much more real somehow."

John had some idea what she was talking about.

"What did you say this was?" she asked.

Father Joe swung his eyes towards John.

"Oh. It's Dream Tree fruit."

"Dream Tree? Never heard of it." To everyone's delight, she took another mouthful, soon followed by a second.

"Don't overdo it," her husband said.

"I'm fine, Dan. Don't worry so much." Her hand was steady now. She continued eating.

John thought Father Joe's eyes looked a little moist. That was forgivable. How was one supposed to react while watching a miracle unfold?

She had graduated to steady consumption. For some reason, she made John think of a child watching Saturday morning cartoons with a bowl of cereal on their lap. The jam was now visibly diminished.

"It's the most she's eaten in a while," her husband said, sounding almost like he was in awe.

"I can hear you, you know." There was strength and defiance behind the humor in her words. She was shovelling it in with gusto now. "This is delicious. Can you get it in the stores? Where is it from?"

"It has limited availability," John replied, since he was the designated expert on the fruit. "We got it directly from the tree."

"How interesting." She ate like a lumberjack until the bowl was empty. Even John, who had more reason to know what was going to happen than the rest, was caught by surprise.

Father Joe reached in. "Here, let me take that, Linda. Looks like you're finished with it."

She looked embarrassed. "I did overindulge, didn't I?"

Joe was smiling. "Not at all."

Her husband looked stunned as he confirmed that the bowl had indeed been emptied by his wife.

"Can I tell you all something?" she asked, speaking in a hushed tone.

Everyone nodded, concern returning to a small degree.

"I am famished. I know I just had a bowl of fruit jam, but I am starving. Dan, this is the weirdest request I've ever made, but could you barbecue something for me?"

His jaw dropped. "Barbecue?"

"Yes. I know it's the middle of the night, but I don't think I can get back to sleep until I have something substantial to eat. Chicken would be fine. Steak if we have some."

"Steak?"

"Yes. And a baked potato."

Her husband took a moment to compose himself. John perceived that he was close to bursting into uncontrolled sobs. "I can do that. Are you sure?"

She nodded. "Oh yes. Positive. Do we have anything to make a salad? What about the rest of you? Is anyone else hungry?"

Father Joe gave up on any pretense of indifference, and wept.

"Father Joe!" she exclaimed when she turned to see him. "Are you all right?"

"Never better in my entire life." He had no problem smiling through the tears.

"I ask because you're blubbering like a baby. Say, somebody give me a hand. I need to stand up and stretch."

Joe had two strong hands, and quickly obliged. Her husband looked on, some degree of worry returning. "Be careful, honey. Don't overdo it now."

She was already swinging her feet out from under the covers and onto the floor. "Oh hush. Don't you have some food to prepare?"

She stood, as if trying out her legs for the first time. She tested them, finding them good. She extended her arms towards the little girl her husband still held.

"Here. Give Lucy to me."

His face couldn't hide his alarm. Lucy was heavy.

"It's all right," his wife insisted. "I'm fine."

He made the switch from his arms to hers.

"Mommy," the little girl said, snuggling into her mother's shoulder.

"There, you see? We're fine, aren't we, Lucy?"

"Yes," came the muffled reply. John realised that he couldn't take much more of this either, or he'd be crying too.

"Go and make me some supper then."

"All right. I'll see what I can find."

"Cook lots," was her parting instruction. She turned her attention to her daughter after he had walked out the door.

John cleared his throat to facilitate conversation. "I should warn you, it is not uncommon to have vivid dreams after eating that much fruit. So, if you experience something like a vision, don't be alarmed. It will pass. There aren't any other side effects that we know of. At least I didn't have any." *Except for reliving the memory of the visions*, he thought but didn't add.

Linda didn't seem fazed by his warning. "Well, I feel like getting out of this room. Want to go for a walk, Lucy?"

"Okay."

"Let's get your sister up. I want to see her too."

Father Joe cleared his throat.

"My friend and I have to go, Linda. Once again, I apologize for the late and unannounced visit."

She gave him a look. "Apologize? Are you serious?"

"If it's all right with you, I would love to stop by some time later tomorrow and see how you're doing. Would that be all right?"

"You are welcome anytime, day or night. Don't you ever doubt it."

"Very good. Enjoy what remains of your night and don't forget to get some sleep."

"Eventually," Linda said. "I feel like I have some catching up to do."

"We'll see ourselves out then."

Linda met John's eyes. "I'm sorry. What was your name again?"

"John."

"Thank you, John."

It was concise, but it was way more than enough. "You're very welcome." Most of what he had been through in the past few weeks just became worth it.

Father Joe was moving. "Come on, John. This day has been long enough."

John followed.

"By the way," Joe said as they walked towards the front door, "you're staying with me tonight."

Beats sleeping in the car again, John thought.

They exited. The garage door was open and the light on. Dan was tinkering with the barbecue, but stopped when they walked past.

"Father Joseph?"

"Yes, Dan."

"What just happened?"

Father Joe hesitated before responding. "Something good, I think."

"Was it a miracle?"

Here came the tricky part. "I hope so. A short-term one at least, wouldn't you say?"

He nodded, his eyes watery.

"I'll be back tomorrow. Let's see how she feels then. Maybe she should go back to her doctor, if she continues to feel good. Maybe they can tell us if it's a genuine miracle or not."

"Good idea."

"Enjoy your night, Dan."

They walked away, tired but fulfilled. John wondered if he'd be getting any sleep, despite the long day.

"It's not far now, but if I nod off along the way," Father Joe asked, "will you give me an elbow?"

John was feeling euphoric and fulfilled. Joe's request didn't instill any sense of panic.

"Since I have a vested interest in your driving skills, I shall commit to keeping you awake."

Joe looked over. "Thank you, John."

"For what? Promising to elbow you in the ribs?"

"No." His tone was serious. "For allowing me to have a small role in the most fascinating thing that I've ever been a part of in my entire life. It's all happened so fast. I don't profess to understand most of it, even now. You and I will have a nice, long talk tomorrow. I intend to pose a multitude of questions."

"I intend to be oblivious to most of the answers."

"I've missed you, John. That dry, sarcastic sense of humor sustains me."

They had reached the car.

"Then you'll have to do with limited sustenance for tonight," John replied. "My brain is mush."

Joe chuckled. "I feel like we've done God's work here tonight. It's a good feeling."

"As is sleep."

"Well then, let's be on our way."

CHAPTER 40

Ghost was not gifted with patience. The response to his call for a strike against the bugs was taking too long. Standing in the midst of the forest in the middle of the night wasn't the problem. It was the inaction that gnawed at him. The victims and emergency responders were all gone now, so he remained alone in the dark.

Overhead, the cover was breaking. Edges of individual clouds were becoming visible, illuminated by the brightness of the full moon now only partially hidden. A large, open section of sky was moving ever closer, bathing the landscape in crisp white light as it came. Ghost watched as the tree was suddenly under the glow of the moon's reflection. He stepped closer, fascinated.

"Not so hidden now, are you?" he asked aloud. The tree was absolutely covered in a living blanket of whatever these things were. There must have been tens of thousands. He continued to move slowly closer.

Relying on instinct, he kept approaching until his senses told him to stop. From this vantage point, he could see movement from the swarm. It was a writhing, undulating entity—a living green blanket choking the last vestiges of life out of the tree. The impact of the lunar illumination hadn't dawned on him. He wasn't experienced enough to know that much movement for the bugs was unusual for night, and heralded a much more demonstrative response.

The tree exploded.

Untold thousands of bugs took to the air simultaneously under the light of the moon, a sight both awesome and terrible. Knowing now that he had ventured too far into the danger zone, all Ghost could do was drop to the ground and cover his head with his hands. The effects of being stung were known to him, and he braced himself for what was about to happen. He wanted to remain strong and stoic, even in the face of unimaginable pain. He stiffened in anticipation and waited.

After a minute or so, the sound of small wings diminished to silence. Inaction rankled Ghost to the point of being willing to risk movement. He stood, although not completely upright—coiled for a burst of speed and action if required.

He saw nothing of the bugs.

The tree was completely barren. It looked like it had been dead for years. Ghost scanned all the nearby trees, looking for signs of the swarm. He could see nothing. The bugs had scattered to the four winds as far as he could tell and who knew where they would end up. Quickly forgetting his good fortune in not getting stung, and mumbling creative curses learned over the course of his military career, Ghost keyed his radio and called off the response team.

It was after ten the next morning when John awoke, the bright sunshine flooding in through the windows. He padded into the kitchen, discovering that he was alone. His eyes sought and found the coffee maker. He was well into his second cup when Father Joseph entered through the side door. His face told John everything before he spoke a word.

"She's wonderful!" he exclaimed.

John figured there was no point in pretending he didn't know who he meant. "That sounds encouraging."

"John, she's up and about. She's eating nonstop. Her color is good. Her strength is returning. It is a genuine miracle! Do you hear me?"

John was both relieved and happy. But he was lacking in Joe's level of enthusiasm.

"Here's to full recoveries," he said, extending his coffee mug in a mock toast.

"Indeed. At least you made a full pot." He headed for the cupboard to seek a mug of his own. He poured, and then sat across the table.

"Linda's husband is thankful. The poor guy has been through hell."

"I'm glad." John meant it.

"You may be interested in knowing that he runs a small accounting firm here in town. He has been growing it since he started several years ago. He has built up a good reputation."

John nodded. "He seemed like a good guy."

Joe took a sip. "He offered you a job."

John almost choked. "What did you say?"

"You came up in the conversation and he offered you a job. Now, you don't have an accounting designation so it would be entry level stuff at first. But you could take evening and weekend courses if you wanted to. You could be a CPA yourself someday if you worked hard at it."

"Is this a serious thing or a knee-jerk reaction to our visit last night?"

"Does it matter to you?"

"Yes, it matters. If it's knee-jerk, then what happens if she relapses in six months? Or six days for that matter. He fires me?"

"No, of course not," Joe said. "My, but you're depressing this morning. Dan isn't like that. If he offers it, he means it."

"Look, Father Joe, I'm happy about her healing and that's an understatement. But I can't help but look down the road at what might be waiting for her and for me. What if my back is a mess again in six months or a year? What if her cancer is still there? What if all this is nothing more than a temporary adrenalin boost of some sort?"

Father Joe had already thought about that. "One way we could find out, you know?"

I stepped into that one, John thought. He had been putting off any plans of getting checked out because he didn't want to face the possibility that he wasn't cured at all.

"Yeah," he said. "That's true."

"Your enthusiasm is overwhelming."

"Joe, what if it's all an illusion? Do we want to know that sooner than later? Do you want to tell nice guy Dan that his wife is still going to die despite the great night she just had?"

"Of course not. Look, John, I understand your reluctance, but what about the flip side of this? What if you find out for certain that this is real and permanent?"

John shrugged.

"Either way, you need to know before you can move forward with your life. Don't you want to do that?"

John sighed. "I'm in a warm, fuzzy, delusional state, and I'm getting rather comfortable here. Painful reality doesn't seem the least bit appealing to me. I don't want to add my spinal deterioration to marital breakdown, loss of home and job, leaving the woman and daughter who had become my new best friends, and bug attacks. But you know what would be even more terrible? Finding out that I just participated in giving false hope to a family that's going through the worst possible scenario that they could have inflicted on them, through no fault of their own."

Father Joe nodded. "I understand, John. Or at least I think I do. In my position, I get involved with all sorts of tragedies. People can't help but have an emotional response. You can't help but be protective of your psyche. The strongest, toughest people in the world do the exact same thing. Either that or they go crazy."

"In my case, I'm not sure that would make a significant difference."

"If you take the job, you can stay here temporarily. I'm sure if we work together, we can find a place of your own that would be suitable. I do have some contacts in this community, you know."

John blew a long stream of air from between pursed lips. "I need a little time, Father Joe. I haven't been able to process everything yet. When I look down the road to what my future will be, all I see is a gigantic question mark."

"That's perfect! Take the job, then find a place here in Plattsburg. If you come to a solid conclusion that this isn't what you want, *then* you can say a polite goodbye, and move on to...whatever."

John sipped his coffee, musing over nothing more than his entire future.

"Of course," Joe said, "you don't have to decide at this moment. As a matter of fact, one should never make major decisions before eating breakfast. I know a little place that makes the best omelets you've ever had. What do you say?"

John had a brief vision of Kemina cooking for him the first time at Casa Comida, and felt a twang of melancholy. He forced it away. "I say that sounds very tempting."

"*Temptation* or any derivative thereof is a poor choice of words considering my profession."

John smiled. "Insert *delicious* in place of tempting."

"There! That's better. Why don't you grab a quick shower while I savor this coffee? Then we'll go out and start the day."

"You are a persuasive negotiator."

"Glad to hear it. I have several other items over which I will be twisting your arm."

John finished his mug with one long draught. "The answer is no. There, I just saved you a lot of wasted time."

"We'll see."

John walked away, feeling a little like this was the first day of the rest of his life.

AFTERWARDS

"Oh no." Allie stared in disbelief.

The tree was dead. All the leaves, or at least those few still clinging to the branches, were brown and dry. A few seed pods, now visible at the top of the tree, were lifeless and shrivelled.

Allie walked over to it as if in a trance, placing the palm of her hand against the trunk. She was openly weeping by now.

"Why?" she asked in anguish. Even now, there was a faint residual aura of something like hate radiating from the dry bark. There would be no more happy visions or healings.

John had sent her a text to inquire about the status of her life, and that of the tree. They still communicated regularly, a fact that delighted Allie. She regularly dropped hints and suggestions that John should return for an in-person visit, an event that had yet to happen or even be agreed to. That didn't mean she wouldn't keep trying.

Her mother had required weeks of nagging, arm-twisting and every other kind of leverage Allie could imagine before permission to visit the tree had been granted. Bug attacks were happening in an ever widening area and the danger was still all too real. But so far, Allie had seen no signs of them on her walk. She had agreed to a quick visit and couldn't linger.

Her new reality stood before her, an immoveable monolith impeding the path of her life. There would be no more healings or pleasant visions. Both John and the tree were gone and she couldn't imagine a substitute for the gaping hole left behind.

School had improved, however. Lonnie was attending elsewhere, and Brad was apparently having trouble recovering from his bug attack—emotionally, not physically. While Allie didn't have first-hand information, abundant rumors suggested that he was receiving treatment from some sort of counsellor. She truly felt some sympathy for him, but mostly relief for herself. The incessant bullying had evaporated and she was slowly allowing herself to interact in healthy ways with other students. Perhaps new friendships were on the horizon. It felt that way.

She turned and walked away, feeling that this was the last time she would walk through the forest. She preferred to remember the Dream Tree as it was. The moment was poignant but she endured it and walked onward.

The Bronx, New York City, Yankee Stadium, one month later

From the upper deck, the view of the city skyline beyond the outfield wall was breathtaking. As the sun set, the lights of the city glowed against the dark, glowering sky. It was supposed to rain, but not until the game was over. The stadium lighting kept the field as bright as day, adding contrast to the towering buildings dominating the horizon.

As the seventh inning stretch unfolded, Bobby Felton noticed something unusual. He had been coming to games here for a little over fifty years, but had never seen anything like it.

"Hey, you seeing what I'm seeing?" he said to his buddy Paul. He pointed to the blue letters that spelled Yankee Stadium left of the big screen in the outfield.

"What is that?" Paul squinted to improve his long-distance focus.

Over the wall, melding around the letters, was a dark cloud. It undulated and flowed past the sign and into the stadium.

"What the heck could it be?" Bobby wondered aloud. He could hear a reaction from the crowd as the cloud poured downward towards the spectators.

Paul took a swig from his cup of beer. "Let's wait and see," he suggested.

That turned out to be a bad idea. People were already being stung. The swarm was spreading outwards through the spectators.

When several of the announcers for the live radio and television broadcasts got stung, any government attempts to downplay the spread of the bugs was instantly negated. This would morph into an international story.

The bugs were destined to become a world-wide event, spreading to every continent except Antarctica.

At this point, a baseball analogy seems appropriate.

Strike three, you're out.

The End

CHECK OUT OTHER GREAT CRYPTID NOVELS

SWAMP MONSTER MASSACRE
by **Hunter Shea**

The swamp belongs to them. Humans are only prey. Deep in the overgrown swamps of Florida, where humans rarely dare to enter, lives a race of creatures long thought to be only the stuff of legend. They walk upright but are stronger, taller and more brutal than any man. And when a small boat of tourists, held captive by a fleeing criminal, accidentally kills one of the swamp dwellers' young, the creatures are filled with a terrifyingly human emotion—a merciless lust for vengeance that will paint the trees red with blood.

TERROR MOUNTAIN
by **Gerry Griffiths**

When Marcus Pike inherits his grandfather's farm and moves his family out to the country, he has no idea there's an unholy terror running rampant about the mountainous farming community. Sheriff Avery Anderson has seen the heinous carnage and the mutilated bodies. He's also seen the giant footprints left in the snow—Bigfoot tracks. Meanwhile, Cole Wagner, and his wife, Kate, are prospecting their gold claim farther up the valley, unaware of the impending dangers lurking in the woods as an early winter storm sets in. Soon the snowy countryside will run red with blood on TERROR MOUNTAIN.

CHECK OUT OTHER GREAT CRYPTID NOVELS

BIGFOOT WAR
by **Eric S. Brown**

Now a feature film from Origin Releasing. For the first time ever, all three core books of the Bigfoot War series have been collected into a single tome of Sasquatch Apocalypse horror. Remastered and reedited this book chronicles the original war between man and beast from the initial battles in Babblecreek through the apocalypse to the wastelands of a dark future world where Sasquatch reigns supreme and mankind struggles to survive. If you think you've experienced Bigfoot Horror before, think again. Bigfoot War sets the bar for the genre and will leave you praying that you never have to go into the woods again.

CRYPTID ZOO
by **Gerry Griffiths**

As a child, rare and unusual animals, especially cryptid creatures, always fascinated Carter Wilde.

Now that he's an eccentric billionaire and runs the largest conglomerate of high-tech companies all over the world, he can finally achieve his wildest dream of building the most incredible theme park ever conceived on the planet...CRYPTID ZOO.

Even though there have been apparent problems with the project, Wilde still decides to send some of his marketing employees and their families on a forced vacation to assess the theme park in preparation for Opening Day.

Nick Wells and his family are some of those chosen and are about to embark on what will become the most terror-filled weekend of their lives—praying they survive.

STEP RIGHT UP AND GET YOUR FREE PASS...

TO CRYPTID ZOO

CHECK OUT OTHER GREAT BIGFOOT NOVELS

THE BEASTS OF STONECLAD MOUNTAIN
by **Gerry Griffiths**

Clay Morgan is overjoyed when he is offered a place to live in a remote wilderness at the base of a notorious mountain. Locals say there are Bigfoot living high up in the dense mountainous forest. Clay is skeptic at first and thinks it's nothing more than tall tales.

But soon Clay becomes a believer when giant creatures invade his new home and snatch his baby boy, Casey.

Now, Clay and his wife, Mia, must rescue their son with the help of Clay's uncle and his dog, a journey up the foreboding mountain that will take them into an unimaginable world...straight into hell!

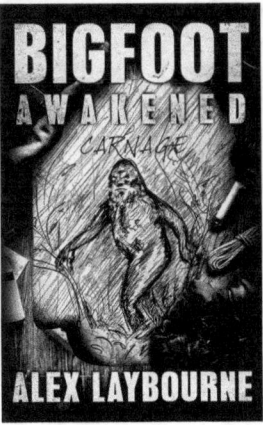

BIGFOOT AWAKENED
by **Alex Laybourne**

A weekend away with friends was supposed to be fun. One last chance for Jamie to blow off some steam before she leaves for college, but when the group make a wrong turn, fun is the last thing they find.

From the moment they pass through a small rural town they are being hunted by whatever abominations live in the woods.

Yet, as the beasts attack and the truth is revealed, they learn that despite everything, man still remains the most terrifying evil of them all.